COPPER CROWN

Lane von Herzen

Thorndike Press • Thorndike, Maine

Library of Congress Cataloging in Publication Data:

Von Herzen, Lane.
Copper crown / Lane von Herzen.
p. cm.
ISBN 1-56054-370-1 (alk. paper : lg. print)
1. Large type books. I. Title.
[PS3572.O45C66 1992] 92-17
813'.54—dc20 CIP

Thorndike Press Large Print edition published in 1992
by arrangement with William Morrow and Company, Inc.

Cover design by Honi Werner.

This book is printed on acid-free, high opacity paper. ∞

For Ida Jesse, mother of Ruby Dell
And Ruby Dell, mother of Janice
And Janice, mother of my own.
Borne by Texas and bearing her again.

❧

PART ONE

❧

1913

A Longing Without Thorns

❧

The grass stretched away from my window in a thousand hot, gold needles. Allie, she came running across it, the sash on her blue smock slapping against her hip. Her bosom shifted under the cloth, swinging low before it rippled back into place. The skin on her face was wetted and shiny, and from the distance, she didn't look colored.

When she came through the door, I heard the sound of her fingers on the latch. Then she was standing in the walkway to the bedroom, hard-breathing and intent. Her hair fell over one shoulder in a dark, curling bush while she leaned over one foot at a time to pick the sharp grass from her heels.

"My mama brung home a new cookbook," she said.

"What kind?" I said.

"Wedding recipes," she said. "But it's only on loan overnight. She got to take it back to Jensen's kitchen tomorrow."

"When you ever going to cook for a wedding?" I said.

She shrugged one shoulder so that it rustled behind the bush of her hair. "Maybe I'll cook for yours," she said. "Seeing as how I won't get invited no other way."

"If I ever was to get married, I don't guess I'd forget you," I said.

"Maybe," Allie said.

"No, I wouldn't," I said.

Me and her both knew that colored girls didn't get invitations to the weddings of white girls. At least not in Copper Crown, even if they did somewhere else. But it wasn't like it mattered to us any, seeing as we neither one of us were engaged to be married. We liked to assure one another over and over again that we weren't old enough to get tied to a man. Men were demanding, we said, especially the good-looking ones. And we didn't put any stock in girls marrying themselves off at no more than fourteen years old, or maybe fifteen like us, just to bear more babies, break more ground, and fight the hard fight till somebody laid them down and put a stone at their heads. Seemed a waste and a shame and a throwing away, and we thought to get out of it if we could.

❧

Allie asked me would I come over to her house to help her copy the recipe book, and I owned as I would. She had gone to school till she was twelve years old, and she could read and write better than most. But there were some words that she couldn't decipher just by looking at them. CINNAMON was one. And MUSHROOMS, even though mushrooms didn't really matter because you couldn't get them in Copper Crown on account of the lack of rain. Allie just left them out of the recipes and sometimes she added a cup of buttered pearl onions instead. She had herself such a talent with her kitchen fixings that she hired herself out for pie-baking and casseroles, and she never had a want of orders.

Allie lived with her mama and her brother in a two-room house on Marston's hill. The wood was grayed and leaning, and three juniper trees covered up gaps in the planks where the dust kept trying to fly through. It was September, and the trees held out bunches of blue-green berries at the ends of their branches, like fruit resting on their fingertips, swollen and delicious. Inside, the floors were earthen, with black roots and rocks knobbing the walkways. Allie's mama had thrown down some circle-weave rugs, which were always clean on account of she beat the dust from them once a day. There was a thick-glassed window in the room where Allie's mama slept, and through it you looked out on a small, sloping field where the bluebells and the crab-grass bristled in the spring.

Me and Allie set down at the kitchen table and copied recipes onto sheets of yellow paper. There were Blush Tarts, and Three-Tier Potato Salad, and Wedding-Ring Casserole and Sweetheart Pie. The ink stained my hands in blotches that were just the size and shape of violets.

"What does your mama want me to bake for her this week?" Allie said.

"Two loaves of that rye bread if you can get the same flour you used the last time," I said. "And a peach pie. We got ripe peaches if you can't find them sweet enough in town."

"I'll see what comes available," she said.

"The pie, it's for my daddy," I said.

Allie got up from the table and walked over to the cook counter. She picked up a hand-sifter and started shaking white streams of flour through the grate at its bottom. In the mixing bowl below, the flour rose in white hills and ridges like it was a land far away and underneath us. "Best to be pleasing your daddy as long as you got one," Allie said.

"I guess you got a daddy, too. Same as everybody," I said.

"Only I don't know who he be," Allie said.

"Won't your mama tell you?" I said.

Allie shook her head. "I asked her twice, but she ain't answered. 'That's all over and done with,' she said, and she wouldn't say no more."

"Maybe she thinks it's better for you if you don't know," I said.

"It's probably some white man close on by," she said.

"Why you think that?" I said.

"Well," she said. "Ain't I the lightest colored you ever did see?"

I looked at her. Even in the dark of Marston's kitchen I saw that her forehead, her neck, the length of her arms all shone. Her skin showed no different from the color of blond horses, or cut wheat stacked in the shade.

"Yes," I said. "You are."

Allie went working herself so hard with her sifting that the whole kitchen filled with a haze of cake flour. Looking through it, I saw that she had grown even whiter than before. A fine layer of paleness had settled on her skin, and even her hair had turned particle-white at the edges, like some thought was making her old way before her time.

"Don't pay me no mind," she said. "It just works on me is all."

❧

In the evenings, my mama and my cousin Lily Mark rolled their black modesty stockings off their legs so I could take them outside to wash in the wide tin tub, along with mine. They turned in the cold, frothy water like six long snakes, open-mouthed and senseless. The dust floated off their skins and colored the suds a milky gray, and in the clear spaces on the water's surface the fireflies reflected white pinpricks of light. From inside the kitchen, there came the sound of Mama soaping the dinner plates and then stacking them in a clean, wet pottery tower. Clackety-clack, like a crayfish skittering over the rocks. I stood up from the washtub and walked away from the house in my bare feet, silently, with the still-warm earth giving way under my toes.

Through Copper Crown, the night air blew a hot, purple breath. A bright haze of heat sank to the lower hollows of the sky and circled there in uneven clouds that took the shapes of fishes and empty-eyed men. When I got to the sweetgum in the Sally River Road, Allie was already there. She had layered over her hair a fine coat of brilliantine that had turned her curls separate and shining and smelling of mint. She was wearing small, cut-glass earrings that winked from the sides of her face.

"You been waiting long?" I said.

"A half hour," she said.

"Supper got put to table late."

"That's all right," she said. "A half hour one way or the other don't make no difference."

"What do you want to do?" I said.

"Let's go look in at Uncle Jensen's."

We made our way by the Sally River. The trees tangled over our heads in a net, and underneath us, the soggy riverbank sucked our feet into its softness and made faint popping noises when we pulled our heels out of the impressions. I could imagine Allie's earrings sparkling in the darkness even when her head was turned away, and I wished I could buy a pair like that for my own self. But my ears weren't even pierced on account of my daddy believed that pierced ears were the mark of a sinful life — even on the little Mexican babies we saw in town, who all wore tiny gold-lacquered studs from the time they were two or three weeks old.

Where the river flowed shallow and we could hear water bubbling over invisible rocks, we turned northward to walk through the weedy stubble of a fallow field. We stepped along carefully, so as not to put a foot in the hole of a rabbit or the crack of a rock, where the rattlesnakes slept. Halfway across the valley, lights blazed in the windows of Jensen's big house. In the lower parlor, a spotted dog was pawing at the paned glass, barking. Me and Allie sat down on a knoll some fifty yards away. We'd seen some of the strangest sights of our lives through those windows; we'd seen my sister, Oloe, dancing with the dummy form she used for her seamstress work. We'd seen Aunt Pauline unwrap her bosom one night and reveal that under the cloth bandeaux and all the stuffing that went inside it, she had only one breast instead of two. And once, not six months past, we'd seen Uncle Jensen kissing a colored girl while he held her wrists behind her back. We didn't consider ourselves peeping Toms. We just considered ourselves curious. There were things we needed to know, and wouldn't anybody teach them to us just for the asking.

Nothing unusual happened that night, though, except for Aunt Pauline appearing herself in the living room wearing her pink velveteen dressing gown. Her hair was piled up on top of her head in a sharp, white bun, like the pointed crest of a bird. She wore half-lensed glasses on the end of her nose, and when she reached upward to kiss Uncle Jensen, she snatched the glasses off, holding them two-fingered and delicate behind her husband's neck — like a glass-winged butterfly.

"Wasn't much of a kiss," Allie said.

"Why not?" I said. "It looked all right to me."

"Wasn't long enough," she said. "Passion kisses last longer than that."

"They do?"

"Mm-hmm."

"How do you know?" I said.

"I seen my brother kissing his girlfriend," she said. "They put their lips together for a half hour at a time."

"A half hour!"

"That's the way they do it," Allie said.

Upstairs, Aunt Pauline rubbed youth-cream on her face, dipping her hand into a porcelain jar that was out of sight.

"Maybe married people don't have time for passion kissing," I said.

"Not amongst themselves, anyway."

"Maybe," I said.

Aunt Pauline, wearing a white mask of cream, stretched her hands towards the ceiling and then disappeared from the window frame to touch her toes. She popped back up ten times and then she went away and the light went out.

"It ain't easy, though," Allie said. "Passion kissing. You got to press your lips together hard and do all your breathing through your nose."

"Have you ever tried it?" I said.

"I's practiced it."

"Show me," I said.

Allie touched her lips to the back of her hand. Her closed eyelids were purple and waxy-looking, and a brilliantine-coated curl dropped across the middle of her forehead. I heard the small, rhythmic sound of air passing through her nostrils.

"Let me try it." I brought my wrist up to my mouth and held it there. The skin smelled sour and soapy, and I remembered the six black leg stockings, submerged in the tin tub. I took my hand down and wiped the place where I'd kissed it on my smock.

"You didn't do it long enough," Allie said.

"It doesn't taste good," I said.

"Try it again."

❧

When I hung the stockings on the washline, water streamed off the soggy toes and hit the ground in fat, uneven drops that sounded like rain. Mama's pale green dress was drying alongside in the heat of the night. A slight wind pushed the bosom outward into two generous-made crests — just the size and shape of Mama when she was wearing it.

Inside the house, the lights were out. A cheesecloth covered a mound of sourdough as soft and plump as a day-old baby. I pinched a piece of raw dough from the underseam and put it on my tongue, where it sat in a bittersweet, buttery lump. Nobody had a sourdough recipe as fine as my mama's. Not even Allie. Mama said the secret was in skimming the starter. Said it put more bubbles into the milk, even if she couldn't explain why.

On the supper table, the Bible yawned open. Its cover was caramel-colored calfskin, cracked and rotted with age. The pages were a see-through onion paper, thin as thoughts and fragile as their gold-painted edgings. The lines were printed large and elegant, and at the beginning of each chapter and psalm, there was an oversized letter with flowers and leaves and sometimes tiny rabbits appearing in the open spaces. *Behold now, thy servant hath found grace in thy sight, and thou hast magnified thy mercy, which thou hast shown unto me in saving my life; and I cannot escape to the mountain lest some evil take me, and I die.* I could read the words well enough, even if their meanings hid themselves from me. I didn't think I lived within the hearing of God, like my mama did, whose prayers floated straight up to heaven and whose dreams turned to prophecy with the days going past. She had what Allie called the second sight, and when she looked at me, her pale gray eyes gone still and unblinking, I had the feeling she was seeing straight through me to my bones, and knew how they'd live and die and rearrange themselves in the earth when time passed over. And it gave me the sense that she was one of heaven's own.

Upstairs, I could hear my mama breathing her sleep in deep, unbroken breaths that skirted over the floorboards. In my room, Lily Mark lay tangled in the bedclothes, whimpering every so often like she always did when she dreamed of men. Her hair bloomed over her pillow in a black, curling rise and underneath it, her neck was as thin as a stem, green-white and succulent and made for early love. I slipped into bed beside her, and was just about to close my eyes when I heard a footstep in the hall. My daddy appeared himself in the doorway, bare from the waist up. His chest was covered with long, gray hairs that swirled outward in a pattern over his ribs. His work shirts had kept him white below the neck and above the wrists. But his hands, where they rested on his hips, were tanned so dark that he looked like he was wearing gloves.

"Cassie," he said.

"Yes sir."

"Where have you been?"

"Out for a walk," I said. "Out to Jensen's."

"Anyone with you?" he said.

"No sir," I said.

"You didn't meet up with that nigra girl?"

"No sir, I didn't," I said.

"If you did, I guess I'd find out about it," he said.

"I know," I said.

He walked away down the hall, his bare feet sticking to the boards. I didn't like to lie to him, but I made a practice of it where Allie was concerned. My daddy had said himself that some things in life were worth a small deceit, and I guess I hoped a true friend was one of them.

❧

On Saturdays, my daddy drove the buckboard into town. Me and Lily Mark, we sat in the back of the flatbed, jouncing over the ruts and stones till a small, hard numbness appeared where our appetites ought to have been. In summertime, Marston's hill and the fields beyond it filled up with copper crown lilies, their thousands of dusk-yellow heads trembling above the green. The town had drawn its name from the blooms of August and late September, when the lilies made their own bright-pointed sea, and people passing through would stop their carriages and stare with wonder at the endlessness of the six-pointed crowns, stiff and golden and filled up inside with stamens as thick as fingers. Blue dragonflies and heavy-bodied bees tripped over the tops of the flowers, drunken and slow in the heat.

We sat in the wagon while the road snaked off towards the edge of the world. Past the last copse of elderberry and juniper, the town appeared itself. Olson's laundering, Callahat's food emporium, G. Joseph's dry goods. Right away, my daddy gave us fifty cents, and Lily Mark and me took it into the emporium and bought ourselves biscuits and fried pork, which was our breakfast every time we rode into town so early. We liked to split the biscuits and lay the bacon down between the two halves. The pork fat soaked into the flour that way, and when we were hungry and it was still early morning, there wasn't much that tasted better. Lily Mark and me, we couldn't agree on many things, but we both knew the best way to eat a biscuit.

Lily Mark liked to stand out by the wagon and lick the last of the meal off of her fingers with the fine, dark neatness of a cat. She wore one of my scoop-cut smock dresses, and I noticed, not for the first time, that she filled it near to overflowing at the top part. Her bosom was pushed upward into two sassy cream-colored globes that drew the men's eyes and held them there. Mama planned to let out some of my calicoes so they would fit her with less of a strain, but letting out took material we wouldn't have till Christmastime. Anyway, Lily Mark didn't complain. She let the men look at her and she didn't blush. She just switched her hair to the back of her shoulders and laughed at them. "They can dream, can't they, cousin," she'd say to me. And I'd say I guessed they could.

❧

Lily Mark came to us by way of fire. She was born to my mama's sister out near Denton. They had themselves acres and acres of high, pale wheat, and come harvesttime, they pulled in a cash crop bigger than anything our family had ever seen. But one August the house caught on fire — probably on account of the papa smoking his cigars in bed, such as Lily Mark told it — and the whole place flamed up and fell down so fast, seemed like it had been waiting years just to get the chance. The wheat crop had been cut the day before, and the sheaves lay stacked, stiff and bundled and waiting for the thresher on the stubbly flats of the field. When the sparks found them, the sheaves bloomed into fire, little pieces and particles of them riding high into the sky in a funnel of smoke before they rained back down to earth as dust and fragrant ash.

Lily Mark, she climbed out her bedroom into a fat-branch blue willow, and slid down to the ground in her bare feet and her nightdress. The mama and the daddy, and the two little boys, they died in their beds, their lips turned gray and sooted, their eyes closed and wet with dreaming. Lily Mark kept yelling up to their windows, "It's fire! Get up, I said! Jason, Simpson! It's fire!" But the four of them were already deaf to her then, their ghosts already caught up in the raging, boiling smoke that ran forward out of the windows before ascending straight upwards past the stained-black debris of the house. After a while, Lily Mark went to sleep under the willow, her knees skinned and splintered with bark, her voice calloused from all her shouting. That's where the neighbors found her later, curled up ragged and black-haired like a beautiful stray.

The first time I laid eyes on Lily Mark, she wasn't fourteen years old, and already she had a face and figure on her like she was twenty. Her hair sprayed past her shoulders, dark and deep and wild. The curve of her bosom surged and circled inwards, leaving below it the frame of her ribs, pointed and ivory-boned, like it might've been a cage made to hold a precious bird.

At the start, Lily Mark went to live with Uncle Jensen and Aunt Pauline. Their house must've had a dozen empty rooms, with fresh-laundered sheets stretched tight across the beds inside them, and not a single child in sight until Lily Mark came along. Aunt Pauline, who claimed she'd been barren all those years on account of a shriveled ovary, thought she might get to be a mother after all. But she hadn't counted on the blue-blackness of Lily Mark's hair, or on the premature swelling of her bosom. She hadn't counted on the woman-curves of her hips and her belly, and the way they showed through her percale dresses in spite of the gathers at the seams. It wasn't a week before men started knocking on Jensen's door, asking was Lily Mark at home and would she be free to visit with them awhile. And Lily Mark didn't discourage them either. She passed time with all three of the Frank brothers, and Aunt Pauline had once found her tangled up inside the long, trembling arms of J. B. Hoag on the far side of the stock barn, her cheeks flushed and wet, and J. B. working her skirt up above her knees. Aunt Pauline had come to see my mama the very next day. There were smudges on her butterfly glasses, and her tongue kept darting forward to lick the chap-lines on her lower lip.

She said, "I don't have any experience raising girls that have mature notions before their time."

Mama said, "I don't guess I do either. Mine are modest, both of them."

"Like they should be," Aunt Pauline said. She pulled her glasses low on her nose, reaching in back of the lenses to rub her eyes. "Maybe if I had got Lily Mark at a younger age, I could've taught her something about it."

"Seems like fourteen ought to be young enough," Mama said.

"You don't know the half of it," Aunt Pauline said. "If I go on like this, with her in my house, she'll get with child before the year is out, and me not having a thing to say about it. She will."

"Pauline, I don't think —"

"She will," Aunt Pauline said.

My mama tucked some stray hairs into the whorl of her chestnut bun. She sipped the last of her tea from her blue stoneware cup, and when she set it down in the saucer, I refilled it, all the tea leaves whirling against each other in a wild-blown, secret storm.

"I would take her if I had the space," Mama said. "But we're full up as it is. Oloe and Cassie, they share the one bed and there isn't any room for a third.

Aunt Pauline's tongue flickered from between her teeth, pink and childish and alive. "Couldn't I take one of your girls?" she said. "In exchange, I mean?"

"Exchange?" Mama said.

"For Lily Mark. It wouldn't be for permanent," she said. "Just till one of them married and that won't be but a year or two at the most."

"You mean you'd take on one of my girls?" Mama said.

"Just for a little while," she said. "And Lily Mark would be so much better with you."

"I don't know," Mama said.

"She'd be so much safer with you guiding her like you would."

"I don't like to let go of one of my own," Mama said.

"But when you think of what might happen," she said. "And it's your sister's only living child."

❧

Oloe was my daddy's favorite, which was natural if only you took the time to think about it. By most families, the first was loved most, and in our family, Oloe was the first. She was tall and graced in her limbs, even from the outset, and when she was five years old and Mama set her to yanking weeds all day from the seedling corn furrows, it nearly broke my daddy's heart. She got herself calloused at the hands and sunburned at the face, but she showed Mama how she was a hard worker who didn't cry for herself. She knew Daddy was already crying for her.

Her and him hadn't to do anything but look one another in the eye to find an understanding. He let her tend the baby ground squirrels she was always finding, set out hurt or lost in the trail of a plow. And later, it was her that went collecting him from Jarley Frank's house on a Saturday night, having drunk too much and torn his shirt out walking somewhere in the wood.

Four years between Oloe and me was too many for us to be rivaling each other. I was mostly too small to be stepping into her clothes before they wore out complete. If shoes for the one cost bread for the other, we weren't ever aware of it. What we had, we shared. What we didn't have, we didn't worry over.

Mama said that when I was three years old I wandered out of the house and lost myself in the forest nearly fifteen or twenty times. Scolding nor shaking nor spanking wouldn't teach me. So Mama tied me with a harness and leashed me to Oloe where she was clearing the corn rows. I watched her hours at a time, reaching down for weeding with those lank, browning arms, her great shocks of chestnut hair falling past her eyes. In time eventual, they cut the harness off me and loosed me altogether. But I still went out fielding with Oloe, walking up the furrows and down the furrows two steps behind her, just like we were tied together by some invisible thread couldn't anybody see but us two.

When Mama arranged for Oloe to go live with Aunt Pauline, me and Daddy sorrowed over it most. I heard Daddy say, "Mother, you're sending out the child that's given you most. She hasn't ever done anything but revered what you've set her to do. Least if we have no choice but to take in Lily Mark, let's bring her in for Cass's place."

"Cass is as good a child as you're going to get," Mama said. "I'd think you would know that by now."

Daddy didn't say anything more. I was lying on my bed, staring at the cracked beams where they traveled up the slant of the roof. I listened for his voice to sound again from its place down the hallway. I imagined him shaking his head from side to side, the small sack of skin under his jaw trembling like a gizzard on an old Cornish bird. "No," he would be saying silently, dully. "That's not the way of it."

❧

Mama said I'd have to give up some of my comforts what with Lily Mark moving in. The porcelain washbowl Daddy had bought me specially at Christmas, half a set of hairbrushes and combs my gramma Sandstrom had saved for Oloe and me, and like that.

"Lily Mark's lost too much to want to give up any more," Mama said. "If she ever did know how to share her comforts, she's probably forgot."

But I don't guess I worried half so much about gaining Lily Mark as I did about losing Oloe. On the day she left us, my sister pinned her hair into a high, loose knot on the top of her head. It was the first time she had ever worn a bun and underneath it, her face looked all the more girlish, her eyes staring out from her soft saucer-lids with the wide, blurry wonder of her nearsightedness. Outside, the sky wept a winter rain, colorless and sweet-smelling, and from our bedroom window, we could watch it falling into the goldness of the fields and disappearing underneath.

Oloe folded her paper dress patterns, every corner of the tissue marked with notes and reminders that she had scrawled there: *Line up edge with contrast bias, add 2 inches to Mrs. Hardester's length.* When the patterns were stacked, they took up half her satchel. In the other half, she laid two work dresses and three pairs of leg stockings, two wrapped cakes of lilac soap, and her black-heeled, lace-up dress shoes. She had saved forty dollars in receipts from her last two years of sewing orders, and I watched her pull out the roll of bills from the center of her bed pillow before plunging it far down into the tunnel of a modesty stocking. Oloe could buckle the satchel only when I leaned onto it, my ribs pressed hard against the handles and all the air gone out of my lungs.

"You'll need me when you pack up to come home again," I said. "There's not one way I can think of that you could get this bag closed all by yourself."

"No, there's not," Oloe said.

"It won't be long, I guess."

"It's just down the road," Oloe said. "You can't call that moving away."

Daddy came in to take Oloe's satchel and went downstairs with it. When we came down after him, he was arguing with Mama over whether to take the horse out in the rain.

"He's off his feed," she said. "That's the way with the start of colic."

"It's less than a mile there and back," Daddy said.

"I don't want him wet," she said.

"Is it better that it's your daughter out there?" he said.

"You said yourself it's only a short way," Mama said. "I would think she could walk."

Mama was standing over the cookstove, stirring something. The heels of both her hands were wrapped tight around a wooden spoon, as if turning the water around in the pot was requiring all the strength she had to give it. Daddy stood behind her, gesturing towards her back. A long piece of hair had fallen down over his ear, leaving his baldness uncovered. When he turned away, there was a shiny, white medallion of skin that made you feel small to look at it, that made you feel you were looking on his nakedness with him unaware.

Oloe walked to the door and picked up her dress form. It was shaped like the torso of a full-figured woman, the bosom rising as square and angled as a shelf above the place where Oloe gripped it.

"I'll be back for the rest," she said, and then she went out. I stood in the mouth of the doorway, watching her go. She hoisted the dress form over her head to keep her hair out of the rain, and I could see the thin linen skin of the dummy blushing a darker pink as the wetness spread across it. Oloe tried to skirt the mud holes in the road, but sometimes she met one, her ankles wobbling beneath her in the dun-colored slipperiness, the hem of her smock darkened by a slick brown tongue of water. From a distance, I couldn't tell anymore that the form in Oloe's arms was only linen and wire. I guess if I had seen her for the first time, struggling over the milkweed and the rocks and the ruts in the road, the rain streaming down her arms and onto the space of her girlish back, I might've thought she was carrying away the dead.

❧

Uncle Jensen, he was family to everybody and to nobody at the same time. He was a first cousin to my daddy and a second cousin to nearly everyone else. Talk was he had fathered two dozen children outside of marriage and not a single child inside of it. But the town said Aunt Pauline was the reason for that last part, seeing as she miscarried once or twice a year.

All the people I knew at that time referred to Jensen as Uncle, and by an afterthought, called his wife Aunt. Most of them could, for a fact, go look up Copper Crown's birthing records and find themselves related to the Jensens after a minor line. But more important to all those cousins once and twice removed was the idea that Uncle Jensen, setting on the best-producing farmland in the county, didn't have himself any legal children to leave his properties to.

And the properties went on for miles. They ran east and north of the milky-green loop of the Sally River. The land was flat and pale there, with not much more than an occasional trace of clay, and when you looked at it from one edge, it appeared like an endless animal hide, skinned and stretched and drying in the sun. In the spring, with the rains, the hide turned darker, and in the fields that Uncle Jensen left fallow, there were the hard backs of armadillos, moving like beads amongst the jimsonweed and the queen's lace.

The house set behind a small cornfield and the smell of the sweet green stalks and the white-kerneled ears drifted up to its door in June and September. The walls were painted-white and peeling, and on the front side, there were twelve glass windows which, when they were opened, got dressed up by their white organdy curtains fanning in the wind. Allie's mama had worked inside that house the last twenty years going, cleaning out the bedrooms, which were mostly empty, and cooking for the harvest hands their noontime meal of spoon bread and chili stew. And when she could, she brought home the cookbooks from the kitchen so that Allie could copy them over. There was *The Homecook's Companion, Recipes from the Old World,* and *Finest Stews and Casseroles,* alongside five or six others. They set on a wide shelf above the cookstove, which was a waste of good space according to Allie's mama, seeing as how none of the hired cooks could read.

Jensen himself was a small-statured man with crab-veined eyes. People said he got satisfaction out of drinking sour liquor and overworking his hired help. The coloreds that worked his fields were likely to get their hands stripped raw from all-day planting, and then have their wages held back for taking five minutes under shade.

As for Oloe, Uncle Jensen promised my daddy he would look after her like she was his own. But Oloe guessed that meant he would take pride in her sewing, her reading, and her keeping quiet in the company of men. She said if that was being Jensen's own, she would thank God to keep her from it.

❧

Allie and me, sometimes we went to Jensen's on the weekends, each of us with our own visiting to do. The fallow field we had walked through all winter was being cut up by two dark bay horses dragging a steel plow. We could hear the underground rocks scraping against the blade. When the plow was through, it left straight, even wounds in the earth. The soil turned over in rich, red clumps that were still cool from being underground, and when Jensen ran water down the furrows, it turned red after the first several feet, looking like pain and the bounty that was to come after it. Allie and me, we went around the long way, lifting our feet over the sandwort and the rockrose at the edge of the wood, and turning north only at the last, where the valley rose into the long, rocky ridges that were bleached the color of bone. Flocks of men, broad-hatted and sweating, picked the fields clean of stones or spread seed from the canvas sacks that swung low and bulging over their bellies. Allie always tried to pick out her brother, Clyde, from among them, but the men in their labor all looked the same, and as often as not, when she called out to him across the hairy squares of the crops, her arms waving, it turned out to be someone else.

When we got to Jensen's big house, I took the path to the front door and Allie took the path to the back. Allie's mama was always waiting for her in the kitchen, her nails stained blue with the berries she had just put into a pie. She was narrow-shouldered and broad-hipped, and she carried herself straight upright, like somewhere inside of her, there was a cup of liquefied gold filled to the edge and she was determined never to spill a drop. Allie called it the height of her pride and wondered out loud where it came from exactly and how she could get some of it for herself.

Meantime, I went upstairs to set by Oloe

while she sewed. She worked in front of the window, the daylight streaming onto her narrow, white fingers and the invisible stitches that lined up underneath them. The fabrics in her hands were always beautiful — dark blue crepes and cream-colored linens — and, held up against her own skirts, they made her look neglected and plain. Once I asked her didn't it ever bother her to turn out dresses for other women that were so much nicer than what she wore. And she just said women didn't want a beautiful seamstress. They wanted a steamstress that did beautiful work.

Allie smiled when I told her about it. "That girl knows her business," she said.

"I wish she'd let her hair down, though," I said. "She's much finer with her hair down."

"What difference would it make?" Allie said.

"Might make a difference to a man," I said.

"She don't need a man," Allie said. "If she's smart, she don't want one."

Allie reached into her smock and pulled her cut-glass earrings out of the pocket there. She felt for the marks in her ears and pushed the wires through, one at a time. She said, "Lord knows I don't want one."

I said, "Lord knows I don't either."

❧

My mama gave advice that seemed like it came straight from the mouth of God. She said, "Don't waste too much time setting up your beliefs about life before you go out and live it." She was right in what she told me, because just when I got sure there was no room for a man in such a tiny heart as mine, I met Murray.

I first saw him that spring, working the old Jackson property just west of Jensen's. He stood in weeds that were as long and white as an old woman's hair, and when he walked, the crickets leaped away from his boots in low, silver arcs, five or six of them at a time. His two brothers stood with him to the one side and the other, each hitching up a sorrel horse to the plow. They all wore wide white cotton work shirts, generous and pleated at the shoulder. The wind played amongst the folds, puckering and releasing them with its hot, bitter breath. Murray would've looked exactly like the others, except his brow was more proud-seeming where it shadowed his eyes. It was slanted outwards in a pale, stony ridge that made me consider his face as a certain and beautiful thing. He turned to look when we rode by.

"New sharecroppers is all," Lily Mark said. She sat riding in the buckboard with me and the hay, while Daddy drove us along the Valley Road, towards home. "They're going to give away half of everything they grow." But her eyes held fast to their backs for the flat quarter mile, looking like they hid an ache behind them somewhere.

I followed her gaze back across the dusty road and the unearthed clots of tangled grass to where the distant forms of the men were standing. One of them was ahead of the horses, breaking up the ground with a long-handled spade. The two others were leaning back on the harness, trying to gauge the plow blade to the right depth.

"They're making a pretty start of it," Lily Mark said.

"They'll do all right," I said. "If they're young enough, they'll do fine."

"Oh, they're young enough," she said. "I saw that much right away."

❧

Lily Mark and my sister, Oloe, and me, we passed Murray's place twice a day on the way to school and back. In the afternoons, the sun swung through the center of the sky, white and blinding and masterful. Vapors rose up out of the ground, making the miniature cottonwood and winterberry trees waver in the distance. The dust gathered in our throats in a thin, chalky layer, and all we could think of was to wash it away with a draft of clear water. So we stopped at Murray's pump, listening to the squeak and suck of the old iron handle, waiting for the wetness to run into the upturned cups of our hands.

Sometimes, Murray walked in from the fields while we were there. His shirt was wetted in a ragged path down the center of his chest, and clear drops of perspiration clung to the ends of his hair. He drank pump water from the ladle, his Adam's apple climbing upward and disappearing each time he swallowed. He liked to point out his brothers to us, each of them walking behind the fork of a plow.

"They're making it shallow for corn," he said.

"Don't they want to come in awhile?" I said.

"I'll take their water out to them," he said.

"How much are you planting?" Oloe said.

"Twenty, this year. Thirty, the next."

"Thirty," Lily Mark said. "I guess a man could do well for himself on thirty acres."

Murray turned to look at her. His eyes opened up underneath his brow, and they were glassy and fast-moving, like the parts of a river where the bed falls away to depth. "Well enough to buy out his share-crop anyway."

Lily Mark was drying her hands on her skirts. She wouldn't look up.

"Where did you get your stock?" I said. I pointed out towards his corral. A yearling pinto moved inside it, dancing along the borders like the dust burned his hooves.

Murray smiled. "Galveston," he said.

"He's fine," I said. Beyond his gate, the pony was thick-necked and proud. His tail flowed white and overlong and two or three inches of it dragged across the ground wherever he went. Over one side of his coat, there was a chestnut marking in the shape of a dove, its wings spread full-feathered.

Murray said, "He needs to be broken with a child on his back. Someone that doesn't weigh any more than a small sack of grain." Then he looked at Lily Mark and Oloe and me, each of us one at a time. "Say, which one of you girls could stand at the other side of a scale from a half bushel of grain?" he said.

Lily Mark laughed. She ran a light hand across her waist. "You know that isn't polite, Mr. Murray. Why anyone just looking at us can see Cass is the only one that doesn't have a figure on her."

Murray's neck flushed a red the color of clay earth. "I didn't mean anything about — what you say," he said.

" 'Course you didn't," Lily Mark said.

❧

That spring, I read *Blackford's History of America, Revised,* and I planted a half acre of jewel tomatoes, the kind that sagged when the fruit started to ripen so that I had to tie the stems to wooden stakes. And while the tomatoes turned out to be so juicy and fat-meated that you could hardly get your fingers around them, I couldn't recall what it was that I had done to tend them, so I wasn't sure I could ever raise them so well again. As to my reading, I remembered all there was about the Revolution and the Civil War, but there were great gaps of blackness in between where I had lost a hundred years of peace in the space of a single daydream.

What I was thinking about was Murray. I was thinking about how, when he rolled up his sleeves, I was surprised by the whiteness of his arms and by the smooth, seamless way they widened to meet his elbows. I was thinking about how his jaw grew dark with beard growth in the afternoon of every day and whether it would feel rough if I ever put my hand up to touch it, with him standing close over me, saying something I'd never heard him say. I was thinking about how my daddy had taken twelve hens to him, huddled and clucking in a crate that was too small, and had come back an hour later with three dollars and a fresh tin of tobacco in his hand, saying Murray was nothing if he wasn't fair. I was thinking about how he'd looked me up and down when I'd said I might help him break his horse, about how I'd felt my neck flush warm when his eyes were on my waist, fixed there, wondering about something.

In the evenings, when I went to meet Allie, I could hear Murray's horse moving through the dark. There was a sound of air rushing from his lungs and of his wedge-bottomed hooves clapping into the dust. And when I went closer I could see him in the blackness — painted and half-angry and sweating over the withers. I stood up on the gate, and he shied to the far side of the corral, making small, tight circles and punching the air out through his nostrils. Once, I was standing like that when Murray came out of his barn. He had a feed bag in his hands, the oats rolling around inside it.

"It's you," he said.

"I just came to see him," I said.

"That's all right," he said. "Come anytime."

Murray leaned over the gate and poured the oats into a bucket. Then he walked over and stood up on the rail next to me. For a second his arm was resting against mine and the skin there felt hot. Then he moved his arm so it was an inch away and I was looking at it and wishing he would move it back.

"Come over often enough to get him used to you, and then it'll be better for you when you ride him," he said.

"Did I say I'd ride him?" I said.

"You said you might."

"There's a lot of wildness in him," I said.

"I'll be right there with you, though," he said.

"You would?"

"The whole time," he said. "I'll be right there at the end of the lead."

"You wouldn't let him run off with me, I guess."

"No," he said. "Not without running after you for as long as I could."

I laughed. Murray sank his head down on his arms and when he brought it back up, he was smiling. There were tiny, fan-shaped furrows at the corners of his eyes.

"That's comforting," I said.

"Don't worry," he said. "I wouldn't let him lose you."

❧

Allie was the only person ever made mention I was pretty for a fifteen-year-old who hadn't got too much figure to her. Said my hair was full of natural curve like the kind ladies went to beauty parlors for and got put in professional. Said my eyes were wise and young both, like that Lillian Gish she saw several times at the silent-picture show. And men were sure taken with *her,* so she didn't see any reason Mr. Murray oughtn't get taken with me. It was true that I was as skinny a girl as she'd ever seen up close, but her mama had told her curves came to every girl given the workings of time. I just wasn't full-extended yet.

"Now, you take someone like me," she said. "Seems like I been extended since I was twelve years old. I popped seams and busted buttons so frequent my mama said, 'I swear seems like I ain't raised you much more than ten years, and already I got to buy you woman clothes.' But she said it good-natured. 'Course I don't know how I might come out. I might change yet. Mama's done all right by herself, but you never can tell about the other half."

It was near past dusk when we were talking.

Two shortcake loaves rose in the oven and we set still in Allie's kitchen-smell of butter and soda and vanilla beans ground fine. Past the propped-out door and down the clay footpath from Marston's, men were walking home from the fall harvesting at Jensen's. They were white men mostly, and Allie and me, we could recognize them easily, even in the half dark. Peder Olson and his brother, Karl, Jarley Frank and his two boys, old man Lobbock, who made a slim living now from hiring himself out.

Allie was saying, "I watch them come by in the morning and I watch them go past at night. Tall mens and short ones, kind mens and otherwise, carrying their hats in their hands, thinking their private things, none of them knowing I's up here looking down, watching them all, considering them all, thinking to myself, 'Which one be my daddy?' "

❧

I spent most of every Saturday kneeling in the vegetable garden. The bright tops of the carrots and the sugar beets shot upwards like small green fountains, and the leaves of the squash grew thick and triangled above their rows. The rabbits liked to sit underneath in the emerald shade where they ate through the waxy, flecked coats of the zucchini to the watery tunnel of seeds at the core. Daddy set iron-jaw traps for the rabbits in every second row, but, as I didn't like the workings of traps, I took them away again before they'd been sprung.

One time I'd had my hands in the earth all morning when Murray came by. I was tying some pea shoots to the trellis, and I didn't even see him until he walked up behind me, angling his work shoes in between two lines of carrots, the greens still trembling from where he passed them by.

"I thought I'd tell your daddy how fine the hens are working out," he said.

"Oh," I said. "Oh." I felt for my hair and found that I'd tied it back and that whole hanks of it had come loose, straggling down onto my neck. The palms of my hands were stained red-brown, and the skin there was cut in two or three places where the nettles had pushed through.

"They're laying two eggs a day, each of them," he said.

"Sounds like they've done well by you," I said.

"They have," he said. Murray looked down at his boots and saw that they had broken the green necks of a spindly carrot top. He pulled back his foot, but the stems stayed where they were, pressed flat in the soil. "Your daddy isn't . . ."

"He isn't home," I said. "Mama either. But you could come inside if you wanted. I could fix you some coffee."

"All right," Murray said.

I followed him back down the garden row, pressing my feet into the wide, flat prints his boots left behind. Inside the house, Murray sat at the kitchen table while I washed my hands and pulled the loose tie out of my hair. I would've changed my dress, too, but there wasn't any time for it with him there waiting. I was just pouring out the coffee when I heard Lily Mark's step on the stair, so I brought out a third saucer and cup.

"Hello, Murray," she said. "Who is it you've come to see?"

❧

Murray said he liked to go fishing in the Sally River, so Allie and me went looking for him there. The water was high with the rains of spring, and that left us to scramble over the knotted legs of the trees when we followed one bend in the river for the next. Up in the branches of the winterberry and the silveroak, the buds had just started to break from their tight, dull coats, washing the air with a passing thought of green. Above them, the sky spread out in the color of hope, so brilliant and new-made that to take your eyes from it was to feel the loss. We went out walking like that every afternoon for two weeks going, but we never found him.

"Let's set down," Allie said. "My feet is worn raw."

"All right," I said.

"You sure he goes fishing here?"

"He told me he did," I said.

"Well, a man shouldn't make himself so hard to find," Allie said.

Allie dropped her feet into the water at the bank, and after I had set myself down beside her, I did the same. The river was warm where it met the air and cooler underneath. In the center, I knew, there were pockets that held the coldest of the underwater currents, swirling over the rocky hollows like an aching, liquid ice. But you had to go swimming to find them, out into the deeps where the river turned green and the trout were long, silver-pink flashes underneath you.

"Want to wash my hair?" Allie said.

"I might."

"You do mine and then I'll do yours," she said.

"We'll have to get the soap at my house," I said.

"I'll get it," she said. "It won't take me a half hour. And my hair needs it, too."

"Okay," I said. "But don't let my daddy see you coming around."

"I won't."

Allie stood up and walked off along the river's edge, back the way we had come. The light was dappled through the trees and she moved in and out of its patterns until I couldn't see her anymore — like a moth on the other side of a screen. I hoped my daddy would be gone from the house when she got there. He had a whip coiled on a hook on the back of the door and once he had said he would use it on someone if he didn't like their kind of people. But I hadn't ever seen him take it down. Men were strange, when I thought about it. Most of the ones I had known I was either looking for or hiding from, and it seemed a heck of a choice. Whether you liked a man or whether you didn't, you had to read his will and then act like it was your own, because that was the way to get by and if you were smart then that was the thought you held inside of your head.

On the close side of the river, there was something making noise in the brush. I thought I would see a buck come out onto the bank, his antlers still hanging with brambles and dried leaves, but instead there were two men, carrying packs and long poles. They were hatless, and one was black-haired and one was light. I thought that it might be Murray and his brother, Harley, and when they came closer I saw that it was.

When Murray caught sight of me, he stopped walking. Under his brow, his eyes were shadowed and wide, and they held on to me for a long time cautiously, like behind them lay the makings of fright or longing and I couldn't tell which one. He spoke something to Harley, and Harley nodded his head. A yellow finch lit on the end of one of their poles, and then jumped off it, flying away low through the trees.

"You look like you're waiting for someone," Murray called out.

"I'm going to wash my hair," I said.

Murray said something again to Harley, and I couldn't hear what it was. Then he handed off his fish pole and watched while Harley walked upstream by himself.

"Aren't you going along?" I said.

"Later on, I will," Murray said. "I thought I'd watch you wash your hair first."

"You can't do that."

"I can't?" he said.

"No."

"Not today or not ever?" he said. Murray was standing above me then, his pack slung over his shoulder. There was laughter spilling over the ends of his voice, and I could imagine his expression all mirthful and dark, the way I had seen it sometimes. I stared straight down at my ankles where the river water lapped them. Underneath, my toes were splayed deep in the silt.

"Don't make fun," I said.

"I'm sorry," he said. "Would you rather I did something else?"

"Yes."

He knelt down next to me, his knees sinking into the leaves, and then he cupped one hand under my chin and he leaned forward. I remember the sight of his mouth that first time and I remember how surprised I was by its softness and the gentle, glassy pressure of the teeth behind it. After I had stopped being frightened, I leaned into it too, and I felt that I was falling a great way through brightness and quiet and the heart of all belonging, so that when Murray pulled away all I wanted was for him to come back.

Murray sat up on his heels, and I saw that he was smiling. "I'd better go find Harley now," he said.

"All right."

When he walked away from me, he was looking back all the time, his head straining over his shoulder.

❧

Come November, my daddy's best plowing horse caught the colic and died inside a week. Daddy expected, what with the loss and all, that we couldn't reap enough crop to carry us through to next harvest. Except one morning, Mama found a package box by the kitchen door that had one hundred dollars stacked up neatly inside. Lily Mark and my sister, Oloe, and me, we swore we knew nothing about where it came from or who might've given us help in such a way.

I never told anybody, but I felt sure it was Murray that had done it. Him and his brothers had made a profit on their first year of corn, and Murray confided to me they were working up the papers to buy the Jackson place outright. But when I asked him about it the next month, he just said, "We've decided to wait on buying till next fall. Harley and Will, they think we might notch down the price by forty or fifty dollars if Jackson gets the idea we're looking at other properties come available. Buyer can't look like he's aching to buy."

I got the indication Mama knew something of his dealings, too, because she started asking after Murray regularly. She let on she thought he was a promising person who might come to a lot of good someday or other. I wanted terribly to know her thinking beyond that, but I never asked. She might've said something I couldn't abide by, something she couldn't take back, and then I'd be sure to live with it the rest of my life when it came out for real.

❧

Allie said, "Don't nobody know what makes two persons fall to loving each the other. Could be they got matching desires for loving in the physical way, could be they got two souls that step inside each the other and know the right fit. But don't nobody know it certain, and best not be pulling so hard at its edges so you pull it full apart."

Murray started coming over to the house for dinner. He kept his shirtsleeves rolled down, and he took his hat off once he got inside the door, and he mostly said "sir" when he talked to my daddy. I liked to slip my fingers into his palm under the table, but I saw that he found it hard to hold my hand and look into my daddy's face at the same time, so I did it less often than I wanted to.

In the autumn afternoons, I went over to the Jackson property to watch Murray break his horse to a bridle and bit. The pinto kept trying to shake the piece out from between his teeth, rocking his head back and forth, and chawing on the gate.

"He won't take it yet," Murray said. "He's got a will."

"It could be you're a matched set," I said, and Murray turned away to laugh.

His was the only two-year-old I ever did see that stood sixteen hands high at the shoulder, and Murray said he'd got plenty more height in him yet. When I asked Murray what name they'd given him he said they hadn't chosen one and why didn't I pick it out myself. So I called him Remy after a dappled, shaggy-headed, small-time racing horse my daddy had once put a bet on, with the result of three fresh dollars being laid in his hand.

I liked to watch Remy toss his head up in the air, clacking the bit in his mouth like it was a piece of hard candy. He shied at the sounds of the wind skimming the earth, rolling his eyes backwards so the whites showed in clear crescents of alarm. But I saw from the first he was just a wild child looking to be loved for his wild ways, and much as I thought to myself about riding his back, I couldn't find it in me to be afraid.

❧

At Christmastime, Murray gave me an imported lace veil. White lace, with a tiny little dove and lily pattern woven in, which showed up delicate against my hair. The design was fine enough so that I could wear it over the front of my face. And when I looked past the screen of doves flying up out of their nests, with heart-shaped leaves resting in their beaks, the world turned softened and fragile for my eyes. Daddy said he didn't see the use for a veil as it was too formal to wear except at Christmas or Eastertime once or twice a year. But Mama said there was sure to be more use in it than that, and most likely, they'd see me wearing it to my own wedding.

"You're acting like he's asked her already," Daddy said, laughing. "He hasn't, has he?"

"He will," Mama said. "Pay attention now, because I'm saying he will."

The day wasn't out before Murray did. It was the same day I climbed up on Remy's back and rode him around the ring so smooth it looked like I'd been doing the same every Saturday my whole life. Remy's gait was even and soundless, and the air parted its lips to let him through. He pulled his hooves high away from the ground and arched his trot like he was getting ready to fly off and me with him.

I said, "God, I wish this horse was mine." My head was thrilling so that I'd forgot my words.

Murray laughed. He was holding on to a ten-foot lead, guiding us inwards when Remy strained for the rail. He said, "Tell me you're going to marry yourself to me and I'll have a mind to make him a present."

"All right, then. I will," I said. Not knowing what love was made up of or how I'd fallen into it, I didn't have myself a choice.

❧

I had to ask my mama what is a hope chest. Oloe said she started to fix me one as soon as she heard about Murray and me. Mama said folks that were better off than us started out hope chests when their girls were no more than five or six years old. They might put in quiltings and linens, embroider work and such like. Some of them set apart bone-china plates or lead crystal even. All so their girls could set up a home when they married themselves. But I was thinking, oughtn't a girl to set up a home even if she never marries herself out? Didn't a solitary girl have any hope to herself, and couldn't she give herself a cedar chest to put hopeful things inside? I couldn't make sense of it.

Oloe figured out a place for it all in her head, though, because she came over to the house once every other day, asking questions about what sort of linens I preferred, and what sort of dishes. What type of thread did I expect running through the embroidered edge of my pillowcases, and like that. Oloe had been making petty monies hiring out her seamstress work since she was sixteen, and what with the fifteen dollars she put towards me and the twenty Mama added from the package box she found, they bought more home goods for me than Murray's house was able to hold swelling out at the sides. I didn't make any objection. Oloe and Mama acted like the way they did for me was nearly as impressive as Murray and me getting together at all.

The worst thing was them making me stand on an old stool chair hours at a time while they were fashioning my wedding dress. There was a thick bolt of ivory sateen leaned up against my leg and everywhere there were snatches of lace, hanging off me in streamers. I'm sure I looked like some kewpie doll stuck full with pins, bending at the arms and the waist whatever way they motioned me, and with a blank look painted on at the face so

I appeared as not to have a single thought of grief or worry working on my mind.

❧

It was completely accidental that I saw Lily Mark riding Remy like she did. The January skies came pale blue and hot, like the center of a flame, and whosoever went without hats showed the tender licks of sunburn across the napes of their necks and down the slopes of their noses. One Saturday, I thought to take myself a rest with Murray under shade, so I packed some hard cheese and sourbread into my carrying sack and I went.

Out at Jackson's property, I saw Lily Mark with Murray, both of them walking out to the corral, one next to the other, and Murray carrying Remy's saddle. From where I stood on the slanted, rocky earth of the drive, they appeared themselves as nothing more than two bright shapes moving in the distance. They could've been anybody, except for the blackness of Lily Mark's hair, which was black like the color of crows in the trees, brilliant and wet-looking even from far away.

Remy arced his neck backwards when Murray put the saddle on him. I didn't hear any of what Lily Mark was saying, but I heard her laughter, turning over in the intervening air, high, then low, then high again. Her dress, which was nothing other than my dress in the beginning, was cut too low on her, so that it bounded her curves. Her bosom, shelved and bountiful, looked like it wished it could get free of its strictures.

When Murray lifted her up to Remy's back, she held to the saddlehorn two-handed, the same as a child. Remy danced his hooves in crazy patterns across the dust, like he would've bucked or reared if Murray hadn't been holding him at the bit. They walked in slow, tense circles around the inside of the ring, concentrating on the movements of Remy's painted legs. I came up to the corral gate and stood on the lower rail, and when Murray turned around the bend and saw me there, he stopped.

"Cass!" he said. "Lily Mark was just saying . . . Lily Mark and me were just . . . we were thinking it would be a shame if Remy was broken to just one individual. He wouldn't be good for anything but pleasure rides if we couldn't accustom him to other people. And when you think of the dollar worth — Cass, think about that — the dollar worth of such an animal as Remy . . ."

I watched Murray's lips working in the heat. They moved darkly, forming the shape of a kiss and then receding away from it again.

"Did you make that horse a present to me?" I said.

"Well, yes," Murray said.

"That's what I thought," I said.

"Of course I did," he said.

"Only he doesn't look like mine just now, what with Lily Mark setting up on top him," I said.

Murray went around to the side of Remy and lifted Lily Mark down off the saddle. Two flush red marks burned in her cheeks, and her eyebrows made a pair of high angry hills, bristly and dark.

"It wasn't but one ride," she said.

"Well, I'll be going home," I said. "Lily Mark, what about you?"

"I'll be along," she said. "In my own time."

When I left them, she was plucking at the folds of her dress, fanning them outwards into the air while she made sure the gathers were free from hay-sticks and burrs.

❧

Tuesday morning, the week before we were to marry ourselves, Murray came over to my house with Remy on a lead and a gold ring in hiding. Remy must have grown two hands in height from when I first saw him, and he followed slowly in back of Murray, walking deliberate and massive in the dust of his own motion.

I was wearing my wedding dress, with Oloe sticking pins to me every side exposed. When she saw Murray through the window, she ran to the door and called out, "You can't talk to her now. She's done up with a dress which you can't see till Saturday."

But I'd already come outside past her. Oloe got a look of shock on her face, at which I smiled outright and said, "It's all right now. The seeing's done."

When Oloe went away, Murray said, "I've brought you one present late and one present early. Remy's overdue — but he's yours, to be ridden by you." Next he produced a thin circle of gold from an inside pocket. I wished he would slide it onto my finger, but he didn't. He just dropped it into my palm, and pressed my hand closed as simple as he might've closed the lid on a box. "And this isn't due till Saturday, but I thought to give it to you now seeing that you might . . . well, I thought to give it now, that's all."

Murray always had right intentions to what he did, so I took the ring from him and I held to Remy's reins like I thought them to be as natural to me as my beating heart. But at the inside I wondered, where did right intentions spark from — and why were they so necessary to a man — and how come Murray's made his face screw up so tight I could barely see that frightened boy running there behind his eyes?

❧

Murray had gone insane with an out-of-control desire, and that's why he did what he did with Lily Mark, most likely. That was the way Oloe told it. She said he had seen those curving shoulders over those cut-low necklines once or twice a week. Frequent enough to drive him over-the-edge crazy with his own secret want. And everybody knew how Lily Mark was angling for him, appearing herself at the Jackson place, saying as how she was just wanting to converse, standing so close under Murray that her plump, pale bosom was all he could look at. It wasn't any surprise to anybody, according to Oloe.

Of course, Oloe coming across the two of them the previous night, that was something she hadn't ever expected. She was almost home to Jensen's, walking by the Sally River, when she nearly fell across them, tangling and clawing one another on the ground so she couldn't tell at the first whether it was love-making or murdering was holding them together. When they caught sight of her standing by, they froze themselves in their motion to the point of holding in their living breath. Oloe didn't let go one word from her mouth. She stepped past them like they were no more than a couple of deer nesting in the dark. But there wasn't any pretending about what was seen or not seen. Oloe was just wretched sorry for me, that was all.

The thing to keep at the front of my mind was that Murray wasn't a man for a lifetime. He didn't have it in him to follow through by his intentions, and that was a dangerous lack in a man by Oloe's experience. If he hadn't broken his honor now with Lily Mark, he would've broken it later with some other fine-looker, and then what mercy would I have found myself? It was true, most likely, that Murray could've held a serious feeling or two for a girl such as me. I was sweet, and diligent-working, and I'd got a fine substance at the inside that Oloe couldn't put a name to. But Murray had shown everybody how he couldn't stand long beside a serious feeling. And I ought to have been grateful for the knowing. To think of me taking vows to that man. To think of how my life would've passed different.

❧

Lily Mark and Murray, they married themselves two days after. Wasn't anything else Murray could do, what with all Copper Crown knowing how he compromised Lily Mark not half a week before he was due to marry himself another. After a month passed, the both of them would decide that the town was too small and its talk was too easy for them to live at the center of its disapproval any longer. They would disappear themselves to north state so far that even fourth- or fifth-hand rumors wouldn't find the ears of us who were desperate for the hearing.

Lily Mark came to the house once. It was directly after the wedding and she was looking to pack up necessities she could call her own — several cotton underslips, two outgrown dresses she brought with her when she first came from Denton, and like that. She talked at me, her voice shaking like she'd kept such a speech boiling inside her years in duration. But her eyes never searched me out. They were hiding a grief she wasn't owning yet. She knew where I was standing by the bedroom door, and she threw her words past her shoulder to me where I caught them full on the breast.

She said, "You got yourself a family that'll take care of you if things go hard. I don't have any of it. I'm all alone and I've had to think that way since I was fourteen years old. Can't anybody blame me for what all I've had to do. I've experienced more on being alone than you're likely to do your whole life. Can't fault me for drawing a man when you don't know anything on maintaining an interest. You're inviting takers and if it hadn't been me, it would've been some other girl that's got more appeal to her ways than you. You can't expect an attracting girl to pass over a man for charity. A man, he has needs, and he can see for himself what girl knows her way around them and what girl doesn't. Consider it, Cass, because if you don't, I swear this isn't the last time chance is going to look you up and down before deciding you don't know anything about what's worth getting yourself and how to keep it for permanent."

❧

For awhile, I thought to myself if only I could talk to Murray one last time, I might come to an understanding as to why things ended up like they did. There were reasons to every turn that swerved a simple life. Had to have been. Sometimes you came into their knowing and sometimes you didn't, and this time I wanted awful bad to have been the other side of ignorant. But Mama said, "Cass, you aren't ever going to get any explanations from Murray, because you aren't ever going to be standing by him face to face. Never again your whole life. I saw it in a dream." So I let that hoping die early.

Mama said I wasn't ever a girl that had the inclining nor the wiles neither to use a man for a selfish direction. She said I was better not to listen to anything Lily Mark had said, because Lily Mark lived by her own code — a code that destroyed most good things around her and would probably end up by destroying her, too. Such a girl expected that the only power the world saw in her was the power of her shape. So she used it like a key or a knife or a word, hoping it would give her something in return, which it hardly ever did.

I said, "But Mama, I'm mourning how Lily Mark said one thing that was true. I know I'm young. I've got time at fifteen years old. But it's true how I don't know anything about lovemaking to a man. How my lips ought to turn for kissing him, how my hands ought to reach for touching him. I don't know any of that and maybe Murray found it out and maybe he —"

"Lack of experience doesn't count for that

much in life." Mama brought her two fingers one beside the other. "You're going to grow up to be the lovingest woman of all in this family. I see it clear. There are going to be many people that show you ways to express it outwards.

"From the time you were a baby, I saw in you how you had a great loving at your heart. And that's something couldn't anybody manufacture might it be missing, and can't anybody steal away now that it's yours for true. Think on it like a present direct from God, because blessed child, that's what it is."

❧

What with Lily Mark gone and Oloe out to Jensen's, I had a sleeping room to myself the first time in my life. Nothing filled it up but the sound of my night breathing, slow and deep-going with the color of my sleep. Sometimes, I woke in the motionless dark to see my empty wedding dress where it was still hanging at the wardrobe door. It looked so old and hollow, it seemed like something I had died inside of. Mama and me, we took it down in time eventual and sealed it in a garment box, with two lace sachets of dried orange rinds and fancy cloves.

Mama said, "You always carry this with

you, Cass, wheresoever you travel in life. Could be you'll need it again."

I said, "Are you saying I will?"

"No," she said, "I'm not." The corners of her full, gray eyes were folded downward, like from sleepiness or pity. "I wish God saw clear for me to get inclinations on everything in life, but He doesn't, and I mostly have to watch the days unfolding ignorant of what all is going to happen, like everybody else."

"I don't have much need for wondering what is going to happen anymore," I said. "Feels like all the big things that can happen to a person have happened to me already."

Mama laughed out. "You're sorrowing," she said. "Sorrowing can't hold up under the stare of time. You're going to see more on life's big things than you know as exist when you think on it now."

Still, Mama thought I'd do better through my sorrowing time if Oloe would move back from Jensen's and give me the old comforts of my sister sleeping beside me in the same room. Oloe had started sewing for a new client, though, who had put in five dresses to order. She said she needed the sewing space the Jensens gave her until the end of summer, when she'd pack up her thread and her bodice frames and move back to home, where I was needing her to remind me of the dreams that used to fill up my nights so that I could get me some of them back.

❧

I tried to think whether anybody I knew was really in love. Not a temporary, hurry-up, sometime kind of love, but a rooted, deathless, ever-on kind. It seemed to me that if I could just find one example of ever-on love, then that would make up for all the people who went through life disappointed. Because part of the disappointment was in thinking that love was just a wish or a dream or a girlish idea and not something you could live with day to day.

I thought about my mama and my daddy. Whatever it was they had between them, it was enough to see them past the dwarfed corn that grew in their fields and the sour pork they lived on all winter, and the blond dust that sifted into and out of their clothes all the day. It was enough to give them tenderness in the quiet moments at night when my daddy would braid my mama's hair into a thick, chestnut chain — his ragged, earth-colored fingers trembling at the very softness they held, his touch gone clumsy in its longing. But I always thought of it as the kind of love that would someday have an end. When they shouted at one another, there was so much simple sincerity about it. There was so much painful vigor. *You've always been this way,* they would say. *I only wonder that I've lived with it so long.* And then there were the silent, fragile days that followed, when all the words my mama held inside welled in the grayness of her eyes, ripening there in a sadness that was no longer young or strange to her.

I would've asked Oloe whether she knew anyone with an ever-on love, but considering she always said she wanted to get married at seventeen, and that was a year past, and there still wasn't any man she would look at a second time, it seemed a selfish question. At that time, she liked to pretend sewing was the only thing she cared about. Her bleary doe's eyes blinked feverishly under sunlight. Her fingertips were pressed into the shapes of her thimbles. Her hair was pulled straight upwards into a pillbox bun, and underneath it her neck was thinner than I remembered — with all the cords showing.

"Are you happy?" I said.

"I guess I'm busier than I've ever been," Oloe said. She put her cloth down in her lap and rubbed her eyes. The veins in her lids stood out like tiny blue rivers, like hairline cracks in porcelain. "The coloreds don't like me here," she said.

"Why not?"

"Because of something last week," Oloe said. "I would've made it right if I could have."

I watched a dragonfly come through the window, its wings going brilliant in the light.

"I'm sure you would have," I said.

❧

It was the Tuesday last, and Oloe was going home to Jensen's. Her shoes were wetted from where she had walked along the edge of the Sally River, and every time she took a step, her laces squeaked. Close on by, in the three-acre cornfield, Jensen and his men were pulling long withered stalks out of the earth and piling together the leafy skeletons. Oloe had just about walked past them when Uncle Jensen called out to her. "Wait a minute," he said. "Oloe, you stay where you're standing." She stopped still at the edge of the road. Over the steep bank, the colored workers continued clearing the corn — their shirts at their waists from all the noon heat. They were acting like they didn't hear anything Jensen said, their eyes drawn down toward the ground like they were concentrating hard on something there — a spray of roots maybe, or a stubborn rock.

"Oloe," Uncle Jensen said, "one of these boys was watching you when you were walking by. Stopping his work, and watching you like you were something fresh for his eyes to get a hold of. Were you aware of that, girl?"

Oloe said, "No sir. I wasn't." There wasn't any telling him he was wrong in what he'd perceived. Uncle Jensen walked down to where the men were turning his earth. His hand took the hair of the man closest by him, and jerked his head back. It was someone Oloe had seen a few times before, Carlyle Lamar.

Jensen said, "Boy, what were you thinking on while you were looking so long on my girl?"

Carlyle had a hundred drops of perspiring making one great shining of his face. His lips were dry at the edges, like they had been salted and turned towards the sun. He said, "Mr. Jensen, I wasn't looking on her."

Uncle Jensen looked up at Oloe where she stood in the road. "All right, Oloe," he said. "You go on and stay to the house now. I've found out the way of it. Don't you worry."

And Oloe went, gathering her skirts in her hands and working her legs at just the under-rhythm of a run. She shut herself in at her bedroom, pulling all her windows to, and working to sew a good ten minutes before she heard it. Carlyle was shouting. Jensen's white men were walking him out to the back field, where the silvergrass grew as high as your shoulder. And Carlyle was shouting, "I ain't done nothing! She'll tell you I ain't. Not looked on, not spoke at, not nothing! She'll tell you if you ask her. She will!"

But Oloe stayed in her room like Uncle Jensen had said for her to. She was afraid of what might come if she spoke out. Uncle Jensen might've got the idea she was partial to Carlyle, when really they hadn't said two words to each other. She knew the coloreds would hate her from that day on — and she was right. They did. They came to hate her with a burning at the soul. For her silence. For her obeying ways. For her uncle. They never knew how she cried for Carlyle like she cried for herself, toiling and lonely in the last winter of her life.

❧

Sometimes, after I left Oloe, I'd go straight to Allie's house, nestled in the juniper and the China trees. My daddy didn't like me going there unless I had a bake order to drop off, but the truth was that Allie's was the only place that eased my abandonment. When I sat inside that kitchen, a stray tabby cat sleeping on my lap and a glass of sun tea in my hands,

I nearly forgot I had been an almost bride and I thought of love again as a longing without thorns, growing somewhere out of sight.

Allie baked until six o'clock, when her mama and her brother, Clyde, came home from Jensen's. They climbed Marston's hill with the small, careful steps of the injured — the toes on her mama's feet pointing inwards like a child's. Clyde stopped every so often and shook his shirt out in the wind, trying to air it dry before he would put it on again at the front door of his new one-room house, sitting twenty yards away from the old one. Inside, his new wife was waiting, her arms sunk to the elbows in the laundry basin, her hair running down her back in a dark waterfall.

"Did you bring that cat with you again?" Allie's mama said.

"I don't know where she came from," I said.

"Well, that's all right," she said. "We like her and she knows it." She ran her hand over the cat's orange-and-cream striped muzzle. "I'm going straight to bed, honey."

"Okay, Mama," Allie said. "You want me to bring something in to you?"

"I ain't hungry for it."

"Some egg bread?" Allie said.

"Not tonight."

Allie's mama walked into the bedroom and

lifted her dress over her head. It was wet through the back and some of the dye had bled blue onto her shoulders. Allie noticed it, and she saw me notice it, too.

"It's bad cloth," she said. And then, a little later, "Let's go outside."

All over the valley, the greens of the Copper Crown lilies were uncurling new leaves. They stained the plain grass with their clusters of brightness, their throats gaping skywards, waiting for the season's rains. The hawks were out, spiraling above the dusk and never coming any lower. I liked the way their wingtips looked like open hands, with the feathers splayed, reaching.

"Do you know anybody in love?" I said.

"What you want to ask me that for?" she said. She took the tabby cat out of my arms and sat down with it in front of the China tree.

"I've been thinking about it and I don't know," I said.

"My brother, he loves Maggie," she said.

"The ever-on kind of love?"

"Ain't that the only kind?" Allie said. The cat was cradled in the crook of her arm, smiling the smile of mice dreams.

"Anyway, it's the best kind," I said.

"Yeah," Allie said. "If anybody got it, they do."

"Tell me how it found them."

"From the start?" she said.

"From wherever."

"Right now?"

"Mm-hmm," I said.

Allie smoothed her skirt underneath her, she pressed her cut-glass earring between two fingers, and then she took her hand away from her face. "All right," she said. "This is the beginning."

❧

Clyde went to Jensen's the day he turned fourteen. My mama said to him don't you do it. Said Jensen going to turn you into a old man before you has even finished being a boy. And it been true. But Clyde, he went his own way. Jensen put him on threshing, the same as if he been full-growed. It wasn't a year before he started in to lose his teeth, whether from fighting or sickening we didn't know what all.

Still, Clyde didn't have any lack for girlfiends, and it been a year ago in summer that he took up with the launder girl from Olson's, Maggie, who most folks agreed was the prettiest woman, white, black, or in between, they'd seen in three counties and thirty years. Maggie looked direct past Clyde's missing front teeth to find there the biggest heart a boy ever growed for a girl, and she never give a thought to his outside looks since. Because that was the type of girl Maggie been. She seen for true.

When Clyde got so's his heart couldn't beat regular no more for swelling with love, he knew he had to marry hisself to her. Her beauty stood before him even when his eyes was closed, so that her rich plum lips like the color of longing, and her acorn eyes, light and wood-grained and clear-seeing to the ends of the world — them things never left him. My mama said later that the one thing Clyde didn't account for was how beauty, whether in man or woman or child, always brung its price.

The week after the wedding, Clyde and his friend, Carlyle, and some of the others from Jensen's harvesting built up the small freestand house for them to live in, there. Clyde and Maggie wasn't moved in two nights before the mens come from up-road, holding their empty rye jugs and their low lanterns. I's sure I recognized the voices of Karl Olson and the Frank boys one Saturday night, but the mens mostly come in twos and threes and every time the voices was different. There wasn't no pinning nobody down.

The mens stood themselves in the yard and hollered, "Nigra boy. We want some of what you got. Nigress like that got to be too much for one run-down dark boy like yourself. We's just looking to share, now. We's fair-minded, ain't we boys? We's going to give her back."

Even at daytimes, when Clyde was working at Jensen's, the yellow-eyed payroll man would ride him about Maggie. He hadn't got any choice but to fight outright, and evenings sometimes brung him home bruised blue and breathing painful for the cracks in his ribs. The more Maggie got aggrieved the more beautiful she growed.

Once she said to me, "God help me, your brother be killing hisself for me and there ain't any way I has found out to turn it around."

❧

It got to be so Maggie couldn't go nowhere without somebody along for protection. Days when Clyde was working, I walked beside her to the mercantile and back. I told her it'd be safer if she stayed to home days and nights both, but Maggie said she wasn't going to die a living death, locked in scared at the house. If fears wasn't getting smaller, they was getting bigger and she wasn't about to help them along in the second direction.

Mens thought on Maggie to such a amount them days, seemed like they had made her into a idea outside herself entire. They drank their narrow eyes full of her long, easy-cut curves, and they decided she been the single location of desire

— dark and untouched like the shapes in their dreams.

If a man could speak to her without anybody hearing, he'd say, "I wants you to come see me about something." But Maggie would act like he'd never spoke, hiding her disgust behind her half-closed eyes, pressing it backwards of the curl in her lips. And then he'd speak out louder, angrier, "Tomorrow. Don't make me send somebody to come get you now."

❧

One time, Maggie and me, we was walking back from town by the River Road when we heard men's voices above the sounds of flowing water. The cottonwoods bent close over us, like the voices might've been coming from the sparrows' holes bored in their trunks, rounded and hollow and wide open as mouths. In the distance, five mens appeared themselves — white, all of them. They had their arms over their shoulders such that, side by side, they covered the road width entire, leaving no ground for nobody to pass by. Tom McAllum was there, and Jensen's mens, Jake and Kemy Frank, too. They all turned quiet when they saw me and Maggie. Kemy Frank whispered something into the ear of his brother, and they both laughed close-mouthed, the air whistling through their noses. They were like little boys with a plan of mischief, holding their breaths with excitement over how it was to turn out.

Maggie said, "They's trouble bad."

I said, "You don't think they going to let us pass by?"

"Not if they has a say about it," Maggie said.

"Then let's go back the way we come."

"They just going to catch us up," Maggie said.

"Well, I ain't going to wait on them," I said.

The mens was coming up all the while. Tom had a pinch of chewing tobacco in his cheek and he spat twice on the dull cover of the road, and then ground out the mark with his shoe.

"You follow along with me," Maggie said. "I might see can I get us out of this yet."

Maggie screamed once before she dropped to the ground, but that was all the warning she give. She thrashed and jerked her limbs like a animal gone rabid, all tremors and sweat and scrambling in the dirt. Her teeth was locked together hard, but a white foam was making its way out between. Her breath hissed over her gums like the sound of a evil wish. The sack of flour she dropped had tore its length and broke open to the road, and before a minute had passed, it was swarmed with ants, red-backed and frantic.

"Maggie! Maggie!" I cried out. Then I turned to the mens. "You going to just stand there looking on, or you going to do something to help her?

She having another fit. The spells! Ain't you ever seen it?! Lord!"

The mens had took their arms down from one the other. I don't think they would've give two cents' care if it hadn't been Maggie, but there was the woman they had been setting their lustings to, writhing from a fit in the filth of the road. One or two of them was alarmed. I could see it in the smallness of their looks.

"Get the doctor to come," I said. "Old man Cannel. He the only one knows what to do."

So the mens, they went away, walking off to Dr. Cannel's, who wasn't a doctor really, but just a old man what owned a medical book and claimed he knowed how to read it. Soon as they had disappeared themselves past a corner of the road, Maggie stopped her flailing, wiped off the spittle from her face, and started off to run home, pulling me beside her.

"How did you get such a idea at your mind?" I said out, lacking from breath.

"I has had a lot of time for thinking to myself," Maggie said. "But don't you imagine they ain't coming back. They going to find them dry goods spilt in the road, with us no ways beside, and they going to know it for a trick. Ain't nothing wrong with tricks except you can't never use the same one twice."

"We'll think us up new ones, then," I said. "Only I use them up as fast as I get them fig-

ured," Maggie said. "Coming a time soon where I's all but run out."

❧

But what I want to tell you is, Clyde and Maggie, they has seen one the other through it. They took all the meanness and the catcalling they could stand, and they come out the other side. Maggie, she going to have a baby in September, and for the first time I can think on, mens is leaving her be. There ain't none following her store by store when she go for supplies into town. There ain't none coming out to the house to shout for her Saturday nights. There ain't even anybody riding Clyde anymore out at Jensen's. Some of his old hurtings is getting the chance to heal themselves whole like they never done previous, and he's standing high on a pride for the works of his seed. This be the closest the two of them has ever got to living in peace, and the way I sees it, it's love of the realest kind that's brung them this far.

❧

Seemed like Allie ought to have kept on talking, but she didn't. That's all there was to tell, I guess. I looked at the shack, twenty yards away, that was Clyde's and Maggie's stand-alone house. Light came from behind the single window, muted and green on the other side of a thin set of curtains. When somebody inside moved a certain way, the curtains turned a shade darker, becoming the color of slash pines, halfway between green and black. The sounds of voices mumbled just over the rhythm of cicadas, private in their meanings. White moths lay flat-winged against the ground, struck still by the last of the day's heat.

Allie tilted her head back against the China tree like she was readying herself for sleep. With her eyes closed, she could've been a mystic, dreamful and removed, looking down on the world from some wise place. I wondered what stories she held inside that she had never spoken. Stories of love or strife she had never even hinted around the edges of. And I'd always thought Allie told me everything.

I went inside and set my glass of sun tea in the kitchen. When I came back out, Allie's lips had drifted apart in her sleep. In her left hand, she clutched the tail of the dozing cat, the fur gone thin and flat under the dampness of her palm.

I touched Allie's arm. "See you tomorrow," I said.

The corner of her mouth twitched once. "Mm-hmm."

Down Marston's hill and through the valley beyond it, the wetness collected in the grass in glassy, glittered drops that caught the light of the sky and threw it back like the eyes of wild things. The trees stood up at the roadside with their green yearnings revealed, their stiff fingers chafing under a small wind. On the oleander trees, the blossoms hung in crumpled, pink rags, scattered over the curtains of leaves like a last-minute thought. Everything held a strangeness inside it that made it somehow new — even my house, with its black-eyed windows and propped-out door, waiting for its homecomings with a wonder that looked like mine.

❧

Mama saw a vision to end the world. It came to her in a dream full with house burnings and night killings and terrors absolute, and when it was all done with, she woke from it crying and shaking like it was to start over complete, but for real this time, as she sat watching.

Daddy was angry at being woken at the death of night. He said, "Mother, there's a war that's been going four months now. You're not seeing anything that hasn't been told in the newspapers already."

"No, no," Mama said. "This isn't the war in Europe. I didn't see that at all. It was Copper Crown that was razed and burned — these lands, these neighbors, these children," she said, holding to me sudden at my shoulders.

Daddy and me, we tried to quiet her mind, but after two hours we realized there was nothing for it. We left her staring out the window by the sitting room, talking to herself and crying softly, like the crazy aged who think no one is hearing. She kept whimpering, "There's a fire, there's a fire burning high and don't anybody see it but me."

After that night, Mama took to herself strange ways. Instead of conversing at supper, she read out loud from horrible chapters of the Bible's judgment book. *And the devil that deceived them was cast into the lake of fire and brimstone, where the beast and the false prophet are, and shall be tormented day and night for ever and ever.* She started blessing everyone who came into or went out of the house, including Remy when I put him back in his ring — drawing an invisible cross in the air with her hand. And she set up late, sometimes into the morning, staring out the downstairs window and speaking her vision over and over.

If I was to bring her upstairs and get her dressed in her sleep clothes, she'd go right on talking. "There's a fire," she'd say. "There's a fire burning high and I can't put it out."

❧

In spite of Mama's predictions, Copper Crown stayed peaceful through spring. The Ladies' Society put up its annual May Day's fair that had a baking contest worked in. Every person who entered was a white lady and a married lady both, but nobody I knew could show you any printed-up rules that said it had to be that way. Me and Mama thought to enter one of Allie's coffee-chocolate cakes for us to measure how her baking compared with others'. I had never seen Allie more thrilled over mischief-making, and she turned her sweet butter, ground her coffee beans, and shaved curls off her chocolate like she was working alchemy with a sure recipe for gold.

At the Ladies' Fair, Allie's cake set three-layer tall and three-chocolate rich next to Aunt Pauline's rum pecan, Mrs. Frank's spicy pound, and such like. The judges walked backwards and forwards tasting so many times I thought they were stalled on their decision. But they ended by picking the choicest cake, even if it was put forward by a girl and her mama who had never baked more than a passable sweet. Allie was crazy happy when I gave her the blue prize ribbon and the ten dollars.

"It was the best one?" she kept asking. "My chocolate was the best one?"

"First place," I said. "Only it's too bad can't everybody know the prize belongs to you."

Allie said, "Don't matter much. Some one of these days, everybody going to know I's the finest cook there is. Don't hurt us none to know it a little while in private first."

❧

Allie's mama fell bad sick that month, with the heat of fever that came along with cholera. Allie stayed by her most every day, sponging her down for cooling, or lying atop the blanket to keep off the chills.

That was the spring, too, when we got thunderstorms that cross-cut the county end to end. Where lightning reached the ground, touch-fires were started, just to flare up and exhaust themselves in the rains following. The livestock were all quick to shy. They smelled the thunder from where it was rolling in, miles away, and there wasn't anything could soothe them till the storm was hours past. Remy had grown so large, Daddy said our ring rail couldn't hope to keep him contained. The fence set at the line of his knees, and he stayed inside it for a sense of the order of things and nothing more. But lightning always pushed him to jump and then disappear himself off at the woods somewhere.

Most often, I'd locate Remy in a sloping field on Marston's hill which had set to full bloom with yellowlace and bluebells. The flowers sprouted out of his mouth in sad bunches when we found him, chewing up his petals like it was hard work but meaningful, and owing to that, he preferred no interruptions.

From where Allie's mama was lying she could look out her narrow window to watch Remy, dwarfing Marston's meadow and eating up all its bluebells, and the vision made her laugh. Allie said she was always calling out to him when she saw him, trying to coax him to come up closer so she might get a better sight. But Remy stayed out to the far end of the clearing, roaming shy and skittery for all his eighteen hands.

Only time he ever came near was the day Allie's mama died, when he walked up to the house like something unseeable was pulling him there, and reached his brown-and-white-patch head full-extended through the frame to hear the dying woman's words, "Oh, Allie, that horse come to touch my soul when it be flying out the window just a minute from now."

❧

Graves never keep their shape. They start off being hills, naked and faceless in the fields where you find them. But then there's the rain that sinks the soil downwards in a collapse that's so filled with sorrow, the eye can never see it. There's the wind that picks up the dust with one hundred senseless hands and carries it to the front paths of as many fresh-painted houses, where it collects in a film on the shoes of the passersby. So that finally the grave is a hollow, a depression where the loved have rested for awhile before seeming to go away again, somewhere, in a form you couldn't dream on.

The thing Allie grieved on most was how her mama took secrets away with her when she died. How she came to Copper Crown in the early years, who she fell to loving once she got there, who Allie's daddy had been, and all like that. Her mama had got herself histories inside that hadn't ever been spoken to her children, and now that she had died, they were likely to be lost forever. Seemed an intolerable waste to Allie. A person dying ought to give more for others to remember them by than flat speakings like, "She was a good woman" or "She raised up her children right."

Allie said, "It's hard to love a person that don't let themselves be knowed. But that's what I done. That's what I still be doing."

I said, "That was what she wanted."

"She didn't leave open no other way," Allie said.

Allie went on like that for several months, talking out sorrows for what wasn't in her knowing. Only subject I tried that made her forget her grief was her sister-in-law. Maggie was showing large with the life inside her, taking on melon-curve lines with the time going past. Allie liked to rub her feet at the end of the day, when the gray, swollen undersides of Maggie's toes would blush pink again and she would loose great sighs of comfort from where she stretched out on her bed. Afterwards, she would let Allie press a hand to her womb to feel the sloshing of the baby rolling over in its quiet sea. Allie always gasped to feel the motion. "It dancing under my palms!" she would say.

Maggie would just lie silent, her arms angled out at her sides, bony and broken-winged. It seemed to me she had grown grieved as her belly had grown wide — her eyes shining out sadder with their splendor than before she'd got big — like she was holding back a secret of her own that the whole world would cry over when she gave it up.

❧

If somebody had asked me, I would have said it'd be a cold day in June before I'd ever see Lily Mark again. And it was. For close on a week we watched as the late storms blew in. The clouds rushed through the sky, tight-fisted and boiling, with sheets of water falling from between their huge, gray fingers. Everyone was saying how if the rains came an inch more heavy or an hour more fast, the earth would wash itself clean with flash floodings that would turn over crops and trees and houses all the same. But the floods didn't come that year. The land opened up its wide, dry mouth and swallowed the water into its sandy, root-crossed depths. And on the same day the land was filled, the sky was suddenly empty. All we had to remember the storms by was a thin-misting shower and a bank of pink-fingered clouds, staining the north horizon.

Lily Mark came in out of the rain like she had only been gone on a temporary walk. Her hair was falling down into her eyes, black and plastered wet. On her skirt, there were patterns of mud curling like brown vines in amongst the folds. Where her waist ought to have been there was a rounded, settled thickness that said she was with child. She looked to be in her sixth month of carrying, though I could've been wrong by two weeks or three. In one hand she held a cloth sack which, when she opened it later, contained a hairbrush and a high-collar blouse, and that was all.

"I'm by myself," she said. "I mean, I'm as you see."

Mama drew the sign of the cross at the air, in front of Lily Mark's face. She said, "Murray?"

Lily Mark motioned her head in a nod. She said, "He left me in city three months back."

Mama said, "You weren't showing any then?" She was finger-combing Lily Mark's hair back from her eyes, drying her face with a towel.

Lily Mark said, "No. I wasn't wanting to tell him about it either."

"I wish you had told him," Mama said. "It would've gone better with you." She was already helping Lily Mark up the stairs, holding an arm around her thickened, wet waist. "Copper Crown isn't a good place to come back to just now. Didn't you know? I've had myself a vision on it . . ."

❧

To my way of thinking, Allie and me were both first-girls-in-waiting to our pregnant women. Allie had got Maggie to do for, and me, I had got Lily Mark. I had never known before that time how little an expecting woman and her food like to be parted one from the other. I couldn't see Lily Mark waking without one hand on a biscuit and the other spooning jam. Some doctor in the city had told her this wasn't any time to hold down on her appetite, so she'd taken him at his word and gone on to expand her dress size to a 20, and then a 22. Towards the end of her time, it got so that half of Mama's bake orders were consisting of special requests put in by Lily Mark. Every time I walked through Allie's door to hand her the bake list, she looked down it and laughed.

"Don't that woman feel guilty about eating your pantry back to front and then cornering up the crumbs off your floor?" Allie said.

"She says she's hungry all the time," I said.

"I believe she is," Allie said. "First it was mens, now it be food. I *guess* she be hungry. And it never be enough for one what's got a hollow at the inside like she's looking to fill. She keeps grabbing out — at peoples, at bakings, at what all she can get — but that hollow, it's going to stay empty."

"I know what you mean," I said. "And I wish it wasn't. I honestly wish she could be filling it."

Allie said, "Ain't you lost too much to Lily Mark to be hoping on that?"

"I thought so when she first came back," I said. "But then she told me how Murray had turned to spite her at the end, how he said he hadn't ever excused her or himself for what they had done initial, and how two people can't build a life when they can't find their own mercy. And I see how she pains under carrying the child of a man who doesn't love her, who won't ever come back, and — I know it's folly, Allie — but I think on all that and I almost forgive her. Isn't it a miracle? But I almost do."

❧

The last time in our lives when Daddy and me passed a whole day together was one occasion that summer. With Lily Mark getting on into her eighth month of carrying, she had got herself a hard pain around the cradle of her swelling. Mama, who had seen a hundred carryings if she had seen one, said it was a tear in the muscle that Dr. Westle ought to give a prescription for. So Daddy and me, we drove Lily Mark out to the doctor's, got her looked after, and were winding home when a wheel on the buckboard split through.

Lily Mark was sitting cushioned in a nest of hay. She was eating dark, ripe persimmons from a sack cloth, and her lips were puckering full and painted-on red, the way persimmons do them. "We going to set here, outside of shade?" Lily Mark said. "This heat's going to crawl all up my neck and cut off my breath."

Daddy climbed down off the driver's seat. He looked out from his stone-blue stare at the hot, flat miles of the narrowing road. He appeared to be impressing the distance onto his mind's eye, like if he concentrated hard enough, he might contain it. Cicadas were thrumming in the fields, and above their heads, a stand of yellow wildflowers wavered. The thrushes and the doves were silent in their nests. Daddy must have stood gazing straight ahead for close on an hour. I thought he was heat-struck, or dream-walking, his eyes full open like they were.

Then he said, "Someone's coming up." Where the road narrowed so far that it reached a point, I saw a round of dust rising. Some time later, the dust grew a horse, and the horse grew a wagon, and the wagon grew a single colored man driving it all forward.

Daddy stopped him at the road and made him change wheels. When we drove off, the man stood staring after us, his hat in his hands, like we might think better of it any minute and go back for him. When Daddy saw me looking after him, he said, "Only a nigra. Some other'n will stop for him."

"I've run through my sack cloth," Lily Mark was saying. "We have any more of those ripe persimmons?"

❧

Hard to think on how that was a time before I knew death. I'd lost people, sure, but I'd lost them to other housings, like Oloe, or to other lovings, like Murray. I still knew they walked the earth's curve, with their own doings and their own ways, with their own dreams that once they had imagined with me. And I knew they weren't lost to me completely that way. Not like I thought death could lose people to me. But I was sixteen then and I hadn't seen half the ways of living and dying that were bound for my eyes.

Mama said I was getting wisdom by spurts and jumps, like some people got aged. They went along for years at a time looking and acting unchanged. And then, in the space of a single night, they grew their gray hairs, spun their webbing wrinkles, and shrunk their height an inch or two — like they were catching up to where they ought to have been all the while.

Me, I was going months without feeling any wiser in my blood, while a time was coming when, under the sky of a few days and nights, I'd get me an understanding I wouldn't ever let go of — an understanding of death and its workings that threw back a light on all living so that it never appeared itself so beautiful.

❧

The world gave up all its fruit at the same time. The second bloom of strawberries fell heavy off the vine when we moved our hands under them, and up at the trees, pink-meat figs and rosy peaches were hanging in their clusters. The air was rich with the last days of summer, and through it flew full-fed blackbirds and glossy finches searching for seed laid to open ground.

Mama started to talk of her visions half the waking day. Most people, including Daddy, thought her mind was disappearing itself from her body — shrinking gradually to the smooth, round shape of a marble that rolled its words of craziness through so many empty rooms. But Oloe and me, we believed in Mama being blessed with the sight, and her words, prophet-sounding and confused, remembered themselves to us in our dreams at night.

Mama said, "It's a time for harvest, but the harvest is empty. It's a time for fruit, but the tree is crooked. People, they're laughing, but their sorrow will follow. Can't a person stop it now. Can't you or me stop it now."

One time Mama was talking that way when Lily Mark cried out from her chair. She looked at Mama as shocked as if someone was coming after her with a kitchen knife. "It's the time," Lily Mark said. Her hands were gripping the table so tight, they started turning white from the nails on up. She said, "Shut up them crazy words! I'm telling you it's the time!"

I took Lily Mark upstairs and put her to bed. She pained horribly for two nights and two days. I stayed up with her, changing her bedclothes and freshening her water stand, and not knowing what all else I ought to have been tending. Mama was staying awake, too, but she didn't help me any. She just sat talking in the empty kitchen, crying now and then about how she couldn't change things anyway, even if she tried.

On the morning of the third day, Mama

came upstairs to where Lily Mark was lying and said, "Two babies will be born this day, breathing in the bastard breath. Their mothers' cries, they reach past the earth, and heaven hears them like one voice — one single, crying voice."

❧

Lily Mark, she held on to her baby so tight, she died trying not to give it up. I remember how, after it was born and suckling at her breast, she looked up at me and said, "Oh, Cass, my life's running out of me. I came through all this, and now my life's running out. Isn't it a wretched thing?"

When the doctor got there three hours later, he said it was a hemorrhage. Couldn't anything have been done for bleeding such as that. He had seen it before and the mothers always died. Double tragic, because then the babies had so little chance of living past the first few days. But then this baby, Lily Mark's baby, looked a good deal stronger than most. Eight plus a half pounds for a birthing weight and fully developed for its nine months' growing. Lily Mark was well fed, that much was sure, and it ended by giving her child a margin's chance for living.

A month or two back, Lily Mark had told

me if she was carrying a girl, she would be naming it Ruby, for her mama. So that's the name I gave. I didn't remember much on my aunt Ruby, but Mama said she had carried a tender heart and a laughing voice, and that we would never find any better name for this child.

Ruby was born with a full head of blue-black hair, which I thought was bound to grow out handsome like Lily Mark's. And her fingers and toes were long and tapering, probably owing to the height of Murray, Mama said. I held her tight to my bosom, thinking a moment on how I might be holding Murray and Lily Mark's night at the Sally River. But it didn't matter any. Ruby was living and breathing and beautiful-made, and while I cradled her there at the inside of my arms, nothing in my world looked more blessed than her.

❧

Baby Ruby lacked desperately for milk. The doctor left Mama and me a powder-mix formula that Ruby ought to have accustomed her taste to after a few days, but in the beginning, she wasn't holding with it. So I took baby Ruby out to Marston's hill, thinking maybe Allie might have herself an idea. I wrapped

Ruby loosely in a broad cotton blanket so she would keep cool under the pressing air. She slept nearly the whole way out, her face in the shadow of the buckboard seat that rocked and creaked over the ruts in the road. I remembered the doctor's warning that if she was sleeping through the day, she had probably lost too much water. And when I leaned over in the seat to check on her, I saw that her lips were chapped and cracking at the edges.

When we came to Marston's, it looked like the whole world had gone to grief. Maggie had delivered herself of her child, and she was sitting up, faded and wailing high, at Allie's place. She was rocking her child in her arms, but he seemed to know how everybody was wretched sad around him, because he cried out like he had been born to a world that was built by sorrow and wished he could've crawled back inside his mother before he ever saw it. Paths of weeping rolled down the sides of Allie's eyes, too, and her hands wrung one the other like they were rags, limp and ragged and raw.

When she saw me standing at the door, with baby Ruby all in a bundle, she came to me crying. She said, "Cassie, oh! Cassie, oh! Maggie's birthed a baby so white at the skin. Sooo white. Not a mark of Clyde on him. Nowheres, oh! Nowheres."

She went on as how Clyde wouldn't suffer Maggie or the child to stay resting in their own bed. He had picked them both up, bedclothes and all, to put crying in the dust outside his door. He'd got a fury working at his mind, and no amount of pleading nor reasons would've calmed it. Only one Clyde would open the door to was Carlyle, and they had kept themselves locked inside for close on four hours.

I had told Allie about Lily Mark, and I was just turning to go home again when Maggie called me back. She said, "The baby's needing me. Ain't that what you come for?" I don't think she gave me time to answer before she took Ruby to her, baring her breast and giving her suckle. Ruby was aching for drink. She held up both her tiny hands to press onto Maggie's full breast, and I watched a single drop of pearly milk escape past her pursing lips and roll down into her hair. Maggie was holding up baby Ruby by the one arm and cradling her own newborn child by the other.

"See how she takes to me?" Maggie said, crying. "God made up babies so wise. They don't know nothing about colorings, but they know all about love. And I got me that to give, ain't I, Allie? Ain't I got me love?"

❧

Here's how it happened. It wasn't but several days after Maggie had possumed that seizure when the men had come for her a second time. It was mid-morning and Clyde had been out to Jensen's several hours already. Maggie was sudsing the town laundry she took in once a week, and she was singing to herself content like she always did when her and Clyde first married themselves. The men walked in through the half-open door, their shoes in their hands so as not to make a sound. The first thing that told Maggie she wasn't by herself was the hand that shut like a closing door across her mouth and nose so that she was fighting for the thinnest air to come pulling through the cracks.

They took her with a hate that made their hands tremble for all its workings. They were burning to wring the life out of whatever living soul fell into their grasp, and that morning, Maggie was the one. "They's making to kill me," Maggie was thinking. "To use me up in all their fury, and to throw me out like a wasted thing." And by God's truth, she did feel like they were wasting her complete — like they were reaching into the furthest corners of her heart and planting a spoil there that wouldn't ever get cleaned out — like they were setting a sickness to her spirit that wouldn't ever get well. All she could do was stare at the soap-filled washing rag she was still gripping tight with her hand, and watch while those suds ran out through her fingers and down onto the floor, where they disappeared themselves through the cracks in the plankings and down into the center of the earth, with all that was good.

Maggie knew if she had told any of it to Clyde, he would've lost his life in the madness that was likely to take hold. So she kept her crying at the inside. And even later, when she found she was carrying child, she couldn't bring herself to steal his happiness out of him.

"How could I break him?" Maggie said, after years were passed, and she was looking back on it. "It was the last goodness his heart was ever to know — and for a man what ain't knowed much, he took it to him like he been making it a nesting place his whole life long."

❧

Sometimes, as the eye of the hell-turned wind passes over, there is a circle of stillness. A center of quiet, of peace almost, that doesn't tell anything about the after-violence that's going to come searing through. We were in it then — the eye, I mean — and you would think the whole town ought to have known it, but scarcely anybody did. Allie and Maggie and Mama and me, maybe. That's all, as I'm guessing it. Nobody that had the powers for convincing or altering. Nobody that could change things the way they were going.

From where I set at home, I could feel how Clyde and Carlyle were still locked in at their house. Door shut hard, windows down tight, and all that rage boiling up at the inside with no way to get out. Their fury was frothing so high, they were changing the air pressure the way I was breathing under it. It was only a matter of hours before we felt their revenge exploding outwards, shaking down our houses, leaving us wandering our sooty, wasted land to find out our own debris.

At home, Daddy had told Mama to get Lily Mark ready for burying, but she wouldn't have any of it. She looked politely in his direction while he was talking, and when he asked her did she understand, she motioned yes, she did. Then she walked solemnly back to her place in the kitchen, set herself back down, and turned to reading the page of the Bible just where she left off.

I said, "Mama, don't you think someone ought to tend to Lily Mark?"

She said, "I'm going to see to her. I've got it in my mind to see to her."

I said, "But Mama, the thing is, she —"

"Not now," she said. "Not just now. You don't know anything about it, but it's too early yet. It's one day too early to be covering up our dead."

❧

Nobody saw Oloe be killed except the ones that did it to her. And God, maybe. It was Murray's brother, Harley, that found her in the edge water — eyes staring to the sky like she was thinking on something there so lovely it had drawn her to a waking dream.

Most folk figured it was Carlyle and Clyde had done it. They had known Jensen's white men were behind the taking of Maggie, and the surest way to twist the knife to Jensen was by Oloe. For myself, I never did see a rage get more logic to it than "an eye for an eye," and I think that was the thought that took hold of them when they saw my Oloe walking home by the Sally River.

The one rape for the other, and that was all. Only, after they ran all their fury dry, and they saw Oloe lying there, weeping on the ground, reaching for her clothes, they knew for the first time what they had done and what was coming from it. Black touching white was the same as setting rope for the hang. And she'd go talking. She'd go crying it all out to Jensen as soon as she got to him. At least if they killed her, it would give them time for the run. Two hours or three. It might've been all they would've needed.

After they did it, they threw Oloe to the river, thinking its windings might have lost her completely. But not long down-current, she drifted up against the fingering roots of a dogwood tree. When Harley fetched me down to the place, I couldn't hardly think Oloe had got the life taken out of her. She lay resting on her back, pink dogwood petals in the water all around. Her face was turned close to the bank and her hair was flowing out behind her like an underwater bloom, rippling forward and back with the lapping of the river — motioning in a liquid amber. I hadn't seen it falling loose so beautifully since she was living at home — home, where if only she had stayed in place of me — brushing it free where she set at the bed, smooth and gleaming in the dark.

❧

Oloe and Lily Mark were laid out naked on the bed, their lips the color of stale grain and ashes, like they had, each of them, kissed their dying full on the mouth. Mama and me, we ran sponges over their wax-pale bosoms, their stiff, soiled legs, their hands holding air. We cried in the same way we breathed, the wetness coming in a rhythm that was thoughtless and constant, and that we could not have lived without.

Oloe's eyes wouldn't close, no matter how we tried. They stared upwards in a wide, doe-eyed supplication to God — quiet and respectful and insistent: Why should You take me now? With the hours going past, a thin veil of dust settled on them, dulling their silent urgency, so that they no longer questioned the cause of their fate. They only mourned it. A necklace of bruises circled her throat, strung in small fingertip-rounds of lilac and blue. But they disappeared when I dressed her in a high-necked blouse, the one fine thing she had ever made for herself, with ivory-bone buttons all the way to the chin.

We put Lily Mark into a white, lace-fronted housecoat that Mama had sewn for herself when she first married Daddy. Mama said she had never once worn it, and anyway it did her heart good to see Lily Mark put to rest in lace, since she had had so little finery in life. She looked dark and generous where she lay, her brilliant black hair frothing onto the bed, her lace-covered bosom still heavy with milk. Her beauty clung to her, even in death.

I don't suppose it would've bothered me if it hadn't been for my sister lying there, too, looking so modest in comparison. Oloe, who was loyal with a fierceness and loving to a fault — who in her skinniness and her half-wrinkled blouse and her glazed-over eyes looked as though we had forgotten her.

"They're ready," Mama said.

"No, not yet," I said.

"What's left to do?"

"Oloe would want her hair pinned up," I said. "High on top of her head. She liked to say it made her feel dignified. She liked to say it made her feel full-grown."

❧

Daddy grew himself an anguish on account of Oloe, she being his special child like she was. During the burying for her and Lily Mark, Daddy looked so webbed-red at the eyes, I thought he had taken to hard drink. But Mama said he just looked that way from his sorrowing. Sorrow that would turn to anger that would turn to killings and so it would circle, round and round.

Mama said, "Used to be a time when I thought revenging had itself an end. When some wise soul would let sorrow be sorrow. But it never happened. Somebody always picked up that grief like a hot stone from the fire that couldn't be held on to, and threw it hard at somebody else. If you asked them why, they said they were just looking for relief from the burning at their hands."

Me, I tried to think about Oloe's death with nothing other than sorrow filling my mind. But I couldn't manage it. A wasting, sightless fury found me and left me in the blank hours of the day. For a time, I wished that I were God and could see across the snarled miles of underbrush and the bald, open spaces to where Clyde and Carlyle hid themselves. I wished I could have punished them with a single thought and never worried about it afterwards. But the wishing itself left me spent and regretful, and when I reached out to touch things, my hands shook with confusion.

The day of the burying, my daddy gathered up a group of men for the hunt. Tom McAllum was with them, and Jarley Frank and his three boys, a dozen of Jensen's men, and Murray's brothers, Harley and Will. They weren't riding six hours before they found out Clyde and Carlyle, hiding in the loft of old man Lubbock's empty barn. They brought the two of them to the Valley Road, south of Copper Crown, and kept them waiting there till night, watching their ropes already hung up on the trees.

The way Mama explained it, the town had got such a taste for hating, they figured they needed themselves more than two lonely black men to get it satisfied. People were saying that colored men would be laying down white women everywhere without a lesson to teach their kind different. So, while Clyde and Carlyle were waiting for the dark, Jensen's men pulled away from their homes every colored man in town between the ages of fifteen and thirty-five years. Everett Parks and his son, Varnell, T. C. Box and Culvert Hillier, Toosie Starling and Perry Deigh. There were seventeen of them altogether, and they all died on the Valley Road, too, that night — straining at the end of as many ropes, their feet shuddering into stillness, their tongues thickening into swollen, dry bulbs that betrayed their amazement.

After on, the town flew up to a kind of frenzy, coloreds and whites the same. Fires were set at Jensen's place and fifteen or twenty others like it, and the settling smoke shut out the daytime sky and made of it a second night. Mama didn't speak her visions anymore. She just stared out the window at all our ruin. But I heard her words in my mind as clear as if they'd been spoken by the voice of all the world. . . . *There's a fire, there's a fire burning high.*

❧

When Daddy got back from his doings, Mama didn't bless him at the door. She said, "God forgive you," with the sound of gravel and sand in her voice, and he didn't take any quarrel with her. He went directly to the washstand and scrubbed his face and neck so long I thought sure that he was leaving behind two layers of skin. "Can't wash that off," Mama said. "It's too dirty a business, Father."

Daddy didn't say anything for a long while. He just set down, bent over at the couch, his hands supporting his forehead like they were trying to catch hold of something there that might save him. When he looked up for my mama, his face was wetted.

He said, "Ol-oe, Ol-oe . . . Ol-oe, Ol-oe," over and over till the word sounded nonsense, till it sounded like the strange language of grief. "Ol-oe, Ol-oe, my Ol-oe . . ."

Mama went to him across the room. She was going to set beside him when he threw himself off his place, arms hooked round her waist, kneeling in front of her and mourning hard to her ribs. She held to him tight, like he was falling down a chasm where she couldn't ever follow. "I know it," Mama said. "I know. And so do all those other daddies tonight — calling out their children's names that aren't going to come anymore."

❧

Mama told me I should get myself away from there. Said Copper Crown was going to be turning anger back on anger for unseeable years after what all had happened and she would be nearer sound sleep if I wasn't living and moving in the cross-fight. Said I should take me the money Oloe had been saving from her sewing work those six years and buy me and baby Ruby a new start somewhere. The city, maybe, or near on by. I asked Mama could she come, too, but she just said maybe after awhile. She had got to see some things through with my daddy first.

"You think you need your mama now, but you're wrong," she said. "You've seen the killed and you've seen the killing and they have both left you trembling at your spirit. But girl — happenings like this, they don't have to break you. A piece of your spirit stays on strong at the inside, whether you know it or whether you don't. Way stronger than these doings you've been living through. You're going to see that, when time passes over far enough to let you. Till then, you've just got to believe in it blind."

I fixed a thick pack for baby Ruby and me, and still, when I threw it up to Remy's back, he carried it like a play toy. When I set up on him, baby Ruby in my arms, I was ten feet off the ground. He was dancing his hooves up under him, anxious from the smell of fire in the air and the layer of soot that clung to his coat. Daddy said good-bye from the house, but Mama walked beside us all the way to Marston's road.

Mama said, "I didn't say anything to you, but I folded the wedding dress in your pack."

I said, "Mama, you know I can't —"

"It's done. It's done," Mama said. "No more talking on it now." She pulled out a lace cloth from her dress sleeve and started in to unwrap it. "You'll be needing this, too," she said. She held up the gold wedding band that Murray gave me, curled and precious where it lay in her palm. "You're on the road alone, and you've got yourself a baby," Mama said. "You're going to be safer if you're wearing it."

"Mama —" I said.

"I can't make you wear it, but I can ask you. For the cause of keeping safe. And I need you to keep safe now, Cass. What with all this burying, you're the only girl I've got myself left."

❧

Allie's place was burned out. I rode to Marston's hill straight from home, but all I found was blackened wood on charred ground, smoke still clinging to the earth like a fog. Maggie's and Clyde's place had been set to flame, too, and I couldn't find anybody standing by, weeping for the ashes. I turned Remy to the Valley Road, thinking to ride south towards Temple. I hadn't gone three miles before I saw Allie walking away to the same direction. The lying smoke was covering her to her waist, and the way I saw her, looked like she was floating over the road with no legs at all, smooth-going like a spirit. I rode beside her ten minutes before she spoke a word.

"You saw the house?" she said.

"Mm-hmm," I said. "Looked like death turned the land to char — and me not knowing if you'd been turned, too."

"I's all right," Allie said. "Maggie, too. Her and her child got out the night before. Olson says he going to take her back to work his laundry."

We went ahead silently awhile. The grayed sky fell even darker so that I couldn't see ahead to the road. But Remy searched out a way, and I drew my mind back from worry. I was just going to ask Allie did she want to ride, too, when we got to the place where the hangings started in, and she turned to me herself.

She said, "I wonder can that horse hold us all."

I said, "For as far as we want."

I pulled her up behind Ruby and me and she held me tight at the waist. Out to both sides of the road, the men were long, black shapes, swaying from the trees. I tried to keep my eyes straight going to the way ahead, but still I saw them, swinging stiff and slow. The air was filled with the sick-sweet smell of the dead. Where the hanged men had been set on fire, there were ashes of hair and work shirts, of skin and shoes underneath, soiling the road in halos of black that the dragonflies rested on in sixes and sevens.

For a moment, I thought there were two women standing out from the dark, too, each one bright under a wide-arcing tree. To the side of my vision, they looked the self-same image of Oloe and Lily Mark, wringing their hands in their dresses and wondering what to do, but when I turned to look directly, they disappeared into rolling smoke under night.

Allie said, "This nothing other from the valley of death."

"I know it," I said.

"I wonder how can we dare pass through," she said.

"Keeping forward on," I said. "Even a valley such as this has got to find itself an ending."

PART TWO

❧

1914

The Heart of the World

❧

The way Allie perceived it, Copper Crown was a world that had started in to spinning so fast that the three of us had been thrown clean off it, like chaff from a threshing blade — shorn off violently from an earth we knew and scattered wide into one we didn't. Wasn't any going back to a place that lived and breathed only by our dreams at night.

I wasn't saying one thing to cross her, but Allie filled up the sky with all her words like she thought I would turn Remy straight around soon as she fell quiet. I swore her lips kept on moving even through her sleep at night, coming close and apart in strange-going shapes. She sounded out her words in a rushing whisper that moved itself like the Sally River — water turning over water in a current patterned by a thought of God, unseeable, with nobody knowing its ending.

Most nights, there weren't any towns to shelter us, and Allie and baby Ruby and me, we rolled out our thin woolen packing under us and turned our faces up towards tree branches that held stars between them like flowers without names. When Ruby cried out under dark, I brought her the doctor's powder formula stirred up with water, and she took it from a hard-cloth nipple tied on over a canning jar. I held the glass up close to my breast, and her and me, we pretended she drew the milk straight from the mama that would've given it freely if she had lived to do it. Sometimes, when I was cradling Ruby all like that — her making those sweet nursing sounds, so needy and asking, I felt sure my own breasts were swelling up with drink enough for all three of us. They stood out pulsing and rich, and so achingly full that when I looked out into the reaching dark, spilling over with its scattered wind, I knew for the first time how it was to be a woman, full-grown and full-loving, standing quiet on her curve of the world, with all the power of life inside her.

❧

The Valley Road, it took on different names. Shiro, Dacus, Montgomery. They all picked up one from the other, and they all threaded south, towards the larger towns as we'd find them, rising up foreign from the flat land. One night, we had reached almost to Conroe, and then stopped short for the dark. The only food we had left was a half loaf of molasses bread that Allie and me had eaten for two days going. At first light, Allie went on ahead with the three dollars I gave her to find out a dry goods store. When four hours passed without her coming back, I took up baby Ruby and went on after.

I came across her not half an hour down the byway, standing stiff and frightened by an idling car. Three men, each of them nineteen or twenty years, were circled close in on her, laughing waggish-like and shoving her at the collarbone where they passed her around one to the other. A wide, dark-browed man was shaking some coin change in his hand. The shortest of them had blond hair that was stuck wet to his head like a helmet and he was holding a sack of bought goods by one hand — a five-pound bag of walnuts and a net sack of dried peaches, it looked like. He had himself a ball of chewing tobacco in his cheek, and he spat towards Allie's feet when he was talking.

He said, "Come on, little girl. Nigra like you has got to belong with *some*body. How come you're out here so lonely?"

When I saw the way of it, I pulled me and Ruby up to Remy's back and rode down on them hard. I said, "Leave off her. Leave off her now."

One of the men tried to catch up the reins, but Remy pulled his head away, twisting his neck into a high, tight arc. The short one let out his surprise, laughing. He said, "Hey, we got us *two* little girls. Two little girls and a baby."

The dark man said, "I didn't know two innocent girls could get themselves a baby all on their own, did you?"

"The colored's with me," I said. "With me and my husband, which if you'd all like to know personally, we're meeting him just down the road." I held out my ring hand to where they could see, and three sets of eyes were stuck fast to the gold there. The small man set down the dry sacks slowly, like they were heavier than he thought when he first took them up.

He said, "Car's running, boys." One of the men let go his hold on Allie and followed the other one to the car. The short man, he smiled wide and crooked while he walked away. He said, "We were concerned. A stranger nigra girl, all to her own self. A dangerous situation, that, being all to her own self. We were just wondering who she belonged with, was all."

"Mm-hmm," I said. "Well, you can get gone out of it now. She belongs with me."

When they drove off, they turned over a thick red dust that hung in the air for seemed like half an hour. Allie appeared herself out of its cloud eventually, standing right where she had been when they left her, frozen by the road. She was looking directly at me and I saw how a faint half smile was playing on her lips.

"One way of looking on it," she said. "All they really stole was our spare change."

❧

I didn't keep count of the fast-falling days. We were traveling through an Indian summer that time had turned away from. The lilac trees sprayed out their blooms generous and sassy, and where they stood up at the roadside, the earth was covered by the splash of purple petals. The color might have held on bright for two weeks or three, if it hadn't been for the high southern wind. It had caught up the blossoms and played on the dust underneath till the air was full with red particle clouds not fit for the breathing. I wrapped baby Ruby with a loose cotton, and held a corner of it up over my own mouth. Allie, she hid her face in her smock, but the dust was so particle fine, it blew through anyhow. I heard her coughing from where she set at Remy's back.

At night, the blowing calmed itself some. Allie and me hung a blanket from a low-branch lilac, and then huddled together at the one side. We took out our sack of walnuts there and fed on the sweet nutmeats till our bellies swelled. The shells cracked open easily under a steel-head hammer Allie brought, and they fell down between us to the night-dark ground, some of the pieces getting hooked up on our skirts like burrs.

Next morning, the wind had disappeared itself entirely, but it had left its color washed over the land like a dye put in for permanent. The grass, the flat land, the tops and undersides of leaves, all of them were covered in a red-dun dust that had turned the whole world to a sepia photograph — still and hot and sleep-like. It wasn't till Allie and me had been rolling the woolens for a quarter hour that we laid our eyes to one another and saw how we were covered, too. Our skirts, our skin, our falling-down hair — all of it was red-dun without seams or stoppings. Even baby Ruby was the same. Allie and me, we started to laughing so deep, we couldn't decide whether we had lost our colors or found them for true. And later, when I saw our walnut coverings scattered all at the ground, I couldn't help but think how they looked like the scales of old skins we stepped out of in the wind.

❧

We held our color for nearly two days. Closer by the towns, carriages and cars started in to pass by regularly, and those people riding as passengers turned their heads hard around to look. The motor sounds, they worked on Remy's nerves, and he weaved and skittered at the roadside when they routed down on him. He had changed himself from a pinto to a roan for all the dust laying on him. His spots appeared to have fallen off his coat like they had been nothing but loose pancakes of color. We wouldn't have known his true coat was still there at all except for the red rising off him like a smoke every time he trotted out the way of an automobile. One time, close on dark, he cantered up a red smoke around us that remembered me to the Valley Road — where me and Allie and Ruby had passed out of Copper Crown for the last time.

I said, "Doesn't the thickened air remind you of that other?"

"Mm-hmm," Allie said. "It does."

"Despite we were crazy griefed then and we probably weren't seeing straight on what all *was* there and what all *wasn't.*"

Allie said, "What you mean we wasn't seeing straight?" She was riding up on Remy with baby Ruby curled in the cloth in her arm, and when she spoke, she drew herself up higher, like from a pull-string at her back.

I said, "Girl, you can't ever tell anybody how I was gone away from my mind. But — I thought I saw Oloe standing there by them dead boys. Oloe and Lily Mark both. Dressed in blue and breathing in the dark."

Allie kept her eyes direct to the road. "Mm-hmm," she said.

I said, "Didn't I say it plain? *Oloe.* And *Lily Mark.* And both of them fresh in the ground, only I saw them standing — standing out under the trees like they were alive, same as you and me."

Allie said, "You seen them because they was there."

I pulled Remy up short and went around to his shoulder, but Allie wouldn't look on me. Her eyes were moving at the distance like it was coming to us fast, and couldn't anybody slow the reckoning.

"They was there," she said. "I know it, because I seen them, too."

❧

I didn't know what were spirits till Allie told me. They are people that have left this life but that miss it so bad, they've got to visit it back. Least that's how Allie's mama told it, and she was seeing spirits every day of her life from the time Allie could first recollect.

Allie said, "When Clyde and me was children, we thought that Mama had got the habit of talking to herself. But later on by, we heard her talking her mama's name, or her brother Jube's — and we knowed how both of them had died before we was born. When I asked Mama the way of it, she explained. She said, 'Them that dies from this life ain't dead to the world. They's changed their shape and they's changed their knowing, but they ain't lost their life. Most of them has took to themselves a way of being stronger than what any of us here knows, and for Mama and Jube, that's the way. They visit me by the kitchen or maybe while I's walking out to Jensen's and we talk like there wasn't never time for when all three of us was alive.'

"I asked her how come, if her mama and her Jube was with her, me and Clyde couldn't see them. She said, 'Child, you can't no ways see a spirit with your eyes. You got to see it with your soul. Some peoples, their soul never gets the proper sight and they walk the world blind for always. Other peoples, their soul gets the vision by unlikely ways — by loving too much or losing too much or both of them put together. But one thing be sure. The visioning peoples, they got their spirits with them their whole life long. That's a thing to remember. I can't say why that's the way, but I know it is. Them that gets to themselves a seeing soul, they can't never unsee again.' "

❧

Our rose-colored skins floated off in the river. The White Oak Bayou, it was called, rolling green and shallow across our path. The stream bottom was a fine mud-silt that swallowed our feet like a wide velvet mouth. And the water, it eased itself past our clothes and held us there with its cool lips in such a way as to feel like a kiss. I rinsed off baby Ruby from the top of her thick-growing hair to the tips of her dust-covered toes. She came out looking bright and new-made as the day Lily Mark gave her up. Allie and me, we watched our color coat the river where it left us, lying at the surface in a sheet of red heat that had been so dry for so long, it couldn't ever get wetted through — not even atop a waterway.

We were close by a town now. People's farms were coming smaller, driving roads were coming wider, and the waysides grew up an occasional business — a dining house or a sleeping cote or a livery barn. Everyplace we stopped at, we asked did the owner need himself some hired help of a kind like Allie and me. But nobody was wanting.

Allie said, "Some folks want colored help. Some folks want white help. But there ain't nobody want one of one kind and one of the other. It ain't regular."

I said, "We're not going to work for two different people, so you put that out of your mind."

Allie said, "That ain't what working on my mind, Cass. I's just saying it ain't regular."

I said, "We're all we've got — you and me and Ruby. Can't any of us hope much on surviving without the others for to take care of them."

"I know, I know. I ain't saying otherwise," Allie said. "But if we keep on begging at the door — black, white, and baby-carrying — we going to step out nowhere by the long road."

I said, "Have we got us a choice?"

"Yeah," Allie said. "We does."

❧

This is the way we did it. The next dining house we came to, I left Allie and Ruby out by the road and walked in by myself. An old man let me pass at the door. He was a Mexican, the size of a child, and he had got an out-of-control head of hair, straw-thick and stark-white and falling all down into his eyes.

"Mr. Skeet, he is owning the business," he said. "He is at the back. Getting ready for the supper, for the cooking. But you go talk to him. You go."

At the other end of the building, I found him. A loud-toiling man, flush red at the face and the bulging chin, stood swearing over eight pots and three stoves and a mountain of raw dumplings at the side. He worked by me closely, smelling of onions and uncooked pork sausages. He spoke without looking up.

"Get out, old man," he said. "You don't know nothing for nothing."

"The old man pointed my direction," I said.

His eyes found me for the first time.

"What — what the sam hill are you, girl?" he said.

"I can cook those up for you," I said, pointing at the dough mountain. "Wouldn't that be a worry off your mind?"

The man set down the pot he was holding. He wiped his hand on a rag slowly, cleaning one finger at a time. His smile was grim, his lips stretched in a dark, uneven line. "Well, ain't you considerate," he said. "Wanting to cook up my supper call just to be a help." He laughed through his thick throat. "You don't mind if I just set down here and watch you while you work," he said.

I fashioned it all. One hundred dumplings and five pans fried onions, forty-seven thick, baked sausages and eleven pots strong black coffee. The child-sized old man filled up plates full of fixings and walked them out to the guests. When he came back in, he was carrying dishes for the stacking or glasses needing water or askings for more. But I saw he had himself a calming way.

"Do not worry about the plates," he'd say. "The plates, they can wait until later."

Mr. Skeet, he set behind me all the while, staring straight into the narrow of my back and making me wish it was narrower. I worked through three hours and a half without taking one breath's rest. When I was nearly finished, Mr. Skeet pulled me up short.

He said, "How old are you, girl, and how come you ain't got a husband with you?"

I said, "Sixteen and he's at the war."

He said, "You bad off for work?"

"Yes sir, I am."

He stood up from his stool and walked closer up. He was standing near on by an electric ceiling light, and for the first time since I walked in, I saw how his skin had the watery mark of a burn scar all on the one side of his neck and down one arm. His hand had three fingers attached by a duck web of skin, like a fire had nearly melted them away.

He said, "You get supper for twenty-five diners seven nights a week, and I'm going to give you all your meals and an upstairs boarding room and two dollars spending money."

I said, "I'm going to earn it, sir."

He said, "Yes, you are."

❧

When first I told Mr. Skeet I had me a colored girl and a one-month baby and a nineteen-hand pony out at the road, he looked at me like I was lost to my mind.

I said, "They're going to be less trouble than they sound. The baby doesn't do anything but sleep all the day — she doesn't have any colic. And the colored, she's the hardest-working hired-out girl you'd ever expect to see."

Mr. Skeet didn't say anything. He didn't

even make any motion that he heard except for the way he was wagging his head back and forth, like he had fallen suddenly drunk and was trying, for all that liquor weighing down his head, to tell me no. I went quietly out the kitchen door and brought back Allie and Ruby and Remy to the yard outside it.

"Won't cost you but a dollar plus by the week," I called out.

We must have stood ourselves in that dark grass patch for fifteen minutes. The grasshoppers whirred high where we stirred them. There wasn't anything for a wind, just a hollow where it ought to have been. A giant blue willow was holding its thousand leaves perfectly still.

The door opened. "I ain't paying a dollar plus for nigra work," Mr. Skeet said. "She's going to work her jobs all day and just *maybe* earn the hay that horse's going to eat."

I said, "All right."

"And I ain't paying you to set upstairs with that baby by the hour neither. You're going to have to carry it with you while you're choring."

"I can do that," I said.

Allie's hand searched out my arm in the dark. Her lips were moving under a whisper, so that I barely caught the sound. She was rolling a phrase over like a sweet thing in her mouth, turning it over and over again. "We got us a job," she was saying. "We got us a job."

❧

Mr. Skeet, he took a dislike to coloreds. I asked him once could Allie help me to cook up the supper call and he said how he didn't tolerate nigra hands dirtying up his food. Said he always considered how nigras were like animals in the wild — some of them tried to keep themselves clean, but none of them managed it. An animal couldn't ever get so clean that he wasn't an animal anymore. Allie said if she was so dirty, how come Skeet had her walking around all day behind a straw broom or an ammonia mop. Seemed like she would be undoing all that shining floor work just to walk across a room. Allie said the mind of a man like Skeet was many amazing things, but logical wasn't one.

I was a passing cook — as good as Skeet by all accounts — but nothing more. I didn't have any sense for the workings of spice. Whether nutmeg or cumin or coriander, they all fell together in a souring way. So, most nights, I didn't use any seasonings at all, outside of table salt and ground peppercorn. Whatever I fixed, a slow-cook beef stew or a pan-fried pullet or a baked side of ham, it came out flat-tasting and bare. I didn't hear complaints, but I didn't draw compliments either. With days going past, I got stove burns on my hands and tomato stains on my smocks, and I couldn't keep my mind on the cooking times.

Allie said, "Girl, you got you gifts, but they ain't for fine fixings."

I said, "Can't I be taught if I've got a mind to?"

She said, "I'd be the first one to learn you how, but a gift can't be got by that way. Can't be begged, nor stole, nor give."

I said, "Can't anything be done with it, then.

"Yeah," she said. "Except be used by them that's got it for their own."

❧

Mr. Skeet, he didn't like to distract a person when she was cooking. He was full of interruptings and crossings and cussing-outs, but he held them to his insides while he walked the kitchen. People said that by the heating stove was where he'd got his arm burned so badly, but he never talked on it. Most evenings, he set silently behind me while I did up the foods. The skin at my back would crawl tight where he was long staring, but Allie said we ought to have thanked God that he was only touching with his eyes and nothing other.

That's the way Allie came to take my place. My dresses were too tight across her bosom, but they fell to a perfect length on her ankle, and looking on from behind, there wasn't any way to tell how she wasn't me. When I was fixing food in the kitchen, I always put my hair up in a twisting bun and covered it all by a triangle kerchief, so Allie did the same. We figured how if she stood in for me every night, we'd likely be caught outright within the month. So we changed our places no oftener than once a week — which gave both me and the diners a break from a middling meal.

When Allie took to the kitchen, she brought a magic with her. She picked up a tough leg of lamb and she turned it to a roast miracle, full and toasted pink and sweet-laying in its flavor. Or she touched a bowl of juice-dry peaches and drew them to a simmering pot with honey and lemon and bits of whole clove, which melted to peach heaven at the tongue. Everybody exclaimed on the difference. Mr. Skeet, too, though Allie said he didn't hold the beginnings of an idea as to why.

She said, "He waits till I be cleaning the dishes, and there ain't no cooking left to do. He sets up at the stool behind me and he says, 'You's an irregular girl. Outside of predicting.

You cook fine when you want to, but most nights you just don't want. Ain't no reason for it I can see. You's far off from predicting. But I guess that's the way you's liking it. Ain't it now.'

"When I don't give no answer to him, he stand it up and walk it out. But them be the words he say, low and deliberate-like, while he's staring into the back he think be yours."

❧

The letters I wrote to my mama didn't keep me from paining in her lack. No matter how grown I got, I was always a child by the woman that bore me — just like Ruby was always going to be a child by me. Allie said, "Mothers, they always be loving, and children, they always be needing. Can't nobody remake the plan from the way God laid it out." I guess I couldn't say it better than that.

I wrote down in my letter,

> Dearest Mama,
>
> So many months passing, and you and me apart. I wonder could you recognize me if we were to walk down the same street. Allie, she says I've got me a more womanly way than before we left Copper Crown — more curves at the waist, she

says, and kind of shining-looking around the eyes. But me, I think the change has come more from my Ruby-girl than from my aging. She's calling me Mama now, and God knows how I love the sound. I don't like to think on how I'm not the one that bore her. I feel like I am. She curls her baby hand around in my hair — she cries out for me when she's afraid in the dark — she laughs when I try on a funny face. I love her like she's my very only girl. I can't help myself from it and I don't even want to try.

Allie and me, we're saving on the week's wage. We didn't use up all of Oloe's sewing money before we got us work, either. All counted, we've got one hundred fourteen dollars put by — plus one dollar additional for the passing week. Isn't it full? We're hoping to buy us a small place after a few years more. Allie's such a good cook, we're thinking how we could start up a dining house of our own — in time eventual, we mean.

Mama, I'm running out of space on which to write, but I've got to ask you something that's been nagging on my mind. Mama, have you ever seen a spirit?

Waiting to hear on it. Your loving girl,

Cass

❧

Mr. Skeet didn't have but two friends to call his own. Allie said it wasn't a puzzle as to why. Skeet was schemer and lecher, and he was robbing his diners blind what with the prices he fixed. He didn't make any exceptions for them he called his friends either. Still, for friend-calling he had himself two. Even a wolf liked to hunt in a pack.

Thane and Mondrow were what they called themselves. The first of them wasn't a day older than me — arch-browed and fine-clothed so that he looked most of the time like he was highly surprised on how rich he'd got. Folks said his daddy had given him a set of cattling ranches that he had let his hireds oversee, and he'd been dancing on the profits ever since.

Mondrow looked to me round and brown and veiny as an onion. He held out his lips in a spotty pucker that made him look like he was tasting the sour ways of his own self and not liking it. People didn't seem to trust him either — but they acted like they all owed him a grudge favor. Word had it he was a money-lender, and those that borrowed from him paid back by double cash or favor-working, whatever one he wanted the more.

Mondrow had himself a love for fine horseflesh. The first time he saw Remy in Mr. Skeet's stable, his eyes set themselves to dancing in his head. I was inside Remy's boarding stall, spreading out some fresh hay, and I saw him staring over the half wall, licking his overfed lips.

He said, "It's a new one you got here."

Skeet appeared himself over the half door. His look got settled somewhere about the base of my neck. "The girl or the horse?" he said.

Mondrow said, "The horse."

Skeet said, "Yeah."

"Looks wild-blooded," Mondrow said.

Skeet said, "Don't she though?"

❧

Baby Ruby was blessed right from the start. She had got the best out of Murray and Lily Mark both, and folks that saw her for the first time knew she had herself a God-made way. Her black hair grew out rich and liquid-like from the top of her head, and underneath it there were her eyes — my baby's magic eyes — which shone like two blue pearls from their black-lashed beds.

Allie said, "She the most beautiful babychild I's ever seen. She got this shining to her face — you know what I mean. It's like a piece of the sky got put to her soul, and she be holding its light inside her."

I tried not to be making fuss over her all the time — holding her to my arms too much or talking constantly on children's stories — but I got used to having her with me. When we first came to Mr. Skeet's, I fashioned myself a broadcloth baby-pouch and cradled Ruby in it all the working day. She rested herself over my stomach, her tiny fingers clutching to my dress, her skipping voice sounding out babies' words to my ears. Her and me, we couldn't separate us one from the other, and I guess I kept on feeling that way a long time after she grew to a little-girl child and could pull herself up off the floor and walk away from me on her own desiring.

She liked best to play with a red-haired rag doll under the blue willow in the yard. Mr. Skeet didn't take any objection, so I let her go outside every evening while the sun was turning blush. I could watch her from the kitchen window while I cut up fresh greens for the supper call. She set still in the stubble of the grass, her black hair spilling over her shoulders in a frenzy of ringlets.

I remember one time, looking up from my shallots, I saw a sight through the window that stole my very breath. Out at the yard where Ruby was playing, that fine old willow had caught a glow. Its leaves shone out silver-blue, like they were swallowed whole by a cooling fire. And under them was standing Lily Mark, bent low in a shimmer, lit-up hands stretching out — reaching hard towards the child she knew for her own.

❧

Ruby couldn't see any of Lily Mark — her cool-fire dress nor her blue-shining hair nor her close-reaching arms. Baby hadn't got her the sight yet, and I thanked God for the lack. She hadn't seen enough of sorrow or hadn't known enough of longing to look deeper at the ways of things. All she perceived was the surface-world — that blue willow, spreading out its kind arms between her and the dusking sky, and her red-haired baby doll, smiling the same smile through her black button eyes.

When I ran outside, I cried out for Ruby to come to me quick. She must have heard the strain of urgent in my voice, because her eyes opened wide with worry — like she was afraid she had done something wrong and I had caught her at it. Lily Mark watched on while Ruby toddled up to my arms — her white socks all falling down and her toes pointing half-inwards — but she wasn't making any motion from under the tree. Only her head was turning, smooth and concentrating, looking after Ruby where she went. I took up my girl and left Lily Mark to standing there, defeated for all her electric color.

When I confided to Allie about it, she closed her black-jewel eyes, like she was expecting as much.

"She be aching for her girl-child," Allie said. "Wanting to know what it's like to hold her."

"She can't — she can't actually *touch* Ruby, can she?" I said.

"Not by the feel," Allie said. "She can try all she wants, but Ruby ain't going to know nothing about it."

"Till she gets the sight," I said.

"Which she might not never get," Allie said.

"She's going to get it," I said. "Just a question of time. She's loving life too much to go through it blind. I see it in her eyes."

❧

Skeet's old man waiter, he called himself Humberto. He didn't stand over five foot high from the top of his shagging white hair. His bone-pointed shoulders lined up straight with his narrowing hips, and he was outsized by most a twelve-year-old boy. Sometimes Skeet called him "old woman," sometimes he called him "stick man." But Humberto didn't ever talk back. He appeared like a man with a peaceable heart — one who was too tired or too wise to take an anger to him for permanent.

When he found out Allie was pretending to be me now and then, trying on my dresses and cooking through my supper call, he didn't say anything about it to Skeet. He didn't say anything about it to anybody for nearly six months, and even then, I don't know what started him confiding to Allie and me. Maybe he wanted to watch over us awhile in private — to see for himself if we were full up with tricks and lies, or if we just took one to ourselves occasionally, when we didn't see any other way.

One time Allie was pulling ragweed from the side yard when Humberto came up on her. He said, "You have a talent with your fixings. I never see one better."

Allie didn't say anything. She shaded her eyes with one hand to see if she could catch a meaning from the lines on Humberto's face. But he was standing directly below the bare sun, and all she could see was the light playing through his crazy white hair.

"It is all right," he said. "It is all right. I am just saying you don't have to be wary of me. Now Mr. Skeet, maybe you are right to be wary of him — but the two of us, we are not the same."

Allie said, "How be it you ain't the same?"

Humberto said, "As for me, I do not say much, but I am thinking all the time. As for Mr. Skeet, he talks a long time after his mind goes off to sleep."

Allie said, "You's talking all right now."

"But I have been thinking half the year. Six months! That is something," Humberto said. "And I kept your secret, did I not? Did I not keep it well?"

❧

Now that I was grown, I still had me dreams of when I wasn't. It didn't make any sense at first, but I came to see eventually that people's lives have stages and startings that don't always line up regular with time. In the one way, Copper Crown was nothing more than a few acres square that had been burned off the map. But in the other way, it was the sweet smell of corn and the woman-curve hills, it was the air I breathed under when I first fell in love, and it was the healing touches of my mama's and my Oloe's hands. That first Copper Crown, it had been maimed and killed and wouldn't anything bring it back. But that second one, it was breathing inside me under a life all its own, and when I closed my eyes at night, it filled up my mind with its visions-making.

I didn't hear anything from Mama for seven months in a line. When her letter finally came, I saw how she'd been holding back on account of how much her life had changed. She wrote out,

Dear Cass,

The Federal Bureau came in after all those hangings were done. They were asking questions of everybody like we all were going to jail for life-term. Your daddy, he up and joined the war. Most of the other white men went with him. Said it was the only way to keep free, even if they had to risk dying by the try. And sure enough, the Bureau cleared out fast after all of our men were enlisted. I haven't been hearing anything from overseas.

I'm doing fine at the house. I'm working me a garden with jewel tomatoes and climbing vine peas, and I sell some of them at the goods store when there are women wanting to buy. Remember how once you nurtured up the fattest, ripest jewel tomatoes we ever did see? (Well, mine aren't quite so choice. But I've never known anybody with a gift on growing like you've got.)

I still have me a money stash from the shoebox supply. Enough so that your daddy didn't take any worry in leaving me. And enough so that I can ask you not to take any worry either. (Don't be sending me any money, Cass, because I'll be sending it straight back.) You do like your mama wants you.

Love you,

Mother

P.S. — Only spirit I know of is my papa. He's been living here at the house for years, but I've never thought it my place to tell. Hope you think I've done right.

❧

When Mr. Skeet was angry, his burn scars bloomed flush like a purple flower. They started to darken up by his neck where his collar was straining, and they ran downwards like a dye — across his shoulder where I couldn't see, and past his thick wrist to find out his fingers — flat and webbed like the foot of a goose.

The scars, they were distracting by a large

fashion. Particularly when they changed colors in plain sight. But the last thing I wanted to do to an angry man was to stare directly at his disfigurement. So when Mr. Skeet shouted at me over a chipped dish or a set of tracks on the floor, I peered straight down to the ground at his grainy shoes — concentrating on them hard, like they were going to show me something I didn't already know. If I had raised my eyes a yard they would've pulled towards Mr. Skeet's scarring like iron shavings to a magnet. That's how much I was trying not to look.

Humberto, seemed like he knew everybody's secrets and most of them he was telling to Allie and me. He said that Mr. Skeet didn't have to be burned severe like he was. But five years back, Mr. Skeet hadn't got any friends. Said he didn't need them. Said friends weren't anything other than people hoping to leech off your properties or your monies or your charity givings. Mr. Mondrow and Mr. Thane, they didn't start coming around till after the accident — and by then Mr. Skeet had changed his perspective. He saw how living all to himself had taken him down, and when he looked to where he had fallen, he was afraid for his soul.

His shirt cuff caught fire in the supper room, the diners with their plates in front of them, their glasses full up with drink. Mr. Skeet was stoking the wood stove with a close touch, and the flame took his hand and all his sleeve in the space of a single breath. He started calling out panic. "Put it out put it out God help me put it out!" he said. And all the while he was tearing on his shirt to jerk it away.

But there wasn't anybody that moved to help him. Not a full-grown, not a child, not an old man like Humberto. They were frozen in their fearings, I guess. Fearings of burning up alongside a man that nobody knew, maybe. Or that nobody cared for. Or that nobody would cry over when the earth parted clean his grave.

❧

I wasn't practiced in the ways of deceiving. I just never learned myself to lie, that's all. Never had to till Skeet came along, when I found out two women to their own selves needed fibbing for protection. But I didn't know anything about sewing up a story tight so that no doubting could get in by the seams. And Skeet nearly hooked me up on my own tale-making with all the questions he put to me.

One time he found me out by the yard. I was sitting on the stoop, shelling a rough sack of peas. Ruby was playing not ten foot distant, making tiny horse tracks in the dust with her fingers. Skeet set down beside me slowly, reaching his hands out under him to ease himself to the step.

He said, "How's that husband of yours?"

I said, "He's all right." I kept on looking down at the peas in my lap. Their pale, waxy shells were staining my fingernails green.

Skeet said, "At the war, ain't he?"

I said, "Yes sir."

He said, "One thing I noticed. You ain't got no letter from him here." Skeet rolled his weight back against the railing post. I watched his good arm where it was stretching out across his stomach. "Now, how could a girl know her husband is all right, when she ain't got no letter from him? That's a puzzle, don't you think?"

My throat started to close on me. I felt like I was making to choke. Half a dozen peas spilled out of my skirt and rolled down the steps. I said, "Not if he don't know where she's at. Like my husband doesn't know where I'm at. He's writing me at my mama's over in Copper Crown, and she's sending on all the news."

"Ah," Skeet said. "You got you a nice system, then. You got it all figured, I guess."

Skeet's voice wasn't moving with his words.

It was riding under them, low and mocking — taking back their meanings and hiding them from me.

I said, "I guess."

He said, "You must be excited on what the news service is saying."

"Excited?" I said.

"Don't you know?" said Skeet. "The newspaper's writing the war's going to be over before the year is out. Your man'll be coming to get you after on, and I guess then I'm going to meet him myself."

❧

Allie started in to churchgoing. I didn't know when nor where she got herself the mind to do it. Somebody in town must've whispered "Come on and see" in her ear. She didn't tell me the way of it. Now, I don't have anything against the doings of the church except maybe how the people that are praying inside it don't let anybody through the doors that doesn't look like themselves. The Book says "Love thy neighbor" and the people say "So long as she's a member at the Ladies' Auxiliary." Where we lived, poor whites stood at the back and coloreds got shut out at the street door. I didn't even know an all-colored church existed till Allie told me she had been setting inside one the last three Sundays going.

She closed her eyes smooth as sleep when she talked on it. "It's a rich-smelling, music-filling, crowd-holding place," she said.

I said, "A coloreds' church? With a steeple and a whitewash and a silver collecting plate?"

"It ain't church-looking by the outside," she said. "Unless a hay barn appears itself like a God place. But at the inside, there be peoples singing like their souls depending on it. You ain't never heard yourself such a filling-up sound. Like the music you hearing and the air you breathing come together."

"It's music start to ending?" I said.

"Nearly," she said. "Even when the preacher man be preaching, he falling in to singing. He says, 'When the last trumpet sound.' Just like that he does it. 'When the last trumpet sound, I be there.' Girl, I love to hear them voicings. They carry me up out of myself."

"And I guess that's good," I said. "Getting carried out from where you are."

"Sometimes," she said. "Sometimes, it's all I got me a need for."

❧

If old man Humberto hadn't slept nights in a cottage extending from the barn, he wouldn't ever have known about what Mondrow did. Him and Skeet and Thane, they got themselves drunk late-nights from hard whiskey or gin-mixings. Humberto said as how sometimes they wandered out to the yard, slurring their sorrow-talk or hollering their conquerings — one or the other, but never anything in between. When they were grieving, Mondrow cried over the wife that left him, Skeet cried over the fire that scarred him, and Thane cried over his being too young to know the ways of mourning for true.

The night after Mondrow had seen Remy at the barn, he dragged Skeet and Thane out there with him. Humberto said he was harping on Skeet to sell the animal outright, and Skeet kept saying back that Remy wasn't for him to sell.

Mondrow said, "Yeah, but he belongs to that little-girl cook of yours. Can't you make her do like you want? A skinny little girl like that?"

Thane said, "She's got a will to her own self, don't she?"

"I just pay her wage," Skeet said. "That don't count for nothing."

Humberto told as how they argued themselves into a half-hour knot, without a one being sober enough to untie it clean. And then Mondrow got himself the idea to ride on Remy's back, to test out his stride. Humberto said how, from where he was lying at his cot, he heard them swinging open the stall door. And then there was a small nothing, a thin silence where all he could hear was his own breath. The exploding voices, they came right after. There was a strong shock of sound, filled up with Remy horse-screaming and Mondrow hollering "Get me out!" and Skeet and Thane laughing raucous, like the drunks they were. A long time after everybody had gone, Remy was still bucking his quarters at the plank wall, flaring his temper to the sound of gunshot hooves and splintering wood.

When Mondrow came to see me two days after, his ribs were taped. He had got himself an uncovered cut on his balding head that he had tried to train a few hair-strings over. Skeet was sitting close on by, pulling at a cigarette.

Mondrow said, "Fifty dollars, that's top price for horseflesh." He spoke carefully, like I was a child, hard put to understand him.

"Horseflesh that's on the market, anyway,"

I said. I watched how Skeet started to smile, wily-looking behind a screen of thick smoke.

"What'll it take for you to put him on the market, then?" Mondrow said. "A little Sunday dress for yourself? Some wrapped-up chocolates for your girl?"

"Nothing for nothing," I said.

Now Skeet was grinning hard. He switched his narrow eyes between me and Mondrow. "And it ain't just because she don't like you," he said.

❧

My daddy got killed a month before armistice. Nobody knew exactly which day. By the time the red-cross lady carried a government letter to my mama, the whole world was celebrating their homecomings. Mama had taken three dollars from her savings and bought her a store-made dress — a lemon-yellow linen with a lining sewn at the inside — along with a fine-weave hat to match. She was thinking to look so smart-citified when her man came walking in by the door.

For all her visions, Mama didn't know anything beforehand on how Daddy would go. There weren't any dreams by night. There weren't any omens by day. She wrote in a letter, "I think on how I might've been training sweet peas when he died, or washing out my hair. Not paying him any mind while his soul was stepping out from life. And I think on how many people have passed just that way. Paining to their own selves under an empty sky. (The world has got so much grieving to catch up to. It's been killing so many of its own.)"

For my part, I tried on remembering my daddy, but his face wouldn't come. I saw his clothes clearly — his tanned field shirt working the drag-plow, his patched duck-pants going hunting — but where his face and hands ought to have been, all I saw was clear air. When I imagined my daddy's voice, it was crying out "Oloe-my-Oloe" at the floor by my mama's feet. But all I saw was a sounding set of clothes — moving by grief and rounded by sorrow, from the heart of a hollow man.

❧

Allie's mama used to say how loving hearts survived all doings. They got harmed and they got broken, but they found the world such a beauty-making place that they always turned out to love it again. Maggie, she was such a one.

She wrote Allie from her place at Olson's, where she had taken up the launder work like she had left off it. Except for her baby, which she'd called Lloyd, she hadn't ever been so alone in all her life. County gossips liked to say that she had lured a white man to her bed — that it had served her right to have a bastard baby by him. All the killings that came after on were God's judgment for a single Jezebel. Whites and coloreds the same said her soul was too dirty to rest your eyes on. Little children, taught by their mamas, threw stones at her when she walked the town.

She wrote,

> i thank to god how lloyd ain't knowing none of this. he's a bright, laughing baby — clapping his hands all the day while i get launder suds messing my smocks. been a time when i was carrying him inside of me, i thought this baby been worse than the hell-keep hisself. how it shames me to remember it now.
>
> the way it come out, he's a child-gift of blessings — sent me by a terrible way — but a child-gift of blessings still. he laughs hisself into my dreaming at night, happy and jabbering, and free from all worry. and I see what he be working at.
>
> he's not leaving me let go from life. he be stubborn-loving, i's coming to know. he's holding on tight for him and me both.

❧

Nothing points out the passing of time like a child. I barely would have known I was getting older if it hadn't been for baby Ruby. She outgrew all her dresses before she wore them three months. When it got so that her skirts were riding close on her knee, I'd tear out the threads and resew the hemmings. She was going to grow up tapered and tall, like Murray had been.

Allie and me, we were at the time of life when the passing years don't make any change of looks. Someone guessing on us would have said we weren't children and we weren't old women. They couldn't have seen any farther than that. We hadn't got us any growing fat and we hadn't got us any whitened hair. We were women living by their prime, which back at Copper Crown had been thought on as the years of men and marrying and family-making.

Instead, we were doing kitchen-cooking and room-by-room cleaning and grounds-tending, which by my thinking wasn't separate from what our mamas had done, except we were doing it for hire.

I said to Allie, "Got to be something better

for girl-children to grow themselves up for."

She said, "Don't you be getting set for toiling all your life. We ain't going to be hiring ourselves out forever. We got us a mark we's aiming at."

"With one dollar adding by the week," I said.

"Two hundred eight-seven counted," she said. "That be half on a start somewheres."

"A start for Ruby," I said.

"For all of us," she said. "For Ruby and you and me."

❧

Ruby wasn't to go wanting for long. When she was six years old, Thane asked me would I mind if he gave her some store-bought clothes. A flouncy blue dress, along with one or two flower prints and such like. Whatever I picked out. I ought to have said no right off, except I saw how she'd worn her smocks patch-bare, and I had been thinking how they couldn't be resewn anymore if they were to keep hanging straight.

I looked at Thane. He was watching Ruby where she set at the yard, pulling up hairs of grass with her fingers. Her dress was spread all about her in a circle, like the cloth of an open parasol that had been moth-bitten or secondhand.

"Why are you wanting to give them?" I said.

Thane laughed. His eyebrows hitched up at the middle like they were especially surprised. "I ain't making any claim on her," he said. "I ain't a man for child-briding, if that's what you're worried on."

I didn't say anything. Thane's smiling strayed over his lips before disappearing itself. "She's got such a gracing look about her," he said. "For a child. And them clothes, they's all right for dirt-playing, but they —"

"They what?" I said.

"They take away from her, anyhow," he said.

I said, "Yes sir, they do that."

Later on I asked Allie did I do the wrong thing. She put her arm circled around my back. She said, "There be a mama and there be her child. The mama, she washes, she heals up, she feeds, she clothes on, she holds — she be doing all she can. And when a stranger man asks can he help, she says yes because she sees a way she can do for her child a little more sweeter. Is you going to be judging on such a one? Is I?"

❧

That fall, Ruby started off to schoolgoing looking like a rich man's only child. Those dresses set on her like ribbons and cake frosting, shiny and bright-colored and store-bought. I wished she had her a mama to match. I kept thinking I would be the embarrassment of Ruby someday. She would be bringing home school friends which would fall to laughing when they saw her raggedy mama in a stained cook dress.

Allie said, "Ruby be too sweet to draw scheming peoples to her. You know that. Now, if she had more of Lily Mark to her, I guess I could see why you'd be fearing. But that girl didn't get nothing more from her birthing mama than her outside looks. God or Murray give her the rest."

It was true. Ruby had got a generous way, like we learned those early years. One time she came home from the schoolhouse missing her red-haired rag doll.

I asked her, "Did you forget her in the coat room, honey?"

She said, "No'm, I didn't."

I said, "Where did you put her down, then?"

She said, "With Maddy Carrol. She asked could she have her, so I said she could."

"To play with overnight?" I said.

She said, "For all the nights."

"You gave her for permanent?"

"Yes'm," she said.

"But why, Ruby girl? Why'd you give her that way?"

"That was the way Maddy Carrol asked," she said. "That was the way she wanted."

❧

Humberto said I had me a way with the yard-tending. Said planting grew up greener under my hand than any other he had ever seen. Said I could bury a jewelweed and coax it to come up a peach tree, if only I had a thought in that direction.

H said, "As for me, I have loved the plantings my entire life, but the affection, it is not mutual. I think to water and I flood instead. I think to prune and I cut back too far. The greens, they fade under my touch and I can never give them back their life."

I said, "It takes a feel for what they're needing."

"Yes," he said. "Concern is not enough. So many them I have ruined. But now you are here, and I see I do not have to worry."

In time passing, Humberto told all. He had himself an idea of planting a grove of trees at the far yard. Tall ones, that would hold off a wind from the house. White oak and beech trees, pecans and firethorn. Folks passing on the road would get themselves a view of great, burly trunks waving all their greens in a row, and they'd be stopping at the dining house just to get a clearer sight. It would be attracting business, if only Mr. Skeet would've taken it into consideration.

"He doesn't want to do it?" I said.

"Mr. Skeet does not know what makes beauty," Humberto said. He ran a child-sized hand through his wiry white hair. "He thinks planting a few trees will make of his lawn a mess, a clutter. He does not want to make a clutter."

"But then, a seedling or two at a time," I said. "They're hardly going to crowd him out."

Humberto, he laughed silently. I could hear the wind passing by the gaps in his teeth. "A seedling or two at a time," he said. "A man like that will not know the difference."

Springtime came, and we did all our plantings at night. I hadn't ever grown up trees from saplings before, but I knew how deep their roots ought to have run. Swimming through the tree tangles in the Sally River water had taught me that. Beech were shallow, pecans were deep — and that was the way we dug the ground hollows. I loved the turn of the earth through my hands — mulchy and crumbling and yielding like the seasons. Bending by the tree, tiny leaves kissed my face, cool and polished where they touched.

After we set the trees in their beds, Humberto always shook my hand. He shook it like I was a doctor that had been helping deliver his children — proud and grateful and trembling with his feeling.

"Thank you," he said. "Thank you much, very much. Nothing is finer than what you do here."

❧

Sometimes, after Humberto and me did our night planting, I would have myself a dream. One dream, a single dream, clear and identical as it came to me every time. I was walking under peach trees and oaks, cottonwoods and willows, all grown leaf-bustling and lush at the heart of Skeet's yard. Looking up to find the sky, all I saw was arcing green — a leaf-pieced dome cloth that was spread to keep me shaded. It was a forest I was walking. A forest that had started at the backyard and that had gone on to cover the world — green-glowing and thick-rising, branches netting and roots webbing — a forest full up with a feeling that life was forever opening up inside it, like a layered blooming, with a stillness for its nurture. The stillness of peace or of dreaming maybe, or of spirits talking through the leaves.

❧

Mr. Skeet, he watched trees grow from under his shoes. Sweet green roots put up knobs in the high grass, pressing playfully against the undersides of our feet. But Skeet didn't make any mention. He strode stiff and wide-legged across his lawn, eyes straight to the far road, never once taking notice of the green hand of the saplings, tracing his leggings as he brushed them by. Seemed like the only time he noticed the trees at all was in the pitch-black of night when he fell across them on account of he had been drinking so hard. Humberto heard him swearing in the dark, cussing on the trees like they were living men that had shoved up against him with a spite.

"Who the hell are *you?*" he shouted, fighting with the needled arms of a southern pine. Or, "Don't fight me," he said, bending back the limbs of a baby white oak. "I's only going to go harder with you if you do."

So far as we could tell, the trees made out

better than Skeet did. The saplings were hardy. They dropped a few needles or lost a few leaves, but their roots held place in the ground, and their branches nearly never got broken. Skeet, on the other side, got bramble scratches on his face and hands, and blue-knot bruises on his knuckles. Some mornings, he couldn't hardly remember where he had been the night before, but other times he'd get after old man Humberto.

"Where we getting all this greenage, stick man?"

Humberto looked down at his shoes. "Greenage?" he said.

"Leafage," Skeet said. "Branches and bushes and the like. They's growing at the yard like they's somebody's garden rows."

Humberto swung his head side to side, his white hair waving crazily on top. "It is puzzling to someone like me," he said.

"What?" Skeet said.

"The ways of nature," Humberto said. "It is puzzling beyond my knowledge. That so much green things could grow up in one place."

The two of them stood looking awhile in silence. Out at the yard, a ground-wind was silvering the tall grass. Humberto pulled a stray wheat weed from his hair, and cupped it in his palm, studying it.

"I suppose you know what you have here," Humberto said. He threw out the weed suddenly, and watched while the wind caught it up.

"What?" said Skeet.

"The fertilest land a man could ever dream to own," Humberto said. "Yes. That is it. That is what I think. The fertilest land."

❧

Nobody knew why Thane did Ruby like he did. Not Allie nor me nor Thane himself. When I asked him why did he buy her all those Christmas toys, all those store-made dresses, all those fine-bound books for reading, he said, "Because I thought she could use them, mostly." But he shrugged up his shoulders while he was saying it, like that answer wasn't good enough for him either.

I said, "It's not that we don't appreciate it, Thane. You're doing Ruby much finer than I could do her."

"Only by outside makings," Thane said. "You're teaching her to grow up right. And I can't think of anyone could teach her good as you."

"You hardly know me," I said. But he just smiled. There wasn't any knowing his reasons.

At the start of the gifting, me and Allie

watched Thane closely. We saw his comings, his goings, his wanderings in the yard. Sometimes, if Ruby was playing in one corner of the property, Thane would walk past her without a single look in her direction, acting like he hardly knew she was there — or maybe like he hardly cared. Other times, mostly when she asked him, he would pretend to be a horse, stomping his feet and neighing through his nose, while Ruby rode up on top of his shoulders, shrieking in her delight. But he always put her down after a minute or two, laughing off her protests and going his own way.

"You don't got to worry yourself for now," Allie said. "That man took a far-off interest in Ruby. Far off and gentle made."

I said, "What do you mean 'far off'?"

She said, "He ain't took a interest in the child so much as he's took a interest in the woman inside her. He's waiting on her, is all . . . waiting on Ruby to grow herself up."

❧

By April of that year, Ruby started in to ask questions couldn't anybody answer, leastwise me. "When is my daddy going to be coming home from overseas?" she said.

I said, "Why are you wondering on that, Ruby girl?"

She said, "Everybody else's daddy has come home already. Excepting the ones that have been killed. That's what Miss Alana says."

"Miss Alana, your teacher?" I said.

"Yes'm," she said. "Miss Alana wants all the parents to go on down to the school Tuesday next. Mamas and daddies the same."

"What for?" I said.

"She calls it an open house," Ruby said. "Mamas and daddies the same, they're all going to come." Ruby stood wringing her hands in her blue-flower skirt. "Excepting the ones that have been killed by the war," she said.

❧

When I asked Thane would he come to Miss Alana's open house, he let a smiling take over his face. I owned as how maybe it wasn't my place to inquire, but he shushed me like I couldn't raise any objection worth the time it took to speak out.

"You only got to ask me once," he said.

"Ruby's been wondering after her daddy," I said.

"You don't have to give any explanations," Thane said.

"I just thought —"

"I don't need to know anything about it,"

he said. A wide smile was still riding his lips. He was setting at the porch in one of Skeet's old rocking chairs, swinging it forwards and back like he was making to travel it somewhere. For awhile, I was thinking he'd forgot I was there. He looked straight out to the night, without speaking a word. There was only his rocking between us — and the sounds it made, like so many doors flying open and shut.

I said, "She's just missing her daddy, I guess."

He said, "I expect she is."

❧

Allie said when a man stood out from his friends so much as Thane did, there had got to be money in it somewhere. "Thane be head and shoulders better than the mens he running with," she said. "Skeet and Mondrow and all them others."

"I don't know why you're saying that," I said. "He drunkens the same as the rest of them."

Allie set down her shovel where she was hay-mucking in the corner of the barn. Her dress was soaked through in a V at the back, and when she turned around, her cheeks were glowing hot. Little sticks of straws were clinging to her hair and down her neck, but she let them lie.

"He don't smoke, he don't swear, and he don't grab on to women skirts," she said.

"From what you've seen," I said.

She shook her head, and I watched the straw come sprinkling out of her hair like rain. "From what I know," she said.

Old man Humberto told as how the only reason Thane took up with Skeet was a bootlegging run. Said their whiskey-making brought them each seventy or eighty dollars a month — and that was counting in Mondrow. But then, Skeet had never been caught with a still. Every time the sheriff came by to look for one, Skeet roared him down laughing. He said, "I ain't no backwoods shine-runner. You know I ain't. I got a business to keep up. How'm I going to do that if I go breaking the law?"

"Something to think on," the sheriff said. "You and your friends."

❧

Next time Lily Mark appeared herself, she stayed on a whole week. If it hadn't been for Ruby's open house, she might've kept herself away. But then there's no predicting the ways of spirits. They come and go whenever they want, and they don't pay a never mind to others. I said to Allie once how it must be mighty fine, running their life whichever way they pleased. And she said yeah, excepting it wasn't *life* they were running exactly. Which was true.

I tried to hold that in my mind the night of the open house, when Thane and Ruby and me stepped off the front porch and ran smack into the image of Lily Mark. She was glowing such a blue as to light up the night, and I still didn't fasten on the sight of her till I was halfway through her — the blueness hanging all about me like a smoke — and me, stopping what I was saying with a half sentence out my mouth, taking a gasp for breath and afraid to do even that — afraid I'd be breathing *her* in and maybe I wouldn't be able to breathe her out again. And then I was past her, looking back, Thane and Ruby asking me was I starting in to choke, and patting their hands at my back like I'd turned into an old woman all of a sudden.

Lily Mark, she followed along behind us the whole way to the schoolhouse. Every time I turned back to look, Ruby pulled at my skirts. She said, "Who are you looking for, Mama?"

"It's nothing honey. I thought I saw someone is all."

"Who?" Ruby said.

"Somebody," I said. "Somebody I once knew."

❧

Allie wasn't expecting a Sunday caller. She told me that herself. She guessed she wouldn't ever have met any men at all if she hadn't gone to church Sunday mornings — no colored men leastwise, and they were the only ones that could've changed her life as much as Warren would do eventually. She dressed herself up proper once a week, putting on the only dress she owned that wasn't made for toiling in. It was patterned with tiny calico flowers of a color Allie said was "bird egg blue," and it had got lace stitched on at the skirt hem and the wrists. Inside it, Allie looked pretty as an iced cake — rich and smooth and promising sweetness underneath.

"It been my mama's dress one time," she said. She stared in the mirror at the full curve of her bosoms, and then, standing sideways, she ran her hand down over their shape. She said, "I guess I fill this out just like she done."

"You're shaped like a time glass," I said, moving my hand through the air to mimic her design. "Those work smocks, they hide you."

She said, "Just as well, what with the mens around here." But she was meaning Skeet and Mondrow and men all like that. I don't know if she ever gave a thought to the decent men she was missing because she didn't ever breathe a word on it to me one way or the other. When Warren showed himself at the kitchen door on a Sunday afternoon, Allie looked more surprised than Humberto and me. Her eyes showed white all around the edges, turning their centers to two black-gleaming stones.

"What he want with me?" she said.

"Shhh," I said, leading her out of the kitchen. "He's still standing at the door."

"What do I do?" she said.

"Pick your skirts up out this room and talk to him," I said.

Allie rolled her jewel eyes around in her head. "I ain't asked him to come," she said.

"So you're going to send him away?" I said. "Big, fine-looking man like that, who came over special for to visit with you."

Allie laughed. "You a matchmaking woman all of a sudden?" She touched her fingers to the tip of her pale pink tongue before she ran her hands over her hair, smoothing it back. "I guess I got to show myself," she said. And then she was gone.

❧

Allie said Warren drove tractor for outlying farms. Sat up atop a Yuba Model 12 and felt the machine-horses pulling. Most of the country he drove in was saved for raising up cattle — Longhorns, Angus, Herefords. But the farmers had set aside parcels of the land for cash crops, and Warren tilled the earth close and deep for seedings of cotton or snap peas or rye. Warren said he was as good a tractor man as God had seen fit to set down in the South, on account of which he got himself work regularly. He guessed the wages were pretty good, too, except two dollars a day wasn't half what the white drivers got.

A couple years back, he'd asked a foreman couldn't he get paid by the work he did, instead of being waged flat-rate. Kind of made sense to give a man a reason to try hard. But the foreman had fired him outright. Said he was a "nigra with dangerous notions," making to outearn the white folk without which he wouldn't have any job at all. So Warren had left it alone after that, keeping his figurings to himself and taking his two-dollar wage with a pasted-on smile.

❧

Warren started appearing himself regular come Sundays, stepping across the kitchen porch with a walk that rung out solid-sounding. He was built head-high and shoulder-wide — six foot by both directions, Allie said. But that was just what it looked like from down below. When he stood next to her, he filled up her whole sky. She said, "When I want to look him in his eyes, I got to stare straight up. It like trying to search out the moon. You know it be up there somewhere, but you can't tell how long you got to look."

Sometimes, Warren brought her penny presents — a sweet-clove orange, a blue hair ribbon, a tiny spray of dried field flowers. One time, he even brought a small stoppered bottle of rosewater perfume. Allie puzzled over it all the evening through. She said, "I ain't got no use for somewhat like this here. You'd think he ought to knowed it, too — what with me scrubbing floors or clearing stalls all the day."

I said, "Hard as you work, you've got to get up off your knees some of the time. He gave you rose water for then — when you're dreaming at night, or for your Sundays maybe, when you're waiting on him to come walking by."

Allie held the glass bottle up to the light and tilted it backwards and front. She set her eye up close to it, like she was expecting she might find something precious at the inside — something she hadn't seen before.

"It ain't practical, though," she said.

"Don't everything have to be practical," I said. "Plenty of things worth having that aren't that."

Allie was still staring into the stoppered bottle — like her mind was riding the tiny-made waves on a rosewater ocean. She said, "I guess Warren ain't exactly a practical man."

"Oh no," I said. "No. He's trying to be much more than that."

❧

The first time Skeet thought to lay hands on me, my whole world got shook up, top to bottom. Later on, Allie said she could see it coming from a long ways off — by how Skeet dropped his looking to my hips when I walked around the room, by how he grabbed me at my wrist when he wanted something, taking the excuse to touch, by how he asked after my husband twice or three times.

The night it happened, Allie was working the stove instead of me. The dinner crowd was an hour past, and Humberto was coming in and out the kitchen as regularly as a windup toy, carrying in scrap-covered plates, carrying out fresh folded napkins. Skeet was setting on a stool, smoking himself a frayed cigar.

"I heard Thane went down to the school with you," he was saying. "The other night, I mean. Something for your Ruby girl."

Allie was stacking plates in a hot-water sink, clapping the stonewares hard together so as to make like she couldn't hear. Skeet's voice got closer then. He must've stood up out his chair and come up from behind.

"How come you couldn't have asked me?" he said. "I would've went with you. It being something for your girl there. Maybe if you would've asked me nice."

Where she was standing, Allie felt a thick finger draw a line down the back of her dress. It pressed hard on the cloth, like it was thinking to cut the cotton clean open. Just then, Humberto came in, his hands full of cups. Skeet turned on him when he wasn't halfway into the room. He said, "Get out, old woman."

"I am not done with clearing," Humberto said.

"You's done with everything," Skeet said. "Don't make me tell you twice."

Allie plunged her arms elbow deep in the sink water, like she was looking for some dish she'd lost in the washing. Her arms and her face were her only parts uncovered, and she'd got to keep them hidden. Skeet must've seen her there — all hunkered down over the sink — and wondered whether she was making to climb inside it. He put a clumsy hand to her waist, pulling her backwards. He said, "Get up out of there. I'm talking nice to you now."

And then he had her, had her by one hand circling her ribs and by the other hand sliding down her soapy arm. He said, "You can't pretend I ain't here, little girl. I ain't going to let you." When he saw her, really saw her — saw the dark stones of her eyes, the curl-wisps of her hair, the thick trembling at her lips — he dropped her as suddenly as if she was the devil wrapped up in a woman's form. He opened his palms wide, like they were dripping with a poison, and up at his neck, his scars flooded red. The skin around his eyes was twitching so bad, looked like a craziness had cut loose inside his head.

"You," he whispered to her. "You."

❧

Skeet must've been wondering would his hands ever come clean again. Next day he spent rocking in a porch chair, Mondrow beside him. He hung his hands outside the armrests, like they weren't any more use to him-even if he couldn't bring himself to throw them out completely.

When I walked past the front-room window, I saw Skeet was shaking his head. "Put my arms clear round her, and still I didn't know what I had," he said.

Mondrow leaned back in his chair. He set his hands across the low curve of his belly and let go a long breath. "Plenty of whites has took themselves a little nigra," he said.

"I ain't took her," Skeet said.

"Ain't got nothing to wash off, then," Mondrow said.

I went around to the pantry, and Allie and me set down by the window. We were starting in to peel a knee-high tub of milky potatoes. Every so often, the wind took up the branches of the dogwood outside and threw wild splashes of sun on the thinning curtains. When Skeet's voice came back to us, it was quieter — shaky like a boy's.

"Been fixing my feed all this time," he said. "My feed — getting worked up by them foul darkie hands."

Mondrow said, "Nigra mammie set my table first twenty years of my life. I ain't none the worse for it."

Skeet said, "Maybe."

Mondrow said, "I ain't."

Allie caught her breath just then, and I looked up to see her pressing at a knife-cut on her thumb.

Skeet's voice came up again. "You hate nigras same as me."

Mondrow said, "Yeah, I do."

I reached my hands down to the bottom of the potato tub and brought up a cupful of spud milk. "Soak that here," I said to Allie. "Soak it clean."

Skeet's talking got caught up with the wind. It seemed to be sounding from under the floor. It said, "Then how come you's going on like a nigra lover?"

Mondrow said, "I just don't hate them for their germs."

❧

Punishment was not long in coming. Skeet and Mondrow, they took themselves a day to think it through. There were limits to what all they could do. If they took a strap to Allie and me, we'd be likely to get up and leave — so it wouldn't be hardly worth the trouble. They had got to be softer-going than that.

In the end, this was what they done. Skeet took away from Allie the mop and ammonia she had been cleaning the floor tiles with, and gave her back a palm-sized scrubbing brush and a ten-gallon bucket of lye. "Don't put no water in there," he said, pointing at the lye tub.

"No sir," Allie said.

"I'll find out if you do," Skeet said.

When Allie got up off her hands and knees from a few hours' working, the lye had burned her skin so bad, she was blistering. We wrapped her hands, one finger at a time, in long strips of cotton gauze — but it only helped her temporary. When she went back to scrubbing, the lye soaked through the bandagings and burned her hands some more.

Allie said, "It be the same as a boiling oil, I guess. It feels slippery slick to your fingers touching, even while it be peeling your skin back. I don't know as I got me any flesh left for it to take."

Allie never cried out in the days, but in the nights she let go a soft moaning in her sleep. Just when I was fixing to ask her could we pack ourselves to go, Skeet took her off of the floor work, giving her hands a chance to heal themselves. Her blisterings closed off and shed themselves, showing marks of pale pink scarring underneath. A few weeks passed and she was rolling her fingertips on the tabletop like she was drumming a tune. She said, "They ain't numb no more. I feel them all moving, every one."

I don't think I knew at that time what Skeet had got in mind for punishing me. Maybe I thought he had set out my suffering by harming Allie before my eyes. But a part of me saw there would be something else. A mind like Skeet's wouldn't go idle on me. There would be something else of its making — something quiet and concealed, waiting, always waiting, to catch me unaware.

❧

The sound of Lily Mark's voice was the sound of words moving under water — thick at the vowels and muffled at the edges, the volume riding over her talking in waves. I don't guess I expected her to say a word to me at all, even though Allie had told as how her mama had talked to spirits all the living day. The way it happened, I heard her voice before I saw her. It was late on a summer night, the blue-black of the sky scoring the edges on my window shade. And me, I was lolling in a cool bath, letting the water run all down my arms and neck in the trail of a soft sponge.

"Cassie," she said. "Mama to my girl."

I turned myself fast around in the tub, hooking my hands over the curled metal lip and kneeling close in the clear water. Lily Mark was setting on a wash stool, looking herself in the wall mirror. She glowed a color somewhere between white and aqua — the color of the highest, thinnest cloud in a cool blue sky.

"You're looking pale," I said.

Lily Mark kept looking herself straight on in the reflecting glass. She drew her hands up to her face and traced them slowly over the hollows in her cheeks. "I've lost weight," she said. "See how it tells on me?"

I said, "Mm-hmm."

My bathwater turned cold while we set there, and looking down, I saw my skin take the shivers. The surface shine on the water trembled in a hundred tiny ripples. Standing up, I pulled a towel down from the linen hook and roughed it over me.

"Ruby all right?" Lily Mark said. Her lips moved themselves around the words before the sound took them up, like she was speaking from a great, uncertain distance, her voice straining over the miles in between us.

I said, "I'm doing the best I can for her."

She nodded her head slow. She said, "You are."

While I was pulling my nightclothes over my head, Lily Mark disappeared herself from the wash stool. I thought maybe she had quit me entirely, when I spied a shining in the corner of the damp rug. It was her dress, sparkling and hollowed where she'd stepped free of it. When I turned full around, I found her. She was setting herself down in the bathwater I'd left over. Her body had turned transparent under the surface, so that it looked like her head and shoulders and her pale blue breasts were all that was left of her — floating like a mermaid in a cool black sea.

"I'm tired," she said to me. "It's been a hot day."

❧

The trees in the yard spread out branches to fill up the sky. With each year going by, they were dwarfing the dinner house all the more — reaching over it so far that from a distance it looked like a doll house — all windowed and sided-up in miniature. Sometimes Ruby brought Remy out of the barn and walked him around under the low-hanging leaves. I spied them out the pantry window — the giant-made horse and the fairy-tale forest, and my little girl playing under it all. The sight of it made my heart take to singing.

Some nights, I looked out to the yard from my bedroom window and saw every tree — every last sprouting leaf — flaming with a blue fire and still not burning up. I kept looking for spirits to appear themselves under the branches, but they only showed irregular, in a passing light. They were like flame on a thousand fireflies — bright-glowing for a second's time, and then gone invisible again. Sometimes, a clear image of one of them would burn itself into my mind, so that I would keep on seeing it, even after its light was out. That's how I saw Oloe the first time since Copper Crown, sudden and flaring under the wide dogwood tree. She had got her broad skirts gathered up in her hands like she always did when she walked open ground. The skin on her face was shining flawless and pearl-blue, and her hair was coiled high on the top of her head. Before she disappeared, her eyes found me at my window and held on to me there.

I stood pressing at the glass in the quiet of the night, till I heard Allie's feet coming upstairs. She waited by my open door, listening for my breathing in the dark.

"I been in the yard," she said. "I seen it all."

❧

When I asked Allie what was she doing walking the yard at night all on her ownsome, she said, "It wasn't only me." Said, "Warren been out there, too. And don't you go asking what him and me been doing by secret, because it ain't nothing like what your mind be working up."

"I'm not asking," I said.

"It's what you *imagining* I be worrying on," she said.

"I'm not imagining," I said.

"Fine," she said.

"Fine." I smiled at her.

Allie let go her voiceless laugh, breathing in thick, rasping breaths that whistled when they came out her throat. I tried to remember myself how close she sounded to the times I'd heard her cry — once when her mama died and once when Maggie's baby had been born. The laughing and the crying, they had both got a note of desperate to them, shaking in her bosom like they were fighting to come out and she was straining to hold them back.

Just now, the breaths were quieting themselves. Allie was using the flat of her palm to wipe away some stray salt from the corner of her eye.

"Have you seen the trees?" I said. "The color that's been touching all of them?"

Allie put her fingertips together in the near-dark, like she was making to pray. "I seen that and more," she said.

"What's happening out there?" I said. I faced the dull glow from the window. My hands were dyed in blue light.

"God has picked a spirit place," Allie said. "Picked it, named it, set it down. Right outside our door."

❧

Skeet tried to shoot Warren once. That's how bad things had got. And if Skeet had hit him, maybe even if he had killed him, there wasn't hardly a law man in the state would have bothered himself about it. That was the feeling of the times. There wasn't any course a colored could take to protect himself excepting to run on away, and Warren had got too much stand-up pride inside him for that. Probably he figured if he'd got to dodge and scrape just to stay alive, then it wasn't a world worth wandering, anyhow.

The day it happened, him and Allie were setting on the pantry porch taking a visit. Warren set up straight in a fraying cane chair, holding his field hat in his hands, and talking on some new idea for a plowing machine that had come to him in the night — same as he'd done every Sunday afternoon for four months going.

The shot came like lightning through a clear sky — wild and deafening loud. From where Skeet was standing, just the other side of the kitchen door, he had fired clean through a leg on Warren's chair. What with his seat spilled, Warren had sprawled flat to the floorboards, cracking one or two where he had fallen. Skeet came outside then. He was swinging his gun free and careless, like he could drop it just as easy as he could fire it a second time.

Skeet said, "Now, I don't run no brood farm for nigras." He waved his gun around toward Warren. "Okay, boy?" he said.

Warren looked up from the groaning planks. He said, "I hear you."

Skeet took in a long breath and closed his eyes, like a man who had come home after a long time away. "Then why you still in my sight?" he said.

❧

Allie found out the ways of love. Not that she didn't know them before, just that she hadn't ever found them out with a man that loved her back. Warren was the first one to touch her with a loving that reached its fingers clear down into her soul. Allie didn't let on about him so much by what she said as by how she appeared herself. The black stones of her eyes would wander out the window to the distant trees, never taking themselves a focus. But she was seeing all the same, seeing the picture of Warren her mind was working up — husky-throated and broad-striding, and filling up the sky above her with face and endless shoulders. He was a giant, the way her heart saw him. And growing larger by two inches or three every day she knew him.

Evenings when Allie came inside from meeting Warren in the yard, her hair was escaped from where she had tied it back. The tiniest beading water shone on the curve of her forehead and the high angle across her cheeks. Her lips were kissed swollen and red, and through the parting between them, she breathed rapid as a sparrow.

One time when Allie came in from the night, she said, "I be foolish and I know it. And I can't hardly get myself to care."

I said, "You got to be careful that Skeet don't catch you out."

She said, "If he catch me, then he catch me. That man got his own doings as I can't no ways worry over."

I said, "I watch for him. Nights when you and Warren are out there. I do."

And Allie twined her arms around my shoulders then, rocking me back and forth like one of us was the mama and the other was the child, only I couldn't tell which way it was, and I don't expect it mattered. "We ain't going to be found out, then," she said. "Not with you watching, we ain't." She was pressing her head to my neck, smelling like wet grass and rose water and the willingest kisses of the man that loved her.

❧

Mama and me, we were writing letters every month. Sometimes, it didn't seem like I'd got the strength to tell her two words more than a scrawl in a diary book — what time I'd woken up in the morning, what Ruby'd said when I walked her down to the school, how the supper call had gone, and all like that. But then there were other times — times when what I'd written down shaped into the sounds of one soul talking to the other, when the longest road between my mama and me groaned and shifted and rearranged itself so that it wasn't any distance at all, and there I was, staring into those faded gray eyes with the sun-folded edges — tender and knowing as the wide heart behind them. I said,

Dear Mama,

Can you see me clear as I see you now? You're kneeling by your garden in your corn-flower dress, bundles of jimweed crowding at your hands. Are you happy where you're working? Your eyes, they don't show. They have folds at their edges from where you've labored under the sun the last ten years going. If I think hard on it now, I can nearly see all the sights they've looked on — your topsoil garden growing wild with tomato vine, the back field long gone to seed with milkweed and black-eyed Susans, the springtime bluebonnets flooding the earth like a sea sprung up from the clay. In spite of all the troubles, isn't it fine to grow old in a land such like this?

If you could see my eyes, Mama, I wonder if you'd see all I've been living through. Can you see me partially, maybe? Your little Cass's face — full woman grown? Allie says I've got myself eyes just like yours — clear like a child's — waiting for a wisdom to find them.

Have I appeared yet, Mama? Have I told you all I know? Can you tell me what it is?

Your loving Cass

❧

Two days off from Ruby's fourteenth birthday, she took sick to her bed. Wouldn't take anything to eat, much as I asked her. When I came to look in on her, I saw her face was drained pale where it nested in her black-mane hair. Her fingers were clutched over the top of the sheets, thin as bird claws. She watched me while I set some beef broth on her water stand, her eyes darting quick and wild. I set myself down at the bedside.

"You look like you're about to fall off the ends of the earth," I said. "About to fall that way or get pushed. Why're you acting so afraid, baby?"

Ruby shook her shoulders like she was throwing off a shiver. "I've got the aches something bad," she said.

"Where?" I said.

Her thin, white arm crawled itself out of the bedclothes and came to rest across the fold of blanket covering up her stomach. "About here," she said. "I think I must've ridden Remy the wrong way. Cut myself somewhat awful at the inside, I guess, because I'm bleeding now, too. Bleeding like nobody could stop it."

Looking on my girl lying there, my mind flew back to Lily Mark, pouring her life out of her after baby Ruby had been born — shivering a storm under the sheets and growing colder even so. Her face was nestled close in her jet-colored hair, just like Ruby's — and they both had about them the look of a raven that had taken a woman's form — glossy and well-curved and blue-black at the crown.

"Oh, Ruby girl," I said. "You aren't sick." I laid my head to her breast and kissed her fingers where they were laying on top of the quilt, one at a time. "I haven't told you what I ought," I said. "It's my fault."

"What?" she said. "Mama, what?"

"You've taken yourself a woman's ways," I said. "You've got yourself the monthly."

❧

Mama never got a letter that she didn't answer back. I had written down questions to her quick as they had come to mind, and with a month or two going past, her answerings would fall into my hands, set out deliberate on sheets of white mail-skin. Her writings fanned out like the wings of paper birds, creased-over and weary, and see-through pale by the reading light.

Dear Cassie,

I've tried to envision you where you're at, but won't any picture come to mind. Isn't it strange, the darkness I'm in? God gave me the sight, but not for seeing what all I want. Much as I argue with Him, He doesn't change the gift.

Maybe if I had been born outside of Copper Crown, I could work my imaginings on some other place. Maybe if I had traveled some before I married your daddy. Truth is, I've seen the same Sally River, the same Valley Road, the same seeded patches on the same parceled farms, from the first day my eyes were opened to the world. My whole way of looking on things, from the reach of the white birches to the color of their shade, has been created by this place itself. (I don't even know if I step outside of Copper Crown in my dreams. Could be I go on walking the same ground, Marston's hill, Jensen's road, over on and over on, all my days and nights.)

I try to imagine you, Cass. I try to imagine your eyes, and the knowings behind them, and all the ways you've grown out from under me. And I wish I could tell you I see you for true. But I can't make you out, baby girl. My vision is dark with the filling-up past and all I can catch on to is your sweet gray eyes looking back on me as you were riding away that last time, baby Ruby in your arms, more than fourteen years ago.

Mama

❧

Skeet and Mondrow boarded some forty mares and sires between them — breeders, mostly, that birthed colts which got sold at rancher's auction. They were a sight, those breeders, short-legged and barrel-chested, and muscled heavy over the hinds, like they were bred for nothing outside of ranch-herding. Ruby took to the shaggy-headed colts like they were the chosen beasts of God. She stroked them over with the curry brush so tender-like, they ran to the gate when they saw her coming, poking their tiny muzzles through the fence slats. Every year, a few of them were foaled with pinto patches splashing their hides. Allie and me suspected that Skeet was loaning out Remy for stud, but there wasn't any way to prove it once the siring was done. And we didn't mind the idea of those colts, chocolate and cream, all high legs and spirit, growing fantastic and tall all over the state.

If Ruby had ever got a horse to call her own, though, it was Remy. She rode him like her skirts were melted down onto his back — close and connected — without rising her seat up off his withers. She didn't ever take a crop to him because she didn't ever have to. He minded her from love, aged and lasting, just like he'd done since she'd been a toddling child.

She took him out for a ride amongst the trees every afternoon, no matter the weather. It could be raining in the dead chill of winter, and still she would ride him. I remember one time in February when it started to snow just as Remy and Ruby appeared themselves out from a grove of beech trees, on their way back to the barn. There was the muffled quietness of cold in the air. The only sounds were Remy's shifting his weight from hoof to hoof, and the squeaking of the saddle leather. Ruby saw me where I was standing on the porch. She raised one hand, palm upwards, to the sky.

"It's white rain," she said. Her breath rolled out thick and foggy over her lips while she spoke.

"No, honey," I said. "It's snow."

"Snow!" she said.

"Yes," I said.

"I never thought I'd get to see it," she said.

She rode closer up. A few flakes were tangled in her hair, separate and bright, like stars in a net.

"Me neither," I said.

"Oh, Mama. It's like a celebration. It's like a parade. It's like confetti falling through the sky."

❧

I wrote,

Dear Mama,

When night comes on, I'm lonely for touching. It's been sixteen years since a man held me in his arms — almost long enough for me to forget how my skin came alive with the twining. And then, Murray was always so reserved with me. Wouldn't hardly reach out his hand to find me unless I took hold of him first — and what did I know about taking hold, me being fifteen years?

The years since, they've grown me wiser. If I found out a man to love — one that would turn around and love me back — I guess I'd be holding him all of the time. My hands would line the tendons at his neck, the narrowing shape of his back, the flat muscling in his calf.

I'd be knowing his hills and hollows so good, I could fashion him the ground up from so many wet bricks of clay.

But I'm just dreaming out loud now, Mama. Don't you pay me a never mind. The way things are, the only man that wants to touch me at night is Skeet — and he hasn't got any love behind his connivings. I've got to dodge me this way and that just to keep my bosom out his hands.

Seems like most women are spending their lives dreaming on one breed of man and running from the other. It isn't true of Allie, I guess, her finding love with Warren like she's done. But who else is there? I can't be looking to Oloe nor Lily Mark nor Aunt Pauline nor Allie's mama neither. Only ones left are you and Daddy, and I don't know as I can say one word about how you all had your loving. Long as I been living, you haven't ever told me anything about it. I figure you either haven't been willing or you've been waiting on me to ask. So now I'm asking.

With love,

your Cassie

❧

Dear girl,

Loving was fine-made between your daddy and me. Didn't I ever tell you how it was? I guess I've done what my own mama did, and figured my daughters would find out about men all for their own selves. Unknowing mamas bring up unknowing children. I didn't know any better, Cass. Isn't it a shaming?

Can't everything between a woman and her man be spoken. Some of it has got to be shown. That's the way your daddy and me were. A man such like him couldn't talk out loud on how he loved me. (He tried a couple times, after I begged for him to do it. But the words just came out his mouth like stones — hard-sounding on his lips and hurting him where he let them go.)

Cass, he made up for it with his touch. Those rough-weathered hands found out my deepest places and loved me slow, determined-like, till they turned me over inside with a joy of their own making. Some men touch you by desperate greed and you know they're taking from you all the while, and other men touch you by simple gift, and all their lovemaking is done for to give to you something gentle, something kind, something like the farthest secret in their soul. (You're going to know the one from the other soon as they put a hand to you. You wait and see.)

Funny thing is, Cass, the touching grows out of what all else you got between you. It can't conjure something that isn't there. Like with your daddy and me. Times were good and then they were bad. After Oloe was killed and your daddy went out to take his revenging, I didn't ever give myself up to his touching again. I felt myself ashamed just to be near him. Did you know? Seems like if I had let him come to me again, I would have been taking a killer to my soul, and I just couldn't let go the thought.

And then he went off to the war, and got killed himself. He left me alone with my high thinking and a small hill of a grave to keep the jimweed clear from.

I didn't ever forgive him, daughter-mine, and it was a sorry thing. I did love him so.

Your mama

❧

I always knew there was a God, and I always felt He watched over all I did my whole life long. But God-faith didn't stop bad times from coming. That was the thing. Allie prayed to God at night — but her mama, she still died, and her brother, he still hanged — and her fingers had still blistered up under the lye bleach when she had scrubbed with it all the day.

When I asked Allie why did she keep saying her prayers when they weren't doing any good to her, she said, "They doing a good to me, girl. It just a good you can't see."

I said, "Like what way?"

She said, "Like I ain't praying that God be changing the world. I's only praying that He be changing the way I wake up to it."

I wished I could've found myself a preacher that thought on God like Allie did, but they were either scarce or hiding when I went to look. Those that preached to poor white folk were red at the face from talking on the devil all the day, and those that preached to the fine-fed folk, they had to pass the collection plate before they knew who all was saved.

I was about thinking God Himself had taken

a rest from churchgoing when I passed Allie's worship house one time. It was a feed barn the way it looked from the outside — red, peeling paint over flat-board walls. The corners were leaning so far to the north, looked like the beams were fixing to pick up their plank skirts and run away. But the sound was what caught me up short, the sound of the singing — like a hundred silver voices ringing underwater — filling up the air with notes till it was all I breathed.

You can hinder me here, but you can't
  do it there
For He sets in the heavens, and He
  answers my prayer
Just going over in the heavenly land.

Way over yonder in the harvest field
The angels, they turning the chariot wheel
Just going over in the heavenly land.

Silver voices. Sounding voices. Music moving through the sea. It was the most holy sound I ever heard. Like God was letting His faithful sing out in their spirit voices before their time had come. Just to know the beauty of it.

❧

Maggie didn't like to write letters regularly. When Allie once asked her how come she didn't send us more news, Maggie wrote back and said, "things don't change that fast. that's all i know." She said,

dear allie,

i hope you's forgive me for all the times i ain't wrote you. the days has come and went and i ain't so much as knowed their passing. copper crown don't seem to change one year to the next, and neither does the people that walks its harden clay. only time i know the years is moving be when I look to my lloyd. last month, he turned sixteen year. sixteen, and i can't hardly believe it.

he so far away from being my baby — my smiling bundle boy — but that's how i see him still. when i first come back to olson's laundering, wouldn't nobody give me a second look but him — the child that needed me for to give him my breast. he was so pale, do you remember? pale as lime-dust when he was birthed, and when he growed to a child, he turned even paler than that.

if i would've left him at the door of some white-folk church, he would've been took in for one of their own, i's guessing. they would've raised him up rich white, most like. they sure would've set more meat to his plate than i's done these passing year. and he wouldn't never have knowed about his mama — how her love had got used up and throwed away and how, after on, she couldn't never get clean again, least not in the eyes of them that remembered. but i couldn't let him go, allie, selfish as i be. i needed him entire. i needed his elf-size feets and his angel hands. i needed them wide, blue-marble eyes with all his love inside them. and now that he be growed, i needing him still. this boy be keeping me alive by love. god help me, but he be.

life has gone easier with me since my looks has finally faded. i's prayed to god for it all these years and he's heard me at last. used to be I thought all my suffering would make me plain. i thought if i cried myself enough tears, there'd be hollows sinking round my eyes — if i kept myself awake enough nights, there'd be wrinkles rooting across my skin. didn't never happen.

i might've never got plain at all without ten hours of hard laundering to keep me striving all the day. mrs. olson, she says i has got too thin to keep up with the work the way i do. she says the thickest part on me be my elbows and my knees, and that it hurts for a person to look on me, the way i's proportioned. but allie, i don't mind. my curves has disappeared themselves. my hips has gone flat, my breasts has gone narrow. my smocks, they hang on me straight like a line from my shoulder to my calf. from the back, i looks like a younger child than lloyd.

all on account of which the mens don't follow me with their eyes no more. the wives of the mens don't scorn me to walk the streets. the children don't throw rocks at my back. the word "jezebel" ain't spat out on me when i passes by.

i's free. i's free. i's plain and withered, god knows, but i's free. oh allie, if only i'd knowed how to do it, i would've give up my looks at the start — so long back, when it still would've mattered. when clyde would've lived to see me — with my bony back, and my spindle legs, and my black-skinned children sprung true from his seed.

maggie

❧

Me and Humberto stopped planting trees when the ground couldn't hold any more. There were birch and white oak and crying willow, sending out their branches like hands, reaching to one another across the gaps in the sky like they were all making to clasp together somewhere when our backs were turned. Humberto saw it too —the life of those wood fingers uncurling against the blue.

"These trees," he said. "There is something about them, something unusual."

"Like how they've been planted," I said.

The old man let out a thin smile. He said, "No. It is not the planting."

"Then, what?" I said.

"It is the growing," he said. He walked to the shade of a Jackson peach and ran his hands across a low-going branch. His fingers, where they moved, were white balsa shoots — swollen with wood-knots where his knuckles ought to have been.

He said, "They grow so fast they hardly have time for water or air. They hardly have time for roots."

"Then they don't have the need," I said.

"They've got to be growing by something other."

Humberto stooped down at the soil and dug his wood fingers into it, feeling for a secret under the earth's clay skin. "I do not know what," he said. "It has got to be something, but I do not know what."

A wind took up the lawn just then, turning it silver under its breath. From out of the grass-hair flew tiny peach leaves, dried and veined from where they had grown old on the ground. They beat the air around us like the turning wings of unseeable birds, brushing past our clothes, settling in our hair with feathers light as ghosts.

"Look," Humberto said, waving his fingers under the rising leaves. "It is a wind from heaven!"

❧

Skeet, he started reaching for me with grasping hands. Nothing anybody would notice, at the first. He might hold me by the wrist or pull me up short by the waist — all the while taking me to task on my chores. But later, he took to touching me personally — pushing me up against a counter when wasn't anybody around, and pressing on me so close that I felt the weight of him from my bosom to my toes. His breath smelled of tobacco and onions, and his scars were darkened to the color of bloodroot where they spread over his neck. Above me, his eyes were two slits, glinting and glittering in their caverns.

"I'm coming after you," he said. "Some one of these nights."

❧

Wasn't anyplace I could hide myself from that man. No box, no shade, no shadow. I saw him coming for me so many times in my dreams, sometimes I woke thinking he had already taken me down.

One time I opened my eyes to see his shape leaning over me in my bed. My heart flew up inside my ribs like a wild sparrow behind a cage. I thought it was beating its wings so hard it was likely to leave me entire. And then I saw that what I thought was Skeet was only Allie come to wake me. She was trying to unglue my hands from their hold on the sheets.

She said, "Girl, what's got you so clinging afraid? I ain't taking the bedclothes for permanent. I just going to wash them is all."

I said, "Don't take them yet, Allie. I can't stand to get uncovered just now."

She let go the linens where she was pulling them. The window was throwing light from behind her, and through the sleeves on her nightdress, I saw the line of her arms falling at her sides — smooth and round as saplings. She brought me the counterpane quilt from the corner, and tucked it in all around my weight.

She said, "That feels safer, don't it?"

I said, "Much as it can while I'm under this roof."

Allie set down at the bed. She took one hand and stroked the hair off my face. She said, "We could leave. We could get us up out of here, away from him."

"And away from Warren, too," I said.

Allie shut her eyes. She was nodding her head slowly, up and down and up. She said, "Loving be one thing — but surviving be another."

"Maybe," I said.

"Mm-hmm."

"But this life isn't worth a go-round without we get us both."

❧

Allie and me, we'd seen danger-making before this. Plenty of times. We'd seen the hate-killings and the living dead they left behind. We'd seen God-churches burning, raped women crying. We'd rocked us to sleep plenty of newborn babies that didn't have any daddy. Allie liked to say how we'd seen every kind of danger-making except The War itself, but I told her if this wasn't a war, I didn't know what was. We were fighting and struggling, and dying too, just like the men'd done overseas — only our trials didn't get written up in the papers. And there wasn't any cease-fire as we could dream on, any time when all the hating would fold itself inwards to an end, when we could pack ourselves up off of killing ground and get on back to a home we knew as peaceful. The place we lived was the same place we were going to die. God didn't make us for anything other.

If I'd had to get through those times all by myself, without Mama nor Allie nor Ruby in my days, I would've given up my life a long while back — would've stepped out my body like a paper skin and turned into a spirit like Oloe or Lily Mark. I thought as how spirits must've still held some feeling inside them-some feeling of everlasting — a feeling that heaven had taken them onto its own land, and that there, finally there, they'd found themselves an acre of peace.

One time I asked Allie, "If you had got to name yourself the color of peaceful, what color would it be?"

"The color of peaceful?" she said. "That

be the same thing as the color of the center of the sky, the way I's thinking. Or maybe the color of bluebonnets when they put a haze on a hill. What you think it be?"

"Could be the color of the Gulf," I said. "Still and wide. Reaching to the curve of the world. Except I haven't ever seen it, so I can't tell for sure."

"The color of peaceful or the color of the Gulf?" she said.

"The Gulf, I guess. The other I have caught sight of by bits and snatches."

"Yeah," she said. "Like lighting up the yard at night."

"Following me down the street."

"Walking upstairs and settling down in your bathwater," she said.

Allie always did see through to the heart of my understanding.

❧

Where we lived, some walls were thick and some walls were thin. I didn't spend all the lifelong day with a hollow glass to my ear. I did my cleaning and my cooking, and I tended to my own business. But sometimes, a floorboard came up loose or an extra door fell itself open, and a conversation came floating down the hallway to my hearing, clear as a song. That's the way it happened when I caught the sound of Allie and Ruby one time jawing in the pantry. They were snipping figs to set on the drying rack outdoors, and just when they made to trim off the last hardened stem, Humberto came in with an extra bushel.

"I found where there are two more trees," he said. "Far behind the yard growth. Hanging to the ground, they were so heavy with fruit."

The wire-mesh door moaned open. "Where you going now?" Allie said.

"I will see if I missed any," he said. "I do not want the fruits wasting at the ground."

Ruby called after him, "Humberto, you're a taskmaster." But she'd got laughter in her voice. She fell quiet for awhile, and then I heard her start up again, low this time. "So what else did he say?"

Allie said, "Wasn't nothing else he *could* say, as I know of. I told him not yet, I ain't ready yet."

Ruby said, "But you are ready, aren't you." It wasn't a question. Allie didn't say anything. "But you do want him, don't you. For marrying, I mean."

Allie laughed then. She said, "Child, you got you such a way."

Ruby said, "You always say that, and then you won't tell."

"I's told him I ain't ready because I got me a family to think on," Allie said.

"A family?"

"Mm-hmm," Allie said. "I got me your mama and you both."

"Allie." Ruby's voice had taken an impatient sound.

"I's lived me thirty year now," Allie said. "The two of you is as close to sistering as I've ever got yet."

❧

I tried hating Skeet one time, but I couldn't keep it up. That kind of venom, it took too much out of me. Maybe I could've stood up under it if I had believed he'd been devil-bought, from his hat to his boots. But the thing was, even bad people weren't bad all the time. And even when they were doing bad things, maybe they weren't damned through and through. Maybe God saw a single, solitary iota of goodness beating in the heart of them somewhere — and maybe that was enough for a person to get themselves a forgiveness.

If all my speculations were true, then it seemed like the question of whether a body was saved or damned was a question of seeing. Like, I couldn't say a person was bad without I looked for the good inside them first — without I looked for it with eyes so wise as the ones of God, which I wasn't ever going to get this side of the Great Divide and maybe not even when I'd crossed over.

Skeet had been wishing harm on me every which way I turned since the day he'd caught Allie cooking in my place. He thought I'd made him out a terrible fool, I guess — thought I'd laughed at all those sweet things he'd spoken to the back of a colored woman that he thought was me. So he'd been shoving me and choke-holding me, grabbing my wrists and pressing my bosom — helping heaven to punish me for my sins, the way he must've figured it. He'd been hating me, straight and simple — hating me with the fury of a man that thought he served up the fury of his God.

Looking back on it now, Skeet must've thought there was such a thing as a righteous killer and that maybe he was one. I'm not sure if I ever knew what "righteous" ways were, but when I thought on them, I never once thought on killing a person. Not Skeet, not anybody. I never once had such a plan in my mind.

❧

Ruby found out my wedding dress. It was hanging in the back shadow of my closet those sixteen years, down at the other side of a spare ironing board. I'd almost forgot it had ever been there at all. But Ruby, she found it out, like she came to find out everything else, in time. When I asked her what she was reaching into the back of my closet for, she said as how Allie had asked her to tote out the ironing board on account of her regular board had got broken.

"I wasn't meaning to find it out," Ruby said. "But when I pulled on the board, I snatched off some lace, and then I thought to — well, I only brought out the dress with a thought to mend what I'd torn."

"I can't see any tear," I said.

"That's the thing," Ruby said. "I couldn't find one either. I guess I must not have torn it exactly."

"Ruby girl."

"Oh, Mama, you're just pretending you're angry. I always know when you're play-acting."

And I was pretending, too. Those yards of lace and organza brought me fresh back to another time, and I didn't mind it any. They brought me back to the quickness of Oloe's long white hands sewing in and out with her fine silk threads — to the sounds of my mama's waking dreams, spoken where she'd stood by the sitting-room window — to the shirt that shifted on my daddy's back while I watched him walking in the trail of our old horse — to the smell of the valley air before fires came running through it, paining my soul and making me wise.

Ruby touched her hands to the cedarwood pendants that I'd strung from the hanger to keep off the moths. "It's sure an ageable dress," she said. "Needlework done so fine — and it hasn't yellowed much, has it? If I hadn't known you'd been married in it, I would've said it hadn't ever been worn."

"You would?"

"*Looks* like it hasn't ever been worn, doesn't it to you?" she said.

"Yes," I said. "I guess it does."

❧

That night was the only time I'd worn the marriage dress since Oloe finished it, so many years ago. It was ten or eleven o'clock at night. The dinner house had gone quiet — so quiet I could scarcely hear any sound at all except the sighing of the rising wind, which could've been the breaths of Allie and Ruby while they dreamed whatever their dreams were full of, or which could've been the breaths of that old supper house itself, respirating through the cracks at the windowsills and past the hinges on the doors. Outside, the cicadas were quiet, playing absent to the thrumming of the wind against the eaves.

That dress was Oloe's finest doing, I guess. I had never seen one she'd sewn that had tinier stitchings to it, nor prettier lacings neither. The waist still fit me where she'd darted it to twenty inches — but my bosom, what all I'd grown of one, was crowded tight at the bodice. I could scarcely get the buttons done up at the back.

Skeet came up on me while I was walking the hallway, up and down, in front of the full-view mirror. Where he stood at the stair landing, his eyes were veined with drink, swollen with tiny red rivers.

"What you doing, little girl?" he said. "Playing dress-up bride?"

I didn't say anything. Talking wouldn't have made a difference then. In one of my nightmares once, I'd seen him coming at me down this hall, just like he was doing now. When I'd envisioned him, he'd been wide and unstoppable as a giant, filling up the passage to its edges so that there wasn't any way I could get around him. And that's how he was just then, no bigger and no smaller than I'd dreamed him — just powerful-built and fast-approaching, his scars flooded blood-black from all his drink.

When he got to me, he threw me under one arm, hitched up alongside his waist, like I was a sheaf of hay or a light set of horse tack, and no more weighted nor fragile than that. He carried me down the stairs to the old cook's kitchen before my chance-fist met up with his brow and left an impression there.

"Damn!" he said. He dropped me all the way to the floor. "What all you hitting with?" He found out the fingers on my left hand and dragged my thin wedding band off the one. "You going to go hurting somebody with that," he said. "Little liar that you is. Acting like you's married, when you ain't. I'll bet you's never even had a man except to fill you up with a baby. Ain't that the way?"

He pulled me over to the kitchen door and opened it up. Outside, the wind had found itself a wild-made force, curving and twisting and changing direction so that all the trees appeared like they were clapping their hands — furious passion-waves of leaves, bringing their veined patterns together — blackjack and spicebush, firethorn and chokeberry —

all gone wild under the breath of God. He threw my ring out into the yard, and the trees, they clapped harder.

We were half inside the door and half out when Skeet took me down. He tore me out of my dress like it was nothing more than a fruit peel, a paper wrapping. Soon as the skirts were off me, the wind picked them up, blowing through the open door, sweeping them deep into the kitchen where they took themselves a life and went flying from wall to wall, like a great lace bird gone blind.

Skeet was on me, fallen on my frame with the weight on a bear — pressing all the air out my lungs. He was fighting to draw himself out of his trousers, but his movements were dumb with liquor, and his fingers had got all thick and tangled with the buttons at his waist.

That was when the stick came down on him — fast and jagged where it cracked him at the temple. His head bobbed forward then, huge and monstrous where it fell. The blood-colored scars at his neck were pressed hot to my mouth so that I couldn't hear my own cries anymore. I thought I was likely to die of panic before I could ever crawl out from under him. I was all the way to my hands and knees by the time I saw Allie standing there, holding a wood plank high as a swinging bat, and hardly knowing what she'd done.

"Allie," I said. "Allie girl." And she came to me, then — dropping to her knees and folding me in her cradling arms.

She called out something, but I couldn't hear what it was for all God's wind. That breath in the trees had taken a voice so strong that Allie and me hardly heard all the plate glass blowing out of the house, hardly knew all the wood shutters were swinging open and shut, hardly would've seen, but for chance, the trail of my wedding dress where it flew out the kitchen window, flapping its drape-lace wings straight into what first appeared like the arms of a dogwood tree, but what turned out to be the arms of Oloe, reached straight out to catch it — like she thought the dress might not have been emptied, but might have been hiding inside it the loosed spirit of me.

❧

Come morning, the air was still. The wind had run away to the sky, and into the stillness it left behind there crept a milky frost. It lacquered the woody forest with a cool, melting sheen, and while I walked amongst the trees, I heard thick drops striking the ground in twos and threes. Plat, plat. Plat, plat, plut. The sound of kisses on the skin of the earth.

Cold white blossoms hung on the dogwood tree like bits of rag cloth. Frozen to the center trunk was my wedding dress, the sleeves thrown wide into the branches. When I plucked it down, it fell stiff like a woman into my arms. On one side of the hem, there was a string of white icicles, weeping from the heat of the sun.

I looked for my wedding ring, trying to remember the direction Skeet had thrown it the night before. I combed my fingers through the grass, and stars of hoarfrost fell into my palms, but I didn't find any ring there, hiding amongst the pieces of cold. It wasn't till I turned to go inside that I spied it, a pale-yellow shining from the branch of the closest tree.

The ring was stuck on the hand of Lily Mark's willow, almost hidden by a spray of sharp crescent leaves. It was edged over a thick-knuckled knot in the wood, now swollen bulbous and grainy from the frost. I pulled at the ring, but it was too small to slip over the willow's joint. And when I pulled harder, the frozen crescent leaves cut into me like tiny knives, drawing pearls of blood from my fingers. I saw that, unless I took a saw to the branch, that ring was going to stay stuck forever.

But I guessed I hadn't any more use for a ring, things being like they were. And Lily

Mark, she was entitled.

❧

Skeet was laid in a downstairs bed. It took Humberto and Allie and me, all three of us, to get him inside. His boots were waggly and dust-filled and they struck loudly against the floor when they passed over the doorjambs. He liked to comb a few long, stray hairs over the top of his smooth balded crown, but in the wind they had gotten mussed and out of place, and they fell like a scraggled cat's tail over the scar on his neck. There was a mark at the back of his head where Allie had struck him with the wood plank. It was raised and blue with a sharp-edged corner, and it looked like a strange, square plum.

The first day, he let go wide, low sounds from the back of his throat. "Aaahhh," he said, and the sound rolled out pained and even from the cavern that was his mouth. "Aaahhh."

"He trying to say something?" I said.

"No," Allie said. "He ain't come awake yet. Maybe he won't never. He just feeling his distant pain."

"You think he's going to die?" I said.

"If he don't see his way around it," Allie said. "He be bleeding from where I brung that board down on him, bleeding inside, where we can't see."

"We're going to have a whole lot of explaining to do," I said.

"What you mean we?" Allie said. "Ain't no reason for you to go involving yourself. It was me that killed him."

"And it was me that made you want to try," I said. "Besides, he isn't dead yet."

"But he going to be," Allie said. She pressed her lips into a thin, down-turning line, and then she let them go. The flesh bloomed back, purpled and wet and injured-looking. "I just know it."

"We're just going to have to wait on him to turn one way or the other," I said.

"Lord-a-mine," Allie said. "Why'd I have to hit him so killing hard?"

❧

Thane and Mondrow were at the door. Through the screen on my window, I could see them — shuffling their feet on the porch planks, their heavy thumbs hooked in their belts. Mondrow pulled his pink, gnarled knuckles from his hip and knocked them against the door for the second time.

"What do you want?" I said, calling out to them. Their two hats swung themselves backwards at the same time, locating my face in the open-shuttered window.

"Where's Skeet?" Mondrow said.

"He's sick," I said.

Mondrow made a sound somewhere between a cough and a laugh. "Wasn't sick yesterday," he said.

"It came on suddenly," I said. "He doesn't want to see anybody on account of it might be catching."

The two hats swung downwards. Underneath them, there were low voices moving back and forth. The occasional words escaped into my hearing, flying upwards on a motionless wind. ". . . but drunk ain't the same as sick . . . all I know . . . what with the drink he had in him . . . I don't remember . . . gin, mostly."

Then the voices stopped and Thane's hat came up. "We'll come back tomorrow," he said.

"You tell him we was here," Mondrow said.

They walked off, taking short strides like aged men, rocking side to side one foot to the other. Shadows from their hats spilled down their backs like water, black and cool-looking over their starched-fancy shirts. Their boots kicked up low clouds of dust that hung in the air, vague and unmoving.

I turned away from the window, back to the blind quiet of the room. After the brightness of the yard, I could hardly see what was in front of me. But then I picked shapes out of the darkness — the sharp corner of a sewing table, the porcelain curve of a washbowl, and Allie setting in a high-back chair, her hands, where they hung at her sides, as still and purposeless as up-pulled roots.

"Do you think they believed me?" I said.

"No," she said. "I don't."

❧

If only we had had more time, we could've figured us a better story as to how it happened, but come morning all our time had run out. Because when I walked into Skeet's bedroom, I found out he had already expired. His mouth was open, same as it had been the night before, but there wasn't any sound coming from inside it — no moan, no breath, no distant pain. His teeth, where they showed, were flat and dry. They looked like shelled nuts or chips of bone, yellowed and easy to break. The square mark where he'd been struck had turned a tender black, like a fruit overripe, and all around it, the skin had been leached of its color. In the air of the room, there was a smell that was both sweet and spoiled — the smell that hangs over stagnant water and ruined beef.

When Thane and Mondrow came by, I

walked them into where Skeet was laid out, gray and unwashed on his bed.

"He died in the night," I said. "None of us know the why of it."

The veins stood out on Mondrow's onion-skin face. His eyes popped from under his brown, peeled lids. "Died?" he said. "Two days ago he wasn't even *sick.*"

"He got sick yesterday," I said. "And he died in the night."

"Not without somebody helped him do it, I'll bet," Mondrow said. His lids sucked up his eyes so they were two wet slits in the brown round of his face.

"Now hold on," Thane said.

"When did he get *this?*" Mondrow said. And his hand appeared itself from his pocket, pressing Skeet's plum mark with the tips of two fingers. "Just the moment before he got sick, ain't that right?"

"He never said anything about it," I said. "And I never asked. It was sometime yesterday that he got sick, and sometime in the night that he passed on. He didn't ask my permission — he just went ahead and did it. And if ever he knew his reasons for dying, he didn't tell me or mine."

❧

Mondrow, he took Skeet's body away with him.

"You all wouldn't know how to bury him respectable," he said. "I'm going to have to see to it myself."

Next day, he came back with the sheriff. They stood in the dining room, the tonic running down their hair in thin, waxy rivers. The sheriff had stepped out of his new, iron-tipped boots on account of they pinched him. At the floor, his toes moved around in his loose cotton socks like small animals shuffling inside of a sack.

"My guess is they killed him while he was sleeping," Mondrow said. "Hit him over the head with a hammer or some kindling or a poker from the fire. Probably one of the nigras. Skeet hated nigras. Didn't even like them to touch his food."

"Slow down, now," the sheriff said. "I just got out of my boots."

"You ask them if it didn't happen like I said. You ask."

"I'm going to ask everything in my good time," the sheriff said. "Provided you stop talking long enough."

Puckers appeared themselves in the round of Mondrow's face, like he was sucking air from the inside of his cheeks.

The sheriff turned towards me. "You want to tell me how it happened?" he said.

So I told it exactly the same way as the day before. Skeet, he was drunk, then he was sick, then he was dead, and I didn't know what all led from one failing to the next. When the sheriff called in Humberto and Allie, they said the story over again. The sheriff reached down to the floor and pulled on his boots.

"Thank you for your time," he said.

"That all you going to do?" Mondrow said. "Thank them that's killed a man?"

"Ain't nobody talked about killing but you," the sheriff said.

"But what about that mark on his head?" Mondrow said.

"Skeet could've done that himself and you know it," the sheriff said. "He been falling-down drunk too many times to count."

"He didn't die accidental," Mondrow said. He puckered his face again, making hollows in his brown-veined cheeks.

"Well, I say he did, and that's all that counts," the sheriff said. "I don't want to hear about it no more. I'm tired. I'm going home. My feet hurt like hell." And he went away, his weight on his heels, the iron toes of his boots never touching the ground, favoring his blisters like a treasure.

❧

We didn't know who all Skeet had named for his inheritance. But we guessed it would be a far-off relative — somebody whose name we hadn't ever heard, whose face we hadn't ever seen, somebody who would sell the property out from under us before our bags were packed, and then go back to whatever nameless place he came from, his pockets full and his laughter loud.

And sure enough, there were men that came to the house to search through Skeet's papers — dull-suited men with dark bow ties who identified themselves by their tasks. *I'm here to look for the legal will and testament,* they said. Or, *I've been authorized to search for the deed to this land.* They learned to come in through the door without knocking, and, at the end of a few hours, to find their way out. They moved themselves through the house like shadows, taking books off the shelves with silent hands and forgetting to put them back. They stepped out of closed closets and locked bulkheads, skittering toward open air with the moths, fresh dust collected on their pinch-nose glasses, their skin the color of water and paste.

But none of them found what they were looking for. County records pulled out their copy of the land deed, but since it wasn't the original, it didn't count for much. And without a will to go by, the city claimed the property for its own, to auction off to a new owner whenever they saw fit. At least, that's how the sheriff explained it to me when he came by the dining house one time that spring with Allie and Ruby and me drinking lemon ices on the porch. He held out a white piece of paper to me, folded in three, like for official business. He was wearing a different pair of boots from the last time I had seen him. They were black and soft-leathered, and they were folded at the ankles in thick, dusty wrinkles, like from age. The sheriff paced back and forth in them while I read the paper in my hands. It said,

Resident: Miss Cass Sandstrom

The property of 137 Halliday Road, Victoria County will be sold at public auction on February the 24th. You are required by county law to terminate your tenancy by the beforesaid date in order that the property may be immediately transferred to new ownership.

I looked up. In the heavy, red-dun dust,

the sheriff was leaving footprints like hooves, pressed round and patient into the earth.

"We have to move out?" I said.

"That's what they tell me," the sheriff said. "Unless you want to buy this old place for yourselves."

❧

"How much cash money you got?" Warren said.

Allie turned her eyes towards me, black and glassy in the near-dark. "It ain't only *my* money," she said. "It's mine and Cass's both."

"How much?" Warren said. He slid his tongue over his lips, fast and shallow, like he was waiting to be fed.

"Seven hundred twenty-one dollar," I said.

"Maybe that be enough," he said.

"Enough for what?" Allie said.

"Enough to buy this property for your own self," he said. "Or enough to bid on it, anyway, when the auction come round."

Allie sat back in her chair. On the porch, there was a breeze that caught her calico skirts, opening the folds outwards like a fan. She looked across the lawn to where fireflies were lighting up the forest with their small white brightnesses, flashing amongst the leaves. In the curve of her glassy eyes, I saw reflected their white points of light, appearing and disappearing, like traveling stars.

"Buy this property?" Allie said. "Us two?"

"Look around you," Warren said. "You got yourself plenty of land, a standing restaurant, ready-made customers . . ."

"Maybe," Allie said. "I'll think on it."

"What's to think?" Warren said. He leaned himself forwards in his seat. The last daylight journeyed over his face in a pale corridor. The white of his teeth was stark and gleaming. "It exactly what you been dreaming on."

❧

Warren came to the house every day now that Skeet was gone. And I noticed he had taken to himself some forward ways. He wasn't forward with me. He was just forward in general. Putting on airs and such. Like one night, and I don't think it had been more than two or three days since Skeet had passed on, I heard Warren up in Skeet's room, rifling around in the bureau drawers, banging his way through the backs of the closets. And when he came out a half hour later, what do you think he was wearing except a suit of Skeet's clothes. His legs were wrapped in black-rib pants, wrinkled and rough-looking and too short where they ended on his calf. They were cinched with a belt of finished leather, a silver buffalo buckling the strap. On his head was a ten-gallon hat, the crown and the brim both looking like furred butter.

Allie said, "I see you been mischief-making."

"Nope," Warren said. "I don't like waste by principle. I just making use of the bounty."

"The bounty of a dead man," Allie said. "Don't you feel no shame?"

"Not hardly," Warren said. "Would you take a pride in me letting them things go to trash?"

"I wouldn't think about it one way or the other," Allie said.

"Then don't think about it now," Warren said. He walked out the door, leaving her staring at his back. The screen swung shut behind him, but through its mesh we could still see that broad yellow hat moving off into the darkness.

"Well, what do you know," Allie said. "I has picked myself a willful man."

❧

Warren had more rebellion in him than I first gave him credit for. With time going by, his shyness dropped away to reveal the pieces of love and anger, want and resentment that fitted together to shape his soul. It was a proud soul and a puzzling one, and the look of it made me a little afraid.

I thought back to the days when Warren was nothing more than a Sunday caller, waiting with his head bowed at the edge of the porch, lacking clean clothes and the shade of a hat, and I wished I hadn't been so eager to take his silences for kindness. Allie would've made up her own mind about him without I pushed her into his arms. I asked myself what had I got us into, and the truth was that I couldn't say.

❧

When Allie said, "We's going to get married," I tried to act pleased. I tried to smile, but my lips were stiff on my face. I tried to laugh, but the sound choked my breath.

"Ain't you going to say nothing?" Allie said. Her hands were open and facing upwards, towards the ceiling. She looked like she expected something might drop into them — a present maybe, or a kiss.

"When?" I said.

"Sunday next," she said. "That's what the reverend told me. Sunday next. Right after the regular church. Everybody's going to stay and watch." Allie stood still for a minute, waiting on me to say something. Then her hands dropped to her sides, delicate and sudden, like birds falling through the air.

"Are you happy?" I said.

"Yes," she said. "But not so much as if you was happy for me, too."

"Don't you pay me any never mind," I said. "You know I'm not satisfied unless I have something to worry myself over."

Allie laughed, but her hands stayed limp at her sides, like broken-necked birds. "That's true," she said. "You always worrying over nothing."

Come Sunday next, me and Ruby were standing in Orlock's field, staring at an old livestock barn with leaning beams and chipping paint. Ruby had on a dress with satin ribbons trailing from the waist. The jimsonweed grew up higher than her hem and the satin ribbons got tangled there, braiding themselves around the sticky stems of burrs and seeds. Over the field, there rose the sound of singing — a hundred voices pouring out like liquid silver.

Ruby said, "How come we can't go inside?"

I said, "It's a church for coloreds only."

Ruby said, "They can't make an exception? Just this once?"

I said, "Honey, maybe they could. But we don't have the right to ask."

❧

Mondrow stayed away. Sometimes I saw him riding by on Halliday Road, slowing up while he rolled down the windows of his car. Even from the distance, I could see his double chin, his swallowed-up eyes. He looked over the land sweeping and slow, like he wanted something from it. To marry it maybe, or to kill it — could have been either one.

Thane said, "You're wrong. Mondrow, he don't want nothing from this land but to own it. He told me so himself."

I said, "What does he want to own it for? There are only trees here. Trees and an old run-down restaurant."

Thane said, "An old run-down restaurant from which people been buying pints of Mondrow's corn liquor the last ten years going."

"Buying it how?" I said. "I haven't ever seen them."

"Them that was wanting to buy give Skeet five dollars on their way in," he said. "Then, when they was leaving, they picked up a jar from a pocket at the coatrack. It was wrapped up in paper and tied with basting string. Looked like a big jar of preserves."

"I remember the customers carrying such," I said.

"It been a big business," he said. "Sometimes brought in fifty dollars a week."

"Fifty dollars split three ways, then, was it?" I said.

Thane grinned, his mouth closed. His mustache sank to where, black and alive, it kissed his lower lip. "I give them the cash to start with," he said. "And they counted me in for the share."

"And now?" I said.

"Now, I don't need the money," Thane said. "I never did when you get right down to it. It was just something to do."

"You won't mind, then, if Allie and me try to buy the place ourselves?" I said.

Thane laughed so all his teeth showed, even-placed and glassy. "No, I won't mind," he said. "Matter of fact, I can't think of nothing with more justice in it. You're likely to make more out of the land than Skeet ever done."

❧

The week before the auction, a man from the county government came to the door. He wore a white-cotton suit with suspenders to match, and in one rounded hand, all the fingernails burled and yellowed, he carried a clipboard.

"For the auction inventory," he said, holding the board up in front of my eyes.

Warren appeared himself from somewhere behind me. I felt the shadow of his tallness on my neck. He was wearing Skeet's hat all the time now, even indoors. It sat on his head in a mountain of buttery calfskin, falling down over his eyes. "What the man want?" he said.

"He's come to take inventory," I said. "On the furniture and such like."

"People got to know what all they're bidding on," the man said. "Only way to bring a fair price."

"Sounds reasonable," Warren said. "You just want to come on inside and make a list of my belongings so's you can sell them out from under me in one week's time."

"Now hold on a minute," the man said. He raised his hand up in front of him, one yellow-nailed finger pointing through the screen at Warren. "This property doesn't belong to you. You're only living on it temporary by the charity of the county, by which generosity you ought to feel yourself beholden."

The man's ears burned pink. He wiped a kerchief across the back of his neck and it came back wet, a few drops of perspiring still clinging to the edges of the cloth. "You going to let me in or am I going to have to come back with the law?"

"Come back with whoever all you like," Warren said. "I don't lock the door on no one but thieves."

While the man walked away Warren laughed after him — tall and shaking in his high buttery hat. And I liked him right then. I remember I did.

❧

The rule was you had to pay cash. That's what the auctioneer said. Ready cash dollar, hot in your pockets. There wasn't any allowing for checks or collateral deposits or promises to make good. The county wanted the money at the time of the sale and not one minute after. They had some use for it, I expect. Like paying all those men in bottle glasses and bow ties that had been spending the last few weeks gathering on Skeet's property.

The auctioneer, he was wearing a bow tie, too. He had a thick, pink neck that bulged into two or three false chins in the space between his collar and his jaw. His lips were drawn into a tight, thin line — bloodless lips — the kind words could come spilling fast from between without hardly a meaning to the sounds. He stood up on a two-foot block of cedarwood, his head pointing out of the crowd. His jowls shook on his neck like the ripe, fatty sides on a pink pork pig.

"If you haven't pre-viewed the dining house

yet, walk on through it now," he said. "Downstairs, there's the kitchen, two washrooms, the pantry, and the dinner hall — all of which comes furnished like you see. Real oak furnishings, too. Going to be antiques in twenty years from now. Upstairs there's five bedrooms and two washrooms more, which makes the place a business and a living house both at the same time."

Somebody in the crowd lifted his hat up off his head. The auctioneer pointed at him. "A man with a question," he said.

"How much land property comes with it?" the man said.

"Seventeen acres, give or take a half," the auctioneer said. "We have posted flags at the corner boundaries. One's north of the barn, one's west of the cluster trees, and one comes up close here, just short of Halliday Road. Mr. Ballard Mondrow owns the land to the outside, there and there." The auctioneer waved his hand towards two flat distances. "And the strip of grass lining the road belongs on his lot, too."

I felt the cash money bulging in my apron pocket. Seven hundred twenty-one dollars, wrapped up to make seven and a half thick, green-papered rolls, a rubber band around each one. The swellings showed through my smock, as big as fists, so Allie stood directly in front of me in order that she might hide them. Folks didn't like to see women and money set so close together. It made them nervous, I guess. It made them think of ruination.

"The bidding is open," the auctioneer said. He drew his hand in a wide arc in front of him, like he was swinging an imaginary gavel through the air. And then words fell out of his mouth all at once and too fast to hear. His lips were twitching over his teeth, and his triple chin was trembling from the motion, but I couldn't understand much of what he said except a few single words he called out slower than the rest. Like I heard it when he said *five fifty,* and I heard it when he said *six even do I have twenty.* And I was just about to raise my hand, but Allie kept me from it.

"Not yet," she said. "Too soon to jump in just yet."

And Mondrow was there, only he was waiting for the bidding to quiet down, same as us. Because he didn't say a word until the auctioneer got to asking for six and twenty, and even then I hardly even saw the lips part in his rough, brown-veined face. They opened just a crack — like a knife-cut in the skin of an onion, almost invisible — while he said, "Here."

A bald man with a Labrador dog bid six thirty, but Mondrow came back with a bid for six forty, and the bald man dropped out, wagging his head.

"Fifty," I said. And the auctioneer pointed at me, a jumble of words coming out between his twitching lips. *Six hundred fifty from the girl in the back do I have sixty.*

Mondrow turned towards Allie and me, his face going a dark boiled brown. He looked back and forth between us like he was trying to figure which one of us had spoken. His eyes were sunk under his brow in two hot points, glimmering wet and red-shot. "Seven even," he said.

The auctioneer's voice was thin and excited, probably on account of the bidding going higher than it should've done. *Seven hundred dollar I've got seven I've got seven somebody give me twenty.*

Allie turned to whisper to me. Her breath blew cool against my face. "Give it all," she said. "All of it."

"Seven twenty-one," I said.

Mondrow's face boiled darker. His hands were sunk in his cash purse, counting. The auctioneer's chins were blushed and trembling and pressed close together.

I've got twenty-one twenty-one twenty-one do I have thirty.

"I'll give a bank check for it," Mondrow said.

No checks. Cash on hand, only cash on hand I have seven twenty-one do I have a raise.

Then there was quiet for a moment. In the house, the weathered floorboards made no sound. In the forest, the leaves held still against the wind. On Halliday Road, no car was moving, no horse, no foot pressed into the hard-baked dust. And then the auctioneer's hand was arcing, moving downwards, down until I thought I could see the gavel swinging with it. *Sold. For seven hundred twenty-one dollars to the girl with the colored.*

Then people in the crowd were turned around to face us. There was a lady with artificial grapes on her hat, and a tall boy eating peanuts from a sack, and there was the bald man with the Labrador dog, and there were plenty of others, too. Most of them looked pleased, I thought, like someone had just told them a funny story and they were remembering the part that made them smile, rolling it around in their minds.

"Come on up here, girl," the auctioneer said. "Come on up and lay out your cash."

❧

So we were propertied. Allie and Ruby and me, and Warren, too, I guess, only I didn't think of the property belonging to him since the cash money we bought it with hadn't been any of his. The county clerk, he wrote my name on the deed, seeing as how he said there could only be one rightful owner of the land and Allie said it might as well be me. But after we got the deed home, I wrote her name in alongside mine. Allie Farrell, in long, loopy letters of script writing, like the kind they taught the children in school if you stayed there enough years to find it out.

We made us preparations to open the dining house again. Only Allie said she didn't like the words "dining house" on account of that's what Skeet had always called the place so why couldn't we name it a restaurant instead. And it was all the same to me so I said yes. In fact, when I turned the word over in my head at night, I saw that it was a definite improvement. Restaurant. It sounded delicate and foreign and it took a long time making its way through your mouth. Men would take off their hats when they walked through its doors and women would set at its tables wearing something other than their work dresses. And the food would be fine and generous — stuffed pullets and jam, sour cheese on top of roast potatoes, black molasses bread and sweet raisin pudding — all fresh from the hands of Allie to be set, steaming and full, onto real porcelain plates.

Maybe we wouldn't have all the niceties from the first, but work and will would bring them, one at a time, to make a gradual glory. We figured there were only two things we couldn't do without at the start. One was fine food ingredients and the other was a clean place to serve them in. Warren gave us half of what he brought home from tractoring, so that we could fill up the larder with spice and fruits, fresh ham and jarred honey. Took us close on a month to stock the shelves right. Meantime, we scrubbed that house clean like it had never been clean before. We took mops to the windows and bee wax to the floors. We laundered the curtains and the table covers and the linens five or six times straight, until they remembered their whiteness. And the dinner plates that had permanent stains baked on them, we threw them out altogether one night, laughing to ourselves while we dropped them into a packing crate and heard them breaking apart, chunked and dullish.

Allie said, "Did you ever know it'd feel so

good to break something apart? I wonder I ain't discovered it before now."

❧

Mornings, after Warren was gone to the fields and Ruby was gone off to school, Allie and me took our breakfast in the forest. We spread a wool sheet over the grass, still wet with night, and set down on top of it with our bread biscuits and our cheese and our two tin cups of chilled milk. The trees stood all around us — the firethorn and the chokeberry and the silveroak — listening to everything we said with the curious ears of the spirits hidden inside them. If the night before had been cold, then there were drops of water that fell off the tips of the leaves. In between the drops, we heard no sound except our own voices, answering back and forth.

"Can I ask you something?" I said.

"What?" Allie said.

"And you don't have to answer if you don't want."

"What?" she said.

"Because it's personal, that's all."

Allie laughed. The bright stones of her eyes rolled back in her head. Her earrings swung in gold-tipped tongs. One of her teeth, where it showed, was whiter than the rest — solid white, like the whitest egg or the whitest heat. I wondered whether Warren had noticed it. "Well, is you going to ask me?" she said.

A bird appeared itself in the firethorn — a red-breasted bird, round, and wet-feathered with black glossy beads for eyes. He danced amongst the branches like the thorns were pricking him, and then he disappeared straight up into the sky, singing with the voice of a child. "What's it like to make love to a man?" I said. "I mean, now that you're married, and seeing as how I might never be, I just thought as I would ask you, is all."

"It's like nothing I know of," Allie said. She stopped her smiling then. Her white-hot tooth was hidden behind her lips, burning there, out of sight. "It's like swallowing a fire and then letting that fire consume you. It's like falling through the air a long ways only you never touch ground at the end. It's like living at the center of the earth."

"Like living where?" I said.

"The center of the earth," she said. "The heart of the world. The lasting location of love."

❧

I'd never seen Allie so happy. On days when there were blossoms in the yard, she would cut one or two to wear them in her hair. Sometimes they were fruit tree blossoms — peach or persimmon. Other times they were bud roses that crept along the wall of the house. They set up on top of her hair bun in a starry yellow or a sunburned pink, and in the evening the petals wilted down onto her neck until she felt them resting there, tickling and cool, and she reached behind her head to take them away.

And another thing. She had taken to singing songs outside of church. Spirituals, she called them. She sang them slow and sweet, like honey on her tongue, and I liked to listen to the soul-touching sounds.

I's no ways weary, I's no ways tired,
Just let me in the Kingdom when the
  world catch fire.
I's going to know my Lord.

When I was a mourner, just like you,
I mourned and mourned till I got through.
I's going to know my Lord.

I guess it was love had wrought the change. Wasn't hardly a time I could came across Allie and Warren together without they were kissing or laughing or whispering into one another's ears. Used to be that, in the early summer, Allie and Humberto and Ruby and me would set up standing ladders under the fruit trees and fill up our four bushel baskets at the same time, the peaches and lemons and plums rolling across our palms while we talked. Now it was Allie and Warren that liked to do the collecting by themselves. And they didn't take any ladders with them either. Instead, Allie set up on top Warren's shoulders, her arms swallowed up by the greenness of the trees, her knees clapped tight against his ears, her skirts spilling down his back in a sagging white flag. She sent the fruit down to him, one at a time. The peaches passed from her hand to his — from the small, dove-colored fingers into the larger darker ones. Sometimes there was a hesitation at the point of handing off, a moment where the fingers touched, overlapped, squeezed a gentle pressure onto each other and into the skin of the fruit. But the fingertip dents were barely noticeable, and when the peaches came to be ripe, their tiny rose-pink bruises tasted like the sweetest part.

❧

We fashioned a sign on a post that we hammered two foot deep into the broken, red earth by Halliday Road. It said,

Restaurant
Opening Saturday
7:00 P.M. Till As long As You Stay
Fine Food For Fine Persons

The sign was white and the lettering was painted-on black. Ruby wrote it out on account of her handwriting was the easiest to decipher, but Allie and me thought up the words. The only problem was that we had a hot, dry wind that day which caught up the dust in its mouth and blew it out again — sepia and particle fine. It covered up our sign within one or two hours so that passersby could only see the sticks and tails of a few of our letters, peeking out from the edges of our words, without any sense to them. Every so often, I took a wet rag out to the roadside and wiped the sign clean.

But once, in the afternoon, I walked outside to find Mondrow's car, stopped and idling. Mondrow himself got out the driver's side, slow and lumbering, and came around to where our sign was, tilting under the wind. He wrapped his rope-veined hands around the post and plucked it out of the ground, like it was no more than a garden stalk. He must have seen me coming towards him from the driveway, but he didn't act like he cared much whether I was there or not. When I came up close enough to shout over the wind, he was sliding the sign into the backseat of his car.

"That signpost belongs to me," I said.

"Not now, it don't," he said. "This piece of land by the road here belongs on my lot. You put up a sign here and you give it away." From where I was standing I saw the brown veins marking his face — tiny interlocking lines, like the center of a web.

"All right," I said. "We'll move it."

"Going to have to make yourselves another one now," he said. "I has took a liking to this one." He got into his car and turned to face me from out the open window. His head hung in the free space like a dying planet, pocked and aged, his two eyes slanted against the wind. "Step back to your own property now or I'll have to pack you up for trespassing," he said.

❧

But the customers, they came anyway, sign or no sign. The first night, there were only eleven that showed up, most of them setting a single person to a table. But ten days after that, there were twenty-six and on the Saturday following, there were forty. Allie figured as we ought to spend half our earnings on improvements, so in June, we went downtown and paid out ten dollars for fifty cloth napkins. Real linen they were, and starched white, with silk-stitched embroidery at the edges. Me, I learned how to fold them in fancy shapes for the place settings. Some nights, they were roses, their pointed petals winding outwards from the center. Some nights, they were crowns, the embroidery climbing up the circled sides like jewels. Some nights, they were doves, their blank wings wide open, like they'd just that minute touched down on the table-tops — all fifty of them, in a giant, silent flock. Every evening we laundered them and every morning we hung them out to dry on a line, where they flapped like wild things caught up in a wind.

❧

It took us a solid month to save up enough money for new wallpaper. The mercantile gave us a sample book to take home so that we could spend some time to find the choicest pattern. There were bells and carriages and field horses and flowers, set to paper in every combination you could think of. Warren, he liked the field horses, but me and Allie and Ruby all liked the flowers, so flowers were what we got. The pattern was called "Sage," and it showed clusters of night-blue blooms on a backing of white. The petals were as thick as bumblebees and at their centers, there were velvety tongues of darkness, like what were at the middle of wild irises, only smaller. We ordered us twenty-three rolls, which was enough to cover every wall a customer was likely to see, plus a few extra. And then, when the paper arrived by the post, we hung it on the walls ourselves, stirring our brushes in buckets of glue, smoothing out the air bubbles from underneath the rolls. Stray bits of paste dried in our hair like snowflakes, starred and separate, and they only disappeared after we washed with shampoo-soap four times.

The customers noticed the way we were

making the restaurant over. They gave us compliments on the new napkins and the fresh wallpaper, and later, on the hanging lamps and the store-bought china. And the men and the women, they started dressing themselves with a bit more care. High collars and suspenders for the one, linen kerchiefs and silk hems for the other.

And Allie's cooking was the reason for it all. The pork side with the cinnamon sauce, the game hen with the apricot stuffing, the flank steak with the soured cream, the apple pie with the bacon and ginger baked inside, the gingerbread with the orange rind, the chocolate shavings on the raspberry custard. Nobody could say as they'd tasted better. The customers that had visited us one time, they came back the next week and they brought their friends. We got to where we served fifty on a slow night and twice that on the weekends. Humberto said that we were on our way to being rich, and all I could answer was I wouldn't turn it down when the money finally caught me up.

❧

The forest grew apricot and peach trees, plums and purple figs. Allie and Warren, they gathered themselves as much fruit as could be made use of in the kitchen, and the rest they left behind. When the leftovers turned ripe enough, they fell from the trees to split open at the ground, the seed stones sending pale, narrow shoots up through the spoiled skin to start up separate trees. In order that the forest didn't get overgrown, I collected all the shoots in a bushel basket for replanting in open ground.

The seeds left a darkness on my hands. The plum skins fell off between my fingers, and the peach meat oozed sticky and black, like sweet-smelling tar. It wasn't long before I was wet to the wrist, the fruit stones sliding out from my slippery hold on them, the pale shoots diving back to the grass like tiny green snakes, trembling towards escape. Then I turned and made for home, cradling my basket on my hip and wondering had I got enough time to plant the new stones before supper.

Matter of fact, I was wondering just that thing the day I came across Oloe, setting below a dogwood tree, her skirts flowing over her knees as smooth as water, blue and depthless. She was making a motion with her hand — a slow rising and a quick falling, over and over — and it took me a minute before I realized she was sewing something. Where all her fingers came together, there was a fine-point needle, and doubled over in the needle's eye, there was a thread no heavier than a passing thought, silk and unseeable.

"You're wearing your hair down," I said. And she was. It poured over both her shoulders in a fine, glossy sheet. She shrugged.

"I haven't had time to put it up today," she said. "I've been working."

"What on?" I said.

"A nightdress," she said. "And I'm just about finished." She snapped the thread between her fists and then spread out the nightdress in front of her. It had a deep-cut collar with lace over the bosom. The waist-sash was covered with stitched-on pearls. And the whole of it was made with spirit cloth, see-through like a veil.

"Oh, Oloe, it's beautiful."

"It's a wedding present," she said. "For Allie. I started on it soon as I heard she had got herself married."

"She's going to love it," I said.

Oloe put the nightdress in my bushel basket full of spoiled fruit and sproutings. "You take it to her, then," she said. "You tell her it's from me."

❧

Allie took to wearing that nightdress once or twice a week. The blueness fell around her in a fog, and her body, growing up out of it, was the dark, solid center of a tree. Her teeth were the stars in between the spread branches. Her bosoms swung like dangling fruit.

"You tell Oloe it's a precious gift," she said. "It makes me feel beautiful. I don't know the why of it."

"And what does Warren say?" I said.

"Warren wants to know why I has took to sleeping naked," she said.

"He doesn't see the nightdress on you?"

"Not a fold nor a seam nor a thread," she said. "I tell him as I ain't naked, but he just shakes his head from side to side. 'If you ain't naked I'd like to know what exactly you is,' he says. He acts like he don't approve it, but the truth be that he do."

"How do you know?" I said.

" 'Cause he can't keep his hands to hisself," she said. "He be passing his fingertips over me, edge to edge. His hands is full up with blue fabric, but he don't see it. 'Your skin be so cool,' he says. 'So beautiful, silkified cool.' "

❧

From across the property line, Mondrow saw us prosper. He saw the restaurant customers lining up outside the porch, maybe some of them the same folk that used to buy his whiskey for five dollars on the bottle. He saw us paint the shutters black and the sidewalls white, like Skeet was always saying he was going to do when he could get a good deal on paint supplies and a cheap hand for labor, only the two never came available at the same time. At night, he smelled Allie's cooking, wafting over the country mile in hints of roast beef red through the center and potatoes split from their jackets, and to him, we were nothing but thieves setting up house.

He looked like he'd been watching all those things happen right in front of him, his onion eyes straining, on the morning he parked his car by Halliday Road and got out, the dust moving under his knees like water turning over. That was the same morning the building trucks appeared themselves, Street Masters Bricklaying painted yellow on the sides. I watched them for a time from my upstairs window, the dozen men in their green-gray overalls behind the wheelbarrows stacked with bricks, sweat traveling down their faces before the sun had even found its way to open sky.

By the time I got out to the road, the first layer of bricks was already set down. It lay one foot wide and thirty foot long, stretched out like a snake in the daylight. On the other side of our driveway, some men were laying another line. They were bent-backed and narrow-shouldered and when they stood up their trowels dripped with brick plaster.

Out on the roadside, Allie was talking to Mondrow. The hem of a pink smock licked her knees and out from under it flowed her spirit-blue nightdress, which she hadn't taken the time to step out of. The tongues of her black shoes wagged loose in the air, like they were fixing on something to say. Her hands were clapped to her waist, brown and birdish, with all the fingers pressed together like the spines of as many feathers.

When I came up close to them, I said, "Mondrow, what you brought out all these bricklayers for?"

Allie said, "He walling us in, honey."

"Wall-building, hmm?" I said.

"Property by the road here belongs on my lot," Mondrow said. "I can put anything on it as pleases me."

"I guess you're looking to put us out of sight

of road traffic," I said.

"Maybe that's right," Mondrow said.

"You thinking to put us out of business?" Allie said.

"Maybe again," Mondrow said.

"Well, I tell you right now it won't work," Allie said. "Not if you put up bars around us and nailed down the sky, it wouldn't work even then." She folded her arms together, slow and certain. Her fingernails were pale and glowing, like tiny moons caught up in her hands. "We's landowners now," she said. "That can't be took away."

❧

The men built for five days straight. Hand over hand, brick over brick, the cement sticking fingers and stones together and shuddering when they came apart again. The men's skin, where it showed, was roasted swollen and red by the sun. The backs of their necks were touched, and so were the curled lips of their ears, where the bits of peeling skin clung, transparent and tender-looking. Over the passing hours, their heads turned wet from all their perspiring. Their hair was slick and oily and close to the head, like boys that had just come away from swimming.

When I asked them, they told me the wall

was meant to be forty-two bricks high, which was upwards of twelve foot when the bricks were laid longwise. And twelve foot would hide from us the better part of the horizon, the part where the flat, thick miles met the creamy edge of the sky and turned into nothing if not an imagining of the distance, an image of the place we were going to end up, which I always prayed was going to be better than where we came from, out of the land of smoke and ashes.

On the day the workers were set to finish the wall, Allie brought out tall lemon ices and spiced mince pies all lined up onto serving trays. The pie pieces were hot, and the raisins and mincemeats steamed where they overflowed their crusts. The men ate them with greedy forkfuls, making funny shapes with their mouths so as not to burn their tongues. Mondrow was nowhere to be seen, so after the men were done eating, they set down in the shade of the wall for a rest, fanning their necks with their unused napkins.

"Seems like you mens have built a wall to be proud of," Allie said. She walked in amongst them while she talked, collecting their empty plates with her little dove-shaped hands.

"We haven't finished it yet," the foreman said. "We have seven more layers to put."

"Seven!" Allie said. "I would've thought that wall was high enough to look at, wouldn't you? It's perfect just like it is."

"It looks perfect enough to me," the foreman said. "But Mr. Mondrow, he wants a wall forty-two bricks high."

"It appear to be forty-two brick high already," Allie said. "Don't you think it do? God knows, it must be twice as high as me."

"At least that," he said.

"And do you know, I can't imagine that Mr. Mondrow would ever stand out here in the sun to count out all them bricks," Allie said. "He a busy man, Mr. Mondrow is."

The man took a step back from the wall. His hair was stuck to his forehead in strings, wet and gritty. From underneath them he was squinting at his handiwork, his eyes moving along the top line of the wall. "You'd think it was forty-two bricks high if you didn't count," he said.

"I know *I* would," Allie said.

The man was grinning then. He had short nubs of teeth lined up across his gums and they were dark, the color of dried corn. "You got any more of that mince pie?" he said.

"Plenty," Allie said. "I just been waiting on someone to ask."

❧

So they never raised the wall to where Mondrow wanted it. Street Masters Bricklaying took their trowels and their wheelbarrows and their leftover bricks away with them and he never knew the difference. Not that that seven layers of brick meant too much. Its being absent gave us two foot extra of sky to look at, that's all. But sky being more precious than bricks, we counted it a small victory.

Mondrow meant to kill our livelihood when he shut us off from view like he did, but the restaurant hardly suffered. Except for a few customers complaining that the wall was an eyesore, we didn't hear it spoken of. Like Allie said, when the food is good, the diners come back. When the food is great, they come back with their friends.

But the wall, it nettled us, all the same. In the morning, the first thing the sun lit on was its wide, eyeless face, looking cold in the way only something manmade can look cold, with an intent behind it, with a malice. And in the evening, the sun sank behind its red teeth, leaving us in early darkness to wonder how our days had escaped, fast-footed and running away. The trees waved their leafy arms over the wall's limit, desperate as prisoners grasping out towards their freedom. And in the treetops, I could always spy a spirit or two, shining in blueness and standing on tiptoe while they watched the sun slide over the curving earth, in a beauty that was ever so distant and appealing.

❧

Some days Warren got work. Some days he didn't. It all depended on how many whites showed up in the mornings. The whites were hired first and the coloreds were hired after that. If a white showed up late, the boss pulled a colored off his tractor. That was the way they did it. None of the farmers wanted it said that they'd loved a colored above their own kind. It hurt the business, that kind of talk did. The grocers didn't like to buy the fruit of a nigra lover. His peaches were tainted, they said. His onions were undersized.

So two or three times a week, Warren came home again within an hour of first setting out. I could see him from the distance, his long legs wavering in the vapors of the hot road, his head turned downwards so that his hat became a yellow dime, rolling low between his shoulders. From one of his hands swung the cloth sack still bulging with his noon meal — a small pork pie, a wedge of molasses bread, two ripe peaches, and a slice of sour cheese.

He spent the afternoons lolling mostly, playing solitaire on the porch or refilling tobacco into the pipe he'd found in Skeet's bedroom. Sometimes he asked Allie would she like to go to Jake Frye's pond with him, and then Allie asked me would I like to go, too, so the three of us piled into Skeet's old Hudson and went. I drove the car most times on account of I was the most careful driver Allie had ever seen, and while Allie never felt partial to riding in cars, she felt more partial to it when it was me doing the steering. I never pushed the foot pedal above twenty miles an hour, and Warren complained that our own dust was overtaking us. Said he drove his tractors through high crops faster than what I would do on the open road. But Allie shushed him.

"Cassie going to get us there on her own time," she said. "Safe and whole and alive."

"Too bad we going to be old by the time she do," Warren said.

"Don't mind me if I just keep to my ways," I said.

"That's right, woman," Allie said. "Don't let him hurry you."

And Jake Frye's pond always came up soon enough — glass-topped and deep, with blond earth lining its edge.

We didn't have swimsuits then, and it wasn't that we couldn't afford them. We just hadn't thought of it, I guess. I turned to look in a distant direction while Allie and Warren stripped down to their underthings. The trees that circled the lip of the pond were silver beech. They were veiny and knotted, like an old woman's hands, and I always thought their crookedness must have been due to the sandy soil they were rooted in. But Humberto said that wasn't the reason. He said trees that were set by the water grew over crooked from sheer vanity, straining to see their own reflection.

I heard the sloshing sounds of Allie and Warren wading in the shallows, their four flat feet gallumphing through the water. And then there was quiet, which meant they were moving deeper, off of the sandy shoals and into the troughs where the pond turned muddy, their legs moving amongst the minnows and the freshwater eels and the beech leaves from last season's shedding. When Allie told me it was all right to look, I turned to find them twenty foot off the shoreline, the pond risen to their shoulders. The white cotton straps of Allie's camisole had slipped off their places and were floating in the water next to her arms. Warren was looking at them, too. He ran his finger along Allie's shoulder where one strap used to be. He looked like he wanted to kiss her there, except I was watching and he knew I was watching and he held off doing it.

Times like that, I tried to mind my own business. God knows I tried. I spread out the blanket I'd brought and I set down on top of it and I tried to think about the restaurant business or Mama's last letter or what was Ruby's life going to be like when she was all grown up. But it wasn't any use, because in the meantime and not much distance away, were Warren and Allie, water-logged and lovemaking, their pillow lips pressed together in a swallowing, silt-tasting kiss, their fingernails gone white and soft as waxpaper, like the fingernails of newborn babies or spirits, fresh from another world.

❧

Humberto said that a man with too much time on his hands was the likeliest candidate for drink. There were all those empty hours to fill up, and most people couldn't stand the prospect of empty hours. It terrified them — that slow turning of the clock, that quiet space inside the mind. At least, that's the way Warren must have felt about it, because he took to drink in the stretch of a few bad months in a year when the harvesting was light and the number of men required to sit a tractor was half what it ought to have been. A good-sized parcel of the county's farming property was turned over to ranching, and where the dust had started to fly in low clouds over the land, there were likely to be seas of cattle underneath, long horns and hooves all flowing together.

Where the liquor came from, I don't know. But I expect Mondrow was continuing to work his sour-mash boilers somewhere in a hidden wrinkle on his land. And even if Mondrow were to shut himself down, there would have been twenty other bootleggers ready to make up the difference in supply. Warren left his empty jars around the house, and they came in every size and shape. Straight-sided canning jars, thin-necked medicine bottles, rounded vases, cornered candy holders — anything that would take a cheesecloth and a rubber band around the top to keep the liquor from draining out. Sometimes Warren didn't quite empty the container, and Allie or me would come around later to find a finger or two of whiskey setting in the bottom of a jar. When I tested a bit of it on the tip of my tongue, it was sour-tasting, like spoiled citrus. And the liquor had a smell to it that started an ache across the bridge of my nose — a smell somewhere between that of hair tonic and gasoline. It smelled like a liquid that would explode under a match. It was that foul. Allie and me always took care not to pour out the remainders in the yard, where they'd poison the green growth. We emptied them down the sink instead, where down by the drain, the white enamel was stained the color of amber from all the times that whiskey had flowed over it.

Seemed like Warren wouldn't have had the money for liquor, being so seldom at a job and all. But the restaurant was doing so good that we none of us had a want for hard dollars. The cashbox was filled to its edges every night, the green bills peeking out from the lid like so many lagging tongues. Warren just took what he needed, and me and Allie banked the rest.

Allie didn't love Warren any the less for his drinking ways. It's even possible she loved him the more. Her heart went out to him in his idleness. It felt the small stings of his defeats. It made up excuses for the changes that were taking him over.

"Used to be that Warren was a ambitious man," Allie said. "But it hard to be ambitious when won't nobody throw a day's work your way."

"I know," I said.

"He having a bad time of it," she said. "But bad times, they pass."

"The drink is consoling him, is all," I said.

"That's right," she said. "It a consolation. Temporary, like. When work come available, he going to put down the drink just as easy as he picked it up."

"Probably," I said.

"I's sure of it," Allie said.

"Hardworking men don't give up easy," I said.

"Not by my account," Allie said.

So Allie and me lied to each the other for the first time in our entire lives. Whether we did it more from need or fear, I couldn't say. The lies didn't stop Warren from drinking, but maybe they helped Allie to sleep better at night, and the way I counted it, a good night's sleep ought to have been worth a small sin.

Hard as it might be for me to say, Warren always was a good-hearted man, even when he *was* thick with his liquor. There was one time I remember — winter season, in the morning — when me and Allie got caught outside in a flash rain. We were hanging out the wash on the line — six bedsheets, and twice that in tablecloths, and fifty square linen napkins. And we were only halfway done when the light went out in the sky. Gray rolled into darker gray and the clouds made hard-fingered fists over our heads. The rain hit us solid as stones, and our skirts turned thick and clung to our legs. The winds pulled the sheets from our hands, and we ran about underneath their white bubble faces, trying to gain them back. Warren saw us from the porch and he came out to help. But he was made stumbling and silly from his whiskey, and when he fell down into the running redness of the mud, he only laughed. He lay back into the coolness of the soil, as simple as a fool or a child, and when Allie finally reached him, he pulled her down, too.

"I fell," he called out to her over the wind.

"I know," Allie said.

"I run out to help you, but I fell," he said.

"Yes," she said.

Warren raised himself up on his elbows and kissed Allie where she set beside him. The water passed over his face in streams that ran to his ears and fell off their curled edges in huge pearly drops, clear as the eyes of fishes.

I turned to go back in the house, and when I looked on them once again from the shelter of the porch, Warren was spread-eagled in the mud, sweeping his arms and legs across the ground surrounding him.

"Look at me!" he said to Allie. "I'm making angels underneath me. Angels in the mud."

And Allie bent over to kiss him again, his arms and legs, still waggling over the earth. "I know it," she said. "I know.

❧

Warren's mud angel stayed with us, printed into the skin of the earth. For a few days straight, its clay wings held the remnants of the rain, and the sparrows came to cool themselves in the clear, shallow pools that spread out like glory from the bowled hollow of the angel's head. Where the angel's legs ought to have been, there were wide skirts in the soil, and on the fifth day, a hundred tender shoots of crabgrass bared their necks to the sun, turning the skirt hem a mossy green color, startling to the eye, even at night. Me and Allie and Ruby took care not to step our feet on the angel's shape. We walked all around it to set out the wash, but we never walked our toes past its borders. Three clothespins had fallen down onto the angel's muddy belly, and we left them where they lay, like great wooden grasshoppers swallowed up inside a messenger of God. Some things were just too mysterious to touch.

❧

That was the season when Warren and me stayed clear of each the other if we could. When he got work, I stayed at the house. When he stayed at the house, I drove the car to town. There were always supplies that needed buying — frying pullets, boiling potatoes, fruits shipped by freight, and like that. It wasn't hard for us to keep clear. We stood ourselves at opposite ends of the roundness of the world. All the lengths of our differences were laid out end to end in a widening distance, and only Allie walked the ground in between. Allie, who loved the both of us without a question as to why.

My objection to Warren was he didn't think things through. He acted out by an impulse or an anger or whatever all seemed right at the time. But he never thought about what would come after on. Or if he thought about it, he never cared. Warren, he wasn't a considerate man. He loved ideas more than he did the necessaries of life. I can't say as I blamed him, but I can't say I admired him for it either.

There was this one time when Warren brought his colored friends over to the restaurant. I knew they had been working all day, because their shirts were stained dark at the collar, the same as on their backs between their shoulder blades. Penny-sized bits of chaff clung to their leggings and spotted the dark, even skin at their ankles. Their eyes were wet and rheumy, swimming in the sympathy that tiredness and whiskey always brought on. There were four or five of them, I think, and they walked through the restaurant doors at suppertime, with fifty chairs full of customers and as many orders placed. Warren took his friends over to an empty table and told them to set down. Him and the others were laughing when they walked in, but now they were serious. An old man, a white-haired one, worked his lips around his toothless gums. He looked like he might have been trying to remember where all his teeth had gone to. Two of the other men were looking at the napkins shaped like doves that they'd set down on their laps. The men worked their brows together, worried on account of they had never seen bird-shaped napkins before and they didn't know the proper way to handle them.

"We want some dinner here," Warren said.

The customers, they got quiet. Two women with high white collars and silver brooches got up to leave, and the men they were with hurried after them. Someone in the back of the room kept on with his eating, and I could hear the thin scrape of his fork as it found and refound his porcelain plate.

I walked over to Warren's table. "If you all come out back, I'll bring you something to eat," I said.

"We don't want to come out back," Warren said. "We's comfortable here."

"I can't serve you here," I said.

"Why not?" Warren said. "I'd like to know why not."

But Warren's friends were losing their daring. The old white-haired man was smiling a toothless smile. "That's all right," he was saying. "That's all right with me." He got up from his place at the table and the other men did the same. They set their dove-shaped napkins on the tablecloth and they walked out, leaving bits of chaff behind them on the floor. "That's all right," the old man said.

When I touched Warren on the arm, he stood up from his chair. He let me lead him to the door, my small, pale hand wrapped around the thickness of his wrist. His breath was hot where it blew over my head, and it smelled like corn and the sourness of sleep. "A man will suffer wrongs, but they won't be forgot," he said. And then he was past the doorway and out of the porch light and moving towards a place I couldn't see.

❧

He held that night against me, Warren did. I had done no less than what had been necessary, since to most of our customers, the sight of a colored at the table was a frightful thing. But to turn a man out from under a roof he called his own — that was a cruel requirement, and I can't say as I felt righteous in doing him that way. There were times I lived by the saying "You got to go along to get along," because sometimes going along was the only chance a person had. Warren ought to have known that saying as good as me, but he acted like he didn't.

In some ways, Warren treated me the same as he did before. When I came into the kitchen in the mornings, he always said me a hello, his hand reaching up to his head like he would've tipped his hat to me, easy and polite, if only he had been wearing it. But Allie was close on by whenever he made the gesture. She was standing over the stove, tending the pan biscuits and pork sides that would come together for Warren's breakfast, and she always kept one eye behind her focused on the man waiting for his meal. She watched him and he knew it, and his actions came off right and respectful, even to me.

Other ways, Warren treated me different. Like, sometimes when Allie wasn't with us, he wouldn't talk to me at all. I might ask him a question about how the tractoring had gone the day before or why was Hiram Henrick letting his eastern acreage go fallow. And Warren would just go on setting there, his brows bulged and knotted together to show how he was concentrating on tamping his new tobacco into the bowl of Skeet's smoking pipe. He set there like nobody had said anything at all — like he had heard no noise except the cicadas stitching their way through the minutes — like my voice had been soundless, and the lips it had come from between were invisible.

Other times, Warren would question me when he hadn't a cause to do it. Like I remember once I decided the walls in Ruby's and my bedrooms were needing a fresh layer of paint. So I bought me four tin gallons of the palest, clearest yellow — yellow like the inside of a banana or like the pitcher of cream before the top has been skimmed. And I was wearing an old smock and a set of tattered garden gloves, standing midway up a stepladder with the paint dripping off my brush, when Warren came to the bedroom door. He looked from one wall to the other. His eyes hollowed themselves out like tunnels, brown and glowing.

"Why you painting?" he said.

"The walls have been needing it," I said.

"Does Allie know what you doing?" he said.

"No," I said. "But she won't mind. I'm not painting more than just the two bedrooms, mine and Ruby's."

"You ought to asked her, all the same," Warren said. "Her or me, you ought to asked one of us."

"I guess I can make a decision or two by private," I said.

"It ain't your private money to be deciding with," Warren said.

He disappeared himself through the doorway, his shoes kissing the floor in their long, sliding strides. When I turned back to my work, I saw that the paint had run down over the handle of my brush, bleeding outwards like a flower past the fingers of my glove and onto the bare skin of my arm. Pale yellow drops dotted the floor below me, hot and painful and strange as tears, or sudden primroses burst open in the cold.

❧

Ruby turned seventeen years old at the end of summer. Seemed like every year since she'd been a baby, her skin grew a shade whiter and her hair grew a shade darker. Allie said even the ravens cried for the blue-black color of Ruby's curls. We could hear the cawing when Ruby went out on horseback, her hat settled onto her shoulders so that her head was bared, her hair turning to liquid darkness under the sun. *Blue hair!* the ravens wept from the tops of the trees. *Blue hair!*

Ruby had filled out faster than the girls she went to school with. Her bosom was pink and generous, and she acted shy about it, hiding it with her hands whenever I helped her change her clothes or draw out her bath. She liked dresses that were high at the collar, made of fine cotton or silk. And she picked out ones with dropped waistlines, their straight, careful seams drawing a loose loop around her hips. I think she would've liked it best if nobody knew she had a figure to her at all. But those wide, hanging dresses didn't fool the boys at school. They watched the way the fabric moved over her curving boundaries, and whatever they couldn't see they worked hard to imagine.

Thane, he kept his eye on her, too. An approving eye, a respectful one. He waited for her every day after school, leaning up against the inside of Mondrow's wall, the afternoon shade spilling over his head. With his fingers, he pinched together the waxed, wiry corners of his fat mustache. He always turned the ends upwards, so that they rested in half curls on the borders of his cheeks. The curve of the whiskers made him look like he was smiling about something, secret and untelling.

When Ruby would turn up the driveway, past Mondrow's wall and all the world beyond it, Thane would fall in step in back of her. He'd set his soft, weathered boots over the childish shoeprints she left behind her in the dust. "I been waiting on you," he would say. And then she would turn around, the air filling the gathers of her skirts for a minute and then sighing itself out of them. "Like you always do," she would say. And there was a gentleness to her voice, a laughter coming just after it.

Ruby liked to ride Remy in the afternoons, so Thane asked could he walk alongside. She said it was all right with her, except Remy was so tall that she didn't hardly see how they could carry on a proper conversation, what with her so far off the ground and all. But he said that the distance didn't matter any so long as they could hear one the other's words. So she rode and he walked. Ruby used to give Remy a loose rein, on account of he chose his own path through the forest, a different one every time, and all of them beautiful. He circled through the dogwood and the elder-trees, the blackbush and the hollyberries, and he always steered away from the broken-up cover of limestone rocks, which shaded snakes under their jagged corners. In one hour or two, he brought her back to where she started from, under the door of the leaning barn, where she could step down off his back to wash her face in the stream of the water spigot, cool and bitter from the underground pipes.

Ruby said, "Remy knows that forest like he's been wandering through it his whole life long."

Thane said, "He chooses his direction for your own safekeeping."

Neither one of them could have known it wasn't Remy that was setting their course, but instead, the spirit of Lily Mark. She appeared herself every day, holding to Remy's reins as she walked on in front of him, all wrapped up in the ground-touching folds of her blue-glowing dress. She moved like a widow, her head bowed, blue hair falling over her eyes like a veil. And all the while, her daughter didn't know she existed. And neither did the man who walked alongside, unseeing and in love, stepping his way gently over the hands of the leaves.

❧

The days rolled over in a burning white heat, lit from the center of the high, flat sky. Those that perspired felt drops as big as glass marbles easing between their shoulder blades or kissing the hollows between their ribs. Those that didn't perspire turned red at the face, their bright cheeks showing whole spider webs of veins, their chapped lips set apart so the coolness of the air could pass across their tongues. Thane asked Ruby would she go swimming with him at Jake Frye's.

"Swimming's the only cure for days such as these," he said. "Cools your very soul like it's the only remedy."

"I can't go swimming," Ruby said.

"What's stopping you?" Thane said.

"I never learned how," Ruby said.

Their voices came to me from the porch, traveling through the screens in the parlor windows. A single rocking chair started crying — soft cries, like a baby in the distant dark — and I couldn't tell whose chair it was, Ruby's or Thane's.

"I'll teach you how," Thane said.

"I don't know —" Ruby said.

"Why not?" Thane said. "You going to go

through your whole life without somebody teaches you?"

"No," she said.

"Might as well be me, then," he said.

"I don't even have myself a swimming suit," she said.

"I'll buy you one," Thane said.

Then I heard both the chairs crying, rocking back and forth on their uneven runners, sounding out their human sighs. I left my seat in the parlor to go find them on the porch. Ruby was swirling a glass of cold tea with a spoon. The melting cubes of ice hit up against one another and made sounds like tiny bells. Ruby looked up at me.

I said, "I expect your mama ought to be the one that buys you swimming clothes."

Ruby said, "All right, Mama."

I said, "We'll drive in to a department store come Saturday. Graham's or J. C. Coop's or whatever one you want."

❧

Allie and me, we had a lot of money in the bank, but we couldn't get used to spending it. We bought us things for the restaurant — fine bone china from overseas, hanging lamps with stained-glass shades, Asian-made carpets with silk tassels on the corners — and we didn't give the spending a second thought. But when it came to buying niceties for ourselves — dresses and hats and pearl combs for our hair and such — that was altogether different. I guess me and Allie had gotten by for so long on so little that we were hard put to understand the ways of luxury. I went to a beauty parlor one time, just to see what it was like. But the sink water was too hot and the hair rollers were too tight, and when I came out the other end of it, my head was covered with finger-sized ringlets that Allie laughed over when she saw them, calling them fancy sausages of hair. She liked me better the other way. Ruby, too. So I never did go back.

J. C. Coop's had a sign under their name that said LUXURY DEPARTMENT STORE EXTRAORDINARY. They carried kitchenwares and hardwares and home necessities. They had a cook's corner with chocolate-covered caramels, and little sticks of cinnamon tied together in bundles, and pickled pearl onions packed inside glass jars. And in the ladies' clothing department, they had button blouses and dobbie-cloth brassieres and silk-woven socks. Ruby tried on five of the bathing suits the saleslady had unfolded from the stock drawers. They all of them had ruffled skirts and sleeveless arm straps. I asked the saleslady didn't she have any stockings so that a girl's bare knees would be covered up modest, but she said modern girls hadn't been covering up their knees for five years or more and if I didn't believe her, I could look through the ladies' magazines and find it out for myself.

I said, "We don't care much about being modern for modern's sake."

"Mama," Ruby said. "Does it hurt us any to know what other girls are wearing?"

"Not so long as they are girls as fine-made as mine," I said.

"Mama."

"And don't tell me I'm being partial, because I know it already," I said.

"So long as you know," Ruby said.

"A mother's got nothing if she hasn't got partial feelings for her own," I said.

Ruby stepped out from behind the dressing-room curtain. She was wearing a navy blue swimsuit with white stripes ringing the skirts. Below the cotton flounces, her knees showed naked and knobbed. Her calves had the beginning of a woman's curves to them, arcing inwards just above the shins, where softness gave way again to bone. The skin covering her ankles turned to a paper on which the blue lines of her veins were drawn, faint and uncertain. The suit's neckline was cut in a scoop, low enough to show the egg-sized hollow at the base of her throat and high enough to cover the separation of her bosom, straight and deep as a wound where it sank into the pinkness of her form. Ruby reached her hands over the flouncy hem and rested them on the tops of her long, shivering legs.

"Mama, is this one too bare?" she said.

I turned to the saleslady. "You say they've been going without stockings for five years now?"

"At least five," the saleslady said.

"Do you like it the best of what there is?" I said to Ruby.

"Yes," she said.

"All right, then," I said. "Looks like we have made up our minds."

❧

If somebody had asked me, I would've said Thane was still biding his time so far as Ruby was concerned. Ruby was just seventeen years old, after all, and Thane must've been three times that. He had never married himself to a woman his whole life long, though the milliner's wife told me he'd come close to it twice. Seemed to me he wasn't the type to run out of patience waiting for a woman of his own.

Of course, Thane had felt something special for Ruby from the very start. The first time he had seen her, playing with her dolls in the dust of the yard, he couldn't hardly speak a word for fear of what truth he might let go of. I expect she was just the most beautiful living thing he had ever hoped to see. He paid for her dresses and bonnets and candies and dolls just so that he could own a piece of that beauty as his — just so that he could look on her like a daddy might look on his child, witnessing all the need of the world in those pale, heart-of-the-sky eyes, and deciding, as if he had himself a choice, to provide her with everything.

The thing is, Ruby was hardly a child anymore, which was obvious. Thane must've first noticed it years back when her bosom started to press the gathers on her smocks, insistent and full, like the breast on a dove. She protruded in spite of herself, her roundness trembling when she walked. Her waist cinched itself inwards, the skin drawn tight across her ribs, and below, her belly turned tender and flat like an empty dish that men thought to fill with the weight of their eyes and the space of their hands. Thane kept on giving Ruby gifts, like he always did, only the gifts changed in their nature. He gave flowers instead of dolls. He gave brooches instead of bonnets. Whereas before, he would carry Ruby around the property riding on his shoulders, her baby's legs dangling down his shirtfront, plump and white, now the two of them hardly touched at all, except if Thane were to lift her off of Remy's back when she came back from her afternoon rides. Some days, she would let him reach up to her waist and float her ever so slowly — such that the eye could hardly tell she was moving downwards — to the ground next to where he stood. Most days, though, she stepped off by herself, her boots landing square in the center of the mounting block, sounding out a crack like the voice of a gun gone off. Either way, Ruby blushed to the roots of her hair. Whether a man was touching her or whether he was only thinking along those lines, she caught hold of his intention and got embarrassed by it. Her face turned the color of blood peaches — pink and smooth-skinned and hot where they were picked from the sunny side of the tree.

I guess I wasn't the only one that had noticed Ruby's shyness, because once, when I was out by the front of the house, on my knees between two rows of carrots, I heard Lily Mark's voice come up from behind me, liquid and heavy with the way she spoke.

"Ruby's too young to be keeping men's company," she said. "It throws her. She doesn't know how to act around them."

I turned to look behind me. Lily Mark was

lying in the arms of the blue willow tree, stretched out like a cat. Her dark hair flowed downwards to the ground, swirling its way around the sharp crescents of the leaves before it passed them by in a current of strands, blue-black and consuming.

"You growing your hair?" I said.

Lily Mark nodded. "Three months now. Oloe says I ought to have done it a good while back. Says long hair makes a person look thinner at the girth."

"It favors you," I said.

"Yes," she said. "It does." She ran her fingers back into her hair so that they all disappeared into its color. "Ruby's got a head of hair just like mine. Have you noticed?"

"Yes," I said.

"The men have noticed, too," she said. "It's part of the reason they come around visiting so often. They want to sink their hands into it, probably. That's the way with men, you know. Always thinking to use their hands."

"Not all of them," I said.

"All of them I have ever come across," she said.

"That doesn't make up the whole world," I said. "Besides, it's not like I'm letting every passerby and his brother in here to visit on Ruby. Only one that comes by regular is Thane."

"Every day regular," she said. "Ruby's too young for that kind of visiting." Lily Mark set up straight. Underneath her, the willow branch started to swaying with the weight.

"As I recall, you were only fifteen when you stepped in with Murray," I said.

"That's right," Lily Mark said. "And didn't it end up killing me?" She put a hand up to her throat. The fingers were plump and blue, swollen at the knuckles.

"What you want me to do, Lily Mark?"

"Run him off," she said. "Tell him never to come back anymore. We don't need him. We don't want him. We can do without."

"I won't," I said.

Lily Mark's face turned dark like the center of a larkspur, hidden and purple. "Why won't you?" she said.

"He's a good man," I said. "He's helped me more than once when I needed helping. If Ruby doesn't want him, she's going to tell him in her own way, in her own time, without you or me to feed her the words."

❧

Jake Frye's pond got its name from a man that had sunk a boat at its center ten years back. The story was that it had been an old boat even when it could float — doublemasted and heavy-keeled, like somebody had built it for ocean-going. It had swamped from a storm maybe or else from plank leakage between the boards — nobody remembered exactly. It sank upright, the hull settling into the green silt at the pond's bottom, the masts standing three or four foot above the line of the water in summertime, and in the winter, when the rains came, sinking just underneath the surface to where no one could see them unless they were swimming over, peering their eyes down into the glassy, deep greenness and looking for strange, out-of-place shapes.

Thane and Ruby went out to Jake Frye's twice a week for swimming lessons, and I went along with them, seeing as how a young girl ought to have had a chaperone. The first few times, they did nothing but practice in the wading shallows. They held their breaths underwater. They floated on their backs for ten minutes at a time. Ruby practiced kicking her feet while Thane circled her at the waist, his arms steady where they disappeared under her belly and came up on the other side. Later on, they tried deeper water. They swam through all the far green hollows where their toes couldn't touch down. Thane kept himself out front and Ruby followed. She held her head high out of the water, like she might've been concentrating on keeping her chin dry. Her hair dragged behind her in thick black ropes that blended together below the waterline. Thane was always calling things out to her, like was she all right — did she want to rest now — did she want to swim to shore.

Me, I stayed at the water's edge, walking up and down in the blond earth and wondering whether Ruby was seeing the kindness in Thane and whether it was making her love him just a little. Of course, she could've been seeing his outer attractions, too. Like the way his mustache came uncurled in the pond, the ends drooping into a frown and holding little drops of water at the tips, suspended and mournful and clear. Or like the way his face got tanned under the sun, deep brown at the cheeks and the brow, and pink on the crown of his forehead where his hat had shaded him for so many years. I don't think I ever admitted it to anybody outside of God, but if Thane had loved me in the slightest way, I would've loved him back without a hesitation. There was just something about him — something about the manner by which he listened when I spoke, his face going still and wide-eyed and respectful — that set him apart from most other men I had known. The fact that he wasn't partial to me, that didn't make any difference. A good man showed kindness all around, no matter his affections. And I didn't begrudge him loving Ruby. I don't guess I could've found a better husband for her if the finding had been left up to me. It was just that Ruby gave no sign she was ready to marry, and I didn't think she considered Thane to be the man that could make her change her mind.

The whole question got settled one Saturday in August out at Jake Frye's pond. Thane and Ruby had swum out to old Frye's sunken boat, and each of them was holding to one of the oaken masts, cracked and swollen with water. Ruby's hair was slicked backwards and her bobbing head looked shiny and streaming, like the head of a seal. They were speaking to one another, but I couldn't hear what they were saying. Their voices rolled across the water like the slow songs of birds, distant and serious. Thane left the mast he had been clinging to and swam over to Ruby's. With both of them putting their weight on it, the oak moaned — low and broken. Thane leaned his head in towards Ruby's and for a second, their foreheads touched and their shadows on the water were joined. Then Ruby moved away, sweeping her arms in a breast stroke like they were thin white wings beating through the water, leaving behind them bubbles and the pale foam of motion. When she walked up through the shallows, the water fell off her in sheets. Under her blue bathing suit, her bosom was heaving with uneven breaths.

"Can we go home now, Mama?" Ruby said.

"All right," I said. "But let's wait till Thane gets in to shore."

"I don't want to wait," she said.

"Why not?"

"It'd be awkward," she said.

"I can't imagine things being awkward with Thane," I said.

Ruby shivered and I caught sight of the trembling where it passed over her shoulders, roughing the skin in its wake. "Mama, he asked me to marry him," she said.

"God in heaven."

"I told him no," she said. "Right away I told him. No, I said. Not ever."

❧

Next day, Ruby stayed home from school. She'd been crying in the night and her eyelids were swollen. They were filled up full with the liquid of her sorrow, and they turned her eyes heavy and spear-shaped, so that you could barely see the blue behind the lashes. Her face was mottled pink and white from going sleepless like she'd done, and on one cheek the pattern of color was so regular, it looked like somebody had drawn it there —

putting six tiny primroses above a scape of thorns. She joined Allie and me for breakfast in the forest. Under a fireberry tree, she held a tin cup to her lips, pretending to drink the milk inside it.

"Seems to me you done the only thing was proper," Allie said. "Told him straight off you wasn't about to marry him."

"It isn't like you ought to have forced yourself to love him," I said. "It wouldn't have come natural and it wouldn't have come lasting."

Ruby's lips trembled so that they shook the rim of the tin cup where it rested between them. She took the cup down away from her face. On the corner of her mouth, there was a single drop of milk, large and still.

"I do love him," she said. "But I love him the same way I've done ever since I can remember."

"What way?" Allie said.

"Like he's my daddy," Ruby said. "Like he's the man that cares for me and looks after me, that buys me clothes for school and candy for the holiday." Ruby's tongue came out between her lips and touched the spot on her cheek where the milk drop had rested.

"You has knowed him too long a time," Allie said.

"I expect so," Ruby said.

"If only he had stayed away when you were younger, maybe you would've seen him different," I said.

"Maybe," Ruby said.

"Too bad about it, but there ain't nothing can be done," Allie said.

Ruby stirred her finger in the tin cup where it rested on the ground cloth. She gazed at the swirling milk, thick and frothy as it moved. "I feel tired," she said. "Tired through to my bones."

"Try a biscuit," Allie said, and she passed a plate of the sourdough rounds, crumbly and steaming. "My biscuits, they have curative powers. That's what everybody says."

❧

I tried to figure how much cash money Thane had spent on Ruby over all the time he had known her. There were six dresses that first year and about as many in all the years following. There were porcelain baby dolls and teddy bears and then later on a silver brooch and an amethyst necklace — and that necklace, it had been dear. Maybe all of it came to three hundred dollars. I asked Allie could we spare that amount and she said, what with the way the restaurant was going, we could've spared twenty times that, maybe more.

Thane came over to the house to say goodbye, just like I expected he would. Said he was going over to Cedarton to oversee his daddy's ranches and didn't know when he might be back. He looked at Mondrow's wall clear and hard while he spoke, like he thought to see straight through the bricks that hid the horizon.

"You don't have to pretend you're coming back," I said. "You can just say it straight out."

"Well, I guess it ain't likely I'll come back," he said. "But I'm trying to stop predicting what seems likely and what don't. Mostly when I take to predicting things, I turn out to be wrong."

Over in the forest, the trees waved their arms against the sky — dark limbs on the pinkness of the disappeared sun. There was no wind, but the trees moved all the same, like by their own thought and will they could toss their leafy heads of hair and point their wooded fingers to something on the other side of Mondrow's wall — a street cat with a round pigeon in its jaws or the two satin-white streamers that trailed off a lady's hat.

"I've been wanting to thank you for all you've done for us," I said. "For Ruby especially." I pulled the roll of cash dollars from my smock and held it out to him.

He shook his head. "Thank me, then. Don't pay me," he said. "Something I have found out — money can't trade on love or grief, either one."

"I only meant to set things right," I said.

"Things is already right," he said. "You and me just don't have the grace to know it yet." He walked off through the opening in Mondrow's wall, not once turning back to look. It wasn't till he had disappeared that I realized he had come to me clean-shaven, his mustache gone, the two waxed curls he liked to twirl with his fingers now lying on the floor of some barber shop more than likely, and how aged he had looked without them.

❧

September was a month of peace. What with Thane gone, we had no one but ourselves to think about, and the bit of selfishness, it did us some good. Allie and Ruby and me took us twenty dollars apiece and hired a dressmaker to fashion us each a dress of our preference. Ruby and me had cut out pictures of the styles we wanted from a ladies' leisure magazine. But Allie had sketched out her own design — a tulip skirt that ended at the calf, and a sleeveless bodice that she had drawn fitted and trim, with a square lace collar draping over the bosom, like it was only to hint at the curves that lay underneath. She picked out a fabric that was green silk on account of she said it moved like water over her hands, slippery and cool.

When all of us were through having our fittings at the dressmaker's shop, we walked down the street to Clifton Grand's House of Photography. Ruby said she had seen a sign in the window that said Clifton Grand was offering a cut-rate on his picture-taking and maybe we could see him about it. The sign was still hanging when we got there. GET TEN PORTRAITS FOR ~~$10.00~~ $7.00 WHILE THE PRICE IS STILL GOOD, it said. IN BUSINESS FOR THREE YEARS. NOBODY TAKES A PICTURE SO GOOD AS ME. So we paid out the seven dollars, and a week later I held the photographs in my hands. All ten of them showed us smiling our serious smiles, our lips closed gently over our teeth, our cheeks rounded like small fruits, high up on our faces. All of our skins were sepia-colored — the same aching yellow shade as the earth and, at the end of the day, as our ankles, where the tongues of the dust had licked us while we walked. We might have been related, it seemed to me, what with the camera finding our glances so forthright and glad, and finding our mouths the quiet keepers of secrets, suspecting more than they would know, and knowing more than they would tell. We all of us had been shaped by the same life, I guess, and the sameness showed in our full-open eyes, our high-collared blouses, the sepia shadows that spilled down onto our necks.

"We's beautiful!" Allie said, when she saw the photographs for herself. "Beautiful every one of us."

"You act surprised," I said.

"Well, I knowed we was good-looking," Allie said. "I just didn't know how *much!*"

"We're going to get full up with conceit if you keep on talking that way," Ruby said.

"That's just fine," Allie said. "I could do with a little conceit. Couldn't you?"

❧

Humberto spent his days tending the forest mostly. He darted through the trees with spades in his hands, or sacks of black mulch. The red maples put out leaves twice the size of Humberto's hands when the fingers were spanned as far as they could reach. When he worked next to the trees, trimming back the firethorn bushes or kneeling between the giant roots of the pecans, he appeared to be more child than man, more treasure-hunter than laborer. The red earth lodged in fine half circles below his nails, and he never quite cleaned it out, not even after spending a half hour leaned over the washbasin with a boar-hair brush and a cake of kitchen soap. Allie inspected his hands every night before she let him handle the food.

"You ain't come clean," she would say.

"The soil has marked me," he would say back. "I cannot wash off the mark of the earth."

"How long has you scrubbed?" she said.

"One hour, I think" he said.

"You lying to me," she said.

"Maybe one half an hour," he said.

"All right," she said. "Get to working."

Humberto and me had stopped planting new saplings about five years back on account of we didn't want the forest to get overgrown. Too much growth and the trees would be fighting one another for groundwater. The barks would weaken and crack, and insects would crawl underneath. But one day that September, Humberto called Allie and me out to the barn. In the corner, leaned up against the tackle, were two silverbell saplings. Their roots were bundled up into two globes of burlap. Their trunks were straight and silvered, like arms reaching for something glorious. Their leaves were the palest green and forked like sparrows' tails. And both of them were in full bloom — one in smoke white and the other in candy pink.

"Humberto!" Allie said. "Where'd you get them?"

"I have never seen a sapling bloom," I said.

"They are rare," he said. "I have found them at the other side of Jake Frye's pond."

"Let's plant them by the house," I said. "I know just the place."

"Set them close together and I think it is true that their branches will braid," Humberto said. "The blooms, they will all come together like this." He laced his earth-covered fingers together and held them up for us to see.

Allie and me dug the holes with spades, sinking the metal heads into the loose, dry soil. I watched her perspire through her dress, so I imagine I did the same. In the small of my back, there was a triangle of wetness, cool when I held it away from my skin. The saplings held up their leaves to the sky and trembled. Their blooms were thin as tissue, veins running through the petals, with sticky pink-tipped wands growing out from their openings.

"Has you ever seen the like?" Allie said. "In full bloom before they even has a set of decent roots."

"Imagine what they're going to be like in ten years or twenty," I said.

"Oh, they are rare trees," Humberto said. "Both of them, they both are rare. That is why I brought them. The bell trees are hard to find."

❧

The thing about those two trees was, they never went out of flower. Every time one set of blossoms was blown away, with so many pink and white petals littering the wind, another set was budding, their colors just showing at the tips of the tight green coats that wrapped them. The trees splashed brightness up against the side of the house, the blossoms lolling on their branches like the heavy heads of dolls, globe-like and dreaming. From inside the restaurant, the customers stared through the quarter-paned windows to see the bell trees standing in the night. How are you keeping your greenery so healthy? they would say. Have you got a hothouse? Have you got a grafter? No, we'd say. It's good land is all. It cares for its own.

Now, if somebody had asked Warren the same question, I expect he would've answered differently. Success with the land seemed unnatural to him. Maybe it seemed impossible. He had ridden over the backs of planting fields for years at a time, shifting from tractor to picker and back again. And always the earth had been stingy — filled up with rocks and clay and roots long dead. The crops that grew up out of it were thorny and meager, and the farmers were always angry over the yield. All the same, they wouldn't listen to Warren's ideas about paying the hired man by the amount of work he did instead of by the day. They stuck to their ways and they made their small profits. Most of them didn't even know enough to rotate their crops. They planted cotton or snap beans on the same acreage year after year, and when the soil turned barren on them, they sold out to the ranchers.

The idea that me and Humberto could've taken a few saplings and turned them into a forest, Warren didn't understand it. He said in my hearing more than once that he figured I had me a system I wasn't letting on about — that maybe I had a secret ingredient I was mixing in with the soil to make it grow things like it did. Allie laughed him off.

"Only secret ingredient she got is a talent with her greenery," Allie said. "God-given, most like."

"Just the same, she be planting on barren land," Warren said.

"If she is, she don't know it," Allie said. "And thank goodness for the ignorance."

But Warren had stopped trusting me, if once

he did. Ever since that night when I had told him and his friends to get out of the restaurant, he looked at me sideways, like I might've been a witch only he wasn't sure how to prove it. One evening, I came into the kitchen to find him and Allie twined together in an embrace. Allie was faced away from me, her hair all falling down her neck where Warren had pulled it loose from its bun. Warren, he was looking me straight on, but he didn't make any move. He kept on talking to Allie like they were alone, with me nowhere close to hear. His eyes were red-shot and half-lidded, dark as wounds at the centers.

"She'll sell you her share if you ask her to," he said.

"Why would I want to ask her?" Allie said. "We has worked together on the restaurant since the very first day."

"The restaurant wouldn't be nothing without you to cook for it," Warren said.

"I just don't see what it's got to do with her," Allie said.

"I don't like her, that's what," Warren said. "She turned me away from my own table."

"Did you give her a choice?" Allie said.

"Was I bound to?" Warren said.

"Don't ask me to do her that way," Allie said. "Me and her has lived too much of life together. We has come too far a distance."

When I left them I was walking on the balls of my feet, the leather on my shoes so soft and worn, it didn't make hardly a sound.

❧

Warren might've gone on fighting me forever if it hadn't been for the time he cut off the hand of a white man in Hiram Henrick's field. Warren never told the story himself, but the man with the missing hand told it all over town in the days that were left to him, and this is the way it went.

Warren had shown up at Henrick's place before eight o'clock and had got himself a place on a tractor. But then a white showed up a half hour later, and Hiram Henrick said that he could take Warren's place. So the white went out to the field where Warren was tilling and gave him the sign to get down off his seat, but Warren wouldn't do it. The man tried to pull him down, but Warren boxed him in the hollow of his jaw. When he fell, his shirt cuff had wedged in the tractor tread, and then when Warren put the engine in gear, the tread had dragged the man's hand straight into the tilling blades. Three or four people were said to have heard the screams from Hiram's house, and that was more than a mile away. Warren ran off, leaving the tractor idling and the man still hung up on the tread, crying. The word was that the man died not two weeks later from an infection of the blood, which the doctor said was a sickness without a cure. And it was probably just as well, he said, because what good was a man without his hand?

❧

It was accidental, the whole business about the man with the cut-off hand. Warren never said as much, but then I don't expect he needed to. We all saw it in the nervous folds of skin setting high up on his forehead. We saw it in the dryness of his lips, which he licked with his tongue to keep from cracking open. We saw it in the shirt he wore day and night for a week without once taking it off to bathe or shave.

He took to following Allie around the house all day. If she was laundering, he would set still by the washing tub, soap bubbles wandering like tiny, lost worlds to lodge on the fiber of his shirt, in the strands of his hair, and him never moving to brush them away. If she was cooking, he would set on Skeet's old stool in the kitchen, his yellow hat pushed low over his eyes so that all he could see was the slat-wood floor and the shiny toes of Allie's new lace-up shoes when she walked from one counter to another, her aprons bulged with peeled white onions or pitted peaches.

He followed her, too, the day she went outside to hang the linens on the line and found five men waiting by Mondrow's wall. Hats and black cloths concealed the whole of their faces except their eyes, shining out cruel and alive like weasels from a hole. Warren didn't try to run. He didn't try to speak. He watched them while they held out their hands towards him and fired, the sound finding him so suddenly that all he knew was the roaring in his ears, rushing him towards deafness in the bright, white, silent afternoon. And when the men turned away, he saw their sunburned necks, their blond, close-cropped hair, the thin layer of sulfur smoke that was twisting in front of Mondrow's bricks, rising into the air above them. He lay down onto the ground at Allie's feet, and she looked at him like she didn't know what had happened or why he was pressing his face to the dust. "What?" she said. "What is it?" She still held the laundry basket propped on her hip. The wind got a hold of the linen napkins that were laying on top. They flew off into the sky like giant moths, first two, then five, then ten, one after the other, mounting Mondrow's wall and disappearing beyond it. And all the while, Allie was looking after them, the wind still dipping into her basket and her not able to stop it. "Oh no," she cried. "Oh no oh no oh no."

❧

Warren, he was shot four times. Thrice through the midsection and once through the throat. There were three dark brown marks over his ribs, frayed at the edges like dried flowers. But Humberto said Warren died from the bullet that passed through his neck, on account of which he lost blood through an artery way, fast and flowing. He poured out his liquid over the dust, and the earth drank greedily from the spreading red stain. Even after Warren was lowered into the ground at the far end of the forest, his knees bent on account of the pine box was too short — even after that, the front yard was still stained with his blood, set in the shape of a four-fingered hand, black and gummy-skinned and covered with flies.

We figured that whoever killed him were friends of the man with the cut-off hand, but there wasn't any way to prove our suspicions. Allie had seen a few sunburned necks, a few guns firing in a few hands and that was all. The sheriff's men stayed just long enough to find out that the murdered man was colored and then they shut their notebooks and went away.

Allie, for her part, she couldn't get over it. She knew Warren had got himself into bad trouble, but I expect she thought the worst that would come from it would be that Warren wouldn't be able to find any more work. If she had thought that he'd be killed, I guess she would've packed up her things and run away with him. She loved him that much.

The days after Warren was buried, they were hard on Allie. Me and her kept running across Warren's half-empty jars of liquor setting about the house. Sour-smelling they were, with a red layer of dust floating on the top of the remaindered whiskey. Allie carried them to the sink like the glass might break in her hands if she wasn't careful. She turned round-shouldered and thin and she stopped going with me for our breakfasts in the forest. Every time I fixed her a plate of food, she pushed it away.

"Only thing I have seen pass your lips since yesterday is a glass of cold tea," I said.

"That's all I wanted," Allie said.

"May be all you wanted, but it's not all you needed," I said.

"Leave me alone."

"I won't," I said. "You need folks around you just now."

"How come you know what I need all of a sudden?" she said. "How come you know it so much better than me?"

"Friends are supposed to know things like that," I said.

"I ain't got no friends," Allie said. "All the friends I had is dead."

She left me where I stood, a plate of stuffed chicken and mashed potato mountains weighing heavy in my hands.

❧

Next day, a letter from my mama came in the post. The words had been written across a torn-off page of newsprint that had turned yellow in the months since it had first been sold. Mama's script was large and wavering, and in more than one place she had forgotten to cross her t's. It said,

> Dear girl of mine,
>
> I hope you'll see your way clear to excuse the scrap I'm writing on. My good paper has run out, and I haven't got myself down to the mercantile to buy some more.
>
> Girl, I'm so proud of you that you have bought that restaurant for your own. I always said if there was one of my children could make a success of leaving

home, it would be you to do it. Oloe, she left home, too, but for some reason God had it in His mind that she should die not long after. I don't pretend to understand why He wanted her so young. I've been puzzling over the possibilities for these last twenty years and still I don't know. Maybe He took her in exchange for my second sight. (Or maybe He's just greedy. Even God has got failings.)

Now that you are in business for yourself, maybe you'll have enough money to come see me some one of these days. I have turned into a white-haired old lady, lying in her bed and lonely for her child. (It isn't so sorry as it sounds. It's just unexpected is all. I never thought to turn aged without I would need to give someone my permission first.)

Missing you,

Mama

❧

I would've shown the letter to Allie except in her age of grief I expect she would've looked at the words without knowing what they meant. She shut herself away in her bedroom all morning, and when I came to check on her, she was still lying between the sheets, her knees curled up to her chest, her shoulders bare except for the see-through folds of the nightgown Oloe had sewn for her when her and Warren were first married.

I guess she would've stayed in her bed all day every day if it wasn't for me reminding her that the meals for the restaurant couldn't prepare themselves without her. The pork and the honey and the dumplings were tasteless without she would put them together with the right spices. It wasn't like I could've taken over from her. I had cooked for Skeet some ten years going and still I couldn't fashion more than a passing meal. Allie would've been the first to say it.

Allie undertook what I call a dry mourning. She watched the world through a wide-eyed and tearless sorrow. The natural curve of her lips turned downwards and bitter-seeming, like she was nursing some sweet private anger that nobody else could taste. The easy conversation that had once come from her died somewhere deep in her throat, and the only words she saw fit to let go of were words of necessity or grief. Me, I expected the mourning to pass by in one month or two, but she held on to it like it was a rare and magic thing. I guess she forgot that Warren had been a man with plain limits and remembered him only as the man that had taught her the ways of love.

Looking back on it now, I ought never to have tried to separate a woman from her grieving. At the time, it was probably just the dearest thing she had, and I set out to take it from her in a thousand ways. I took it from her when I pulled her out of bed in the mornings and helped her to dress, buttoning up the backs of her smocks over the knobs on her spine and telling her how fine she looked, how cheerful. I took it from her when I tied ribbons in her hair and slid rings on her fingers while I told her folks were noticing how she had improved. I took it from her when I sang songs in her kitchen and asked her to sing along, because her voice was so sweet and I didn't want to go another day without hearing it.

" 'Oh Danny boy,' " I sang. " 'The pipes, the pipes are calling.' "

Allie stood behind me, whipping potatoes and cream in a four-quart bowl. Her hand beaters clacked against the bowl's sides, rhythmic and tinny-sounding. I couldn't tell whether she was singing along with me or not.

" 'From glen to glen, and down the mountainside,' " I called.

Behind me, the beaters stopped clacking.

" 'The summer's gone, and all the roses falling.' "

Allie drew in a long breath.

" 'It's you, it's you must go and I must bide,' " I sang.

"You ain't sorry he's dead," Allie said.

The notes of the song died in my throat. In my hands, I held a peeled potato, small and creamy-colored as an egg. It felt cold where it rested in my palm.

"You don't have to say nothing," Allie said. "But I knows you ain't sorry."

"You're making it sound like I killed him myself," I said. I turned to face Allie where she stood. She was still gripping the hand beaters, peaks of whipped potatoes rising off the tines as smooth as buttercream frosting.

"How he died got nothing to do with it," she said.

"Well, then, I don't know what you're trying to say," I said.

"It's just that I can't stand being with you is all," she said. "Not when I know you don't grieve him, not even a little bit."

"Allie," I said. She shook her head, single strands of her flyaway hair waving in the air when she did it.

"You got to leave me on my ownsome for awhile," she said. "You got to go your own way for awhile and it's got to be a separate way from mine."

The peeled potato I held felt so cold that the bones in my hand were full of ache.

"You're asking me to go?" I said.

"Yes," she said.

❧

So Ruby and me packed up our things. Our dresses filled a hanging suitcase. Our hollow shoes made clunking sounds where they rattled in the bottom of a packing crate that'd once held turnips. Humberto helped us to load the bags in the trunk of Skeet's old Hudson, dull and dust-covered in the driveway. I worried out loud about how Allie would manage without a car, but she said she wouldn't go lacking for long. She'd buy herself a new one if it came to that.

There wasn't any doubt in my mind as to where we would go. Back in Copper Crown, Mama was lonely and ailing, living in the old house all by her ownsome, except for the spirit of her daddy, which she said had never left her side since the day he passed on. There, in the place of all our beginnings, we'd find us shelter again. There, in the arms of my mama, we'd find us rest.

When we were just about ready to drive away, Allie came out of the house with a roll of green bills in her hand. Must've been three or four hundred dollars altogether, because when she held them out to me, I saw they were faced with tens and twenties.

"You'll be needing this," Allie said. The wind fanned the bills like they were leaves, fresh-fallen and dry.

"We won't be gone that long," I said.

"The money's yours," Allie said. "That and much more. You own half of everything, and I ain't forgot it."

"Then you keep it whole for me till I get back," I said.

Allie turned and went back in the house, her hair streaming loose over her coatdress, the flat pucks of her heels showing pink. I started the car rolling down the drive, listening to the sounds of the small stones popping under the wheels. In the rearview mirror, I caught sight of the silverbell trees, bright pink and white under the spread of their new blooms. Above them, the windows of the house were eyes, curtained and hollow, inside of which I kept thinking Allie would appear herself, arms waving, the green sash of her coatdress spilling over the sill. But she never came, and then I turned out onto Halliday Road, where the sight of the house was blocked by Mondrow's wall and its row after row of plaster and bricks that looked like they were doing the job of keeping people away or trapping people inside only I couldn't tell which one, then or now.

PART THREE

❧

1932

Emerald Arms

❧

When I first saw my mama again, I knew she wouldn't be long for this world. Ruby and me found her out where she was lying upstairs, swaddled up as tiny as a child at the center of the master bed. Her hair had gone silver-white from the roots to the ends, and it lay out loose on the pillowcase, glinting and curl-less. Her scalp was warm and pink, and when she was lying down, the skin rested smoothly against her cheeks and the wrinkles were made gentle. Something about her looked just like a newborn baby.

When she saw me, she said, "Cassie, my Cassie. I have waited for you."

I said, "Mama, we've come back to you. Did you ever think we would?"

At the first, I could tell, she didn't know what all I meant by saying "we." She looked from Ruby to me, and then back to Ruby again.

"Who . . ." she said. "Who . . . ?"

I said, "I brought Ruby with me."

Mama closed her eyes a minute. I saw two half moons of white eyelashes laying flat against her cheeks.

"Baby Ruby?" she said.

"Baby Ruby," I said. "And you haven't seen her all these years." Ruby set down at the bedside and put her hand over the bony hill of Mama's leg.

Mama said, "All these months, God has been putting off my dying, and I never knew why till right this minute."

❧

I swore I wouldn't ever come back to the town I grew up in. And I swore I wouldn't ever let Ruby come back either. And still I did it all the same. There was a time when I thought my life was mine to do with like I pleased, but now, when I look back, I see that I hadn't done enough living then to understand what all shapes the years. People do a little of the shaping, but only a little. Because the passing time and God Himself both shape you in ways you can't predict. Once, I thought to stay away from Copper Crown because I'd known too much sorrow there, but eighteen years later, standing at the bedside of my mama, and stroking my hands across the streaming silver of her hair, all I knew was love.

I said, "Mama, I shouldn't have stayed away from you so long."

She said, "Shhh. Don't say it. A good life

doesn't leave room for regret."

I said, "Have I had me a good life?"

She said, "I can't be the one that tells you. A good life might have been somewhat different for you than it's been for me."

I said, "Then tell me what it's been for you."

She said, "It's been giving away so much love there have been times I thought I'd die from the outpouring. It's been listening to the spirit of my daddy while he's kept me company these last thirty years. It's been raising up my children the best ways I knew how, and it's been watching Oloe die without hate taking hold of my soul. It's been the quieting of my anger and the rising of my peace — even when war has been going on all around. I don't know as I could call it the life I would've chosen, but maybe God — when I stand before Him, with all my days and nights laid out plain for Him to see — maybe God will call it good."

❧

So then I asked myself again, "Have I had me a good life?" But I didn't know what to answer. Seemed like I tried to be good to others here and there, but then I came to thinking about Allie, and I couldn't say for sure whether or not I had been good to her. The two of us, we were so kind one to another for so many years, and then it seemed like all the kindness just dried up and blew away overnight. Seemed her preferences turned coloreder and my preferences turned whiter, and all we could do was gape at the skin on the other one like it was the worst surprise we ever got. How could we have not seen how God had made us different from the get-go?

But then sometimes, I'd think about what had happened between us, and I'd think it didn't have to do with our skins so much as what was underneath them. It wasn't prejudiced. It was just personal. And I told myself these things and I tried to let them lie. Allie just didn't care for me anymore. You would think I had killed Warren myself the way her caring for me stopped so suddenly like it did. But the fact of it was, she didn't act like she had a bit of caring for me left — not a smidgen of it resting at the bottom of her soul. Not a grain. So I tried to get shut of my caring for her, too. I tried to pass an entire day without me thinking on her, and there were a couple of times when I almost did it. I left all my pictures of her and me back at the restaurant, so that I wouldn't have to be looking on them to jar my remembrance. But still in my mind I knew all the pictures that were ever taken with us two in them — some of them with Ruby, too — and they stood up in front of my eyes when I woke in the morning and then through the rest of the day — just the same as if I'd been toting them with me from one room to the next. And sometimes I thought I heard her voice, high and clear, calling in my soul, calling me to come to her. And I tried to be deaf to it, but it sounded all the same.

❧

Allie sent me twenty dollars through the mail. There was a note, too. It said,

> Cass,
>
> I know you probably be needing money, and now that the restaurant's going so good, I got me money to spare. Here's twenty dollars. Next week, I be sending you more.
>
> Allie

Maybe it was true that I was getting low on cash, but I wasn't ready to take a loan or a handout or whatever name Allie would've put to it. Ruby said I ought to have kept the money. Said we ought to have sent for the doctor for Mama and a good doctor wouldn't put off being paid. On which account maybe I would've kept some of the money with the intention of paying it back later, only when I asked Mama about it she said doctors were best for the living and not for the dying and she didn't want any old man to come set by her bedside and preach to her about the best way to leave this world because she figured she'd just have to find that out for herself.

So I sent the money back with a note of my own.

> Allie,
>
> Ruby and Mama and me are making out just fine. So take back the twenty dollars and please don't send us any more after it either. We've got no use for lucre that isn't our own. Like the Bible says. But I know you were trying to do right by us all the same. Anyway I'm sure you can give it to people that need it more than us.
>
> Cass

❧

There were times when Mama could scarcely breathe. The wind moved through her throat fast and shallow, and I could hear it whistling in the low well of her lungs. Ruby said it was pneumonia, and I couldn't imagine it being much else. We all knew she was dying, most of all Mama herself. But I expect Mama had a different view towards dying than most. It never gave her a moment's fear.

One time she said, "I don't want you giving me any funeral service after I'm gone."

I said, "But everybody gets a funeral."

She said, "A burying maybe, but not a funeral."

I said, "Don't you want something for people to remember you by?"

She said, "If they're not disposed to remember me by my life, I don't expect that any amount of singing or crying or flower-gathering would change it."

Ruby said, "But it always seemed to me that funerals weren't for the dead so much as they were for the living that have suffered the loss."

Mama said, "But Ruby girl, dying isn't a loss at all."

Ruby said, "Gramma, you talk like you're looking forward to leaving us. Don't you like the company you've been keeping?"

Mama said, "You know I do. Your mama and you are all I've been breathing for, minute by minute."

I said, "Then you just get it in your mind

to stay with us a while longer."

"Well," Mama said. "As long as I can."

❧

Every morning, Ruby found a warm tea cozy on the table by Mama's bed. There would be two empty cups setting close by, drained to the stray leaves resting at the bottom — and a half-empty sugar bowl, with a teaspoon or two of the fine white crystals scattered to the floor, where we heard them gritting under our heels like sand. At first, Ruby got upset over it.

She said, "Gramma, you can't hardly sit up straight without getting the dizziness to your head. What do you mean by getting out of bed and walking downstairs? Can't you ask me to fix your tea? And what do you do with two cups every morning? Can't you just drink out of the one cup at a time? Gramma, you are a puzzle and a confounding, I swear you are."

Mama said, "I like fixing my own tea, and I can't do without."

But when Ruby had gone out of the room, the cozy at her side, and the cups and saucers all trembling on a tray, Mama turned to me where she lay in the bed. She was biting her pale white lip.

She said, "I don't like to lie to the girl, but I just can't see my way around it."

I said, "You never leave your bed anymore at all, do you?"

Mama shook her head. "I haven't the strength," she said. "My legs are all withered."

"Then who is doing you the tea?" I said.

"My papa," she said. "He steeps out the best tea you've ever tasted."

"Your papa?"

"Isn't it funny?" she said. "He never even drank tea while he was alive. He never even knew he liked it."

"Well, there aren't many men that do," I said.

"Oh, but Papa does," she said. "And now we have it every morning, before the house wakes up." Mama's hand splayed like a rake, pulling the thin sheet up across her shoulders. "I don't guess Ruby would understand it — my papa being a spirit and all."

"I don't guess so," I said. "She hasn't got the sight yet."

"It's too bad," Mama said. "Because Papa's taken a liking to you and Ruby both. He asked me would I make you all an introduction."

❧

My grandaddy was a shy, retiring spirit. That's what my mama said after he disappeared himself from view, his teacup rattling in his lap on the morning I saw him for the first time. It was five o'clock, and the pale sun was just slanting through the window over the close half of my mama's aged-young face. Setting on the table was a third cup of tea. Mama pointed at it with her pink-knobbed hand.

"We have poured you out your cup," she said. "Still hot for the taking."

Where I walked past him in his high wicker-backed chair, my grandaddy faded to one or two blue-gray lines, hanging in the air like smoke. And his teacup and saucer were suspended in the middle of the air, rattling against one another like they might have been trembling in the breeze.

"Papa, this is my Cassie," Mama said. "Cassie, this here's your grandaddy."

The lines of blue smoke got thick for a time, and I saw a wide straw hat and two glass-blue eyes, and a beard that flowed like water to his knee. The wide hat nodded itself towards me.

"Hello, Grandaddy," I said.

The teacup raised up and lowered from an invisible pair of lips. He didn't say anything.

"Papa's shy and retiring," Mama said. "That's his way."

"All right," I said. I drank my tea and it streamed in a sweet, spicy river down my throat.

"He might not be wanting to speak to you right away," Mama said.

So we set and drank our tea in the quiet and Grandaddy said no word to me and cast no glance on me, and I wouldn't have thought he knew I was there at all, except when my cup was empty, the blue lines that were my grandaddy's spirit pulled themselves out of their chair to pour me a new cup of his wild, sweet tea.

❧

Dear Cass,

Here's twenty dollars. If you don't take it for yourself I can't be making you. But I hope you will take it for Ruby, seeing as how I helped to raise her from the very start and so by some accounting, she's part my child. Just part, like I said, and it can be whatever part you want. But she always going to be in my prayers at night, and if you want to let my mind rest easy by knowing that Ruby ain't lacking for food nor drink nor what all she need, you won't never let me see this twenty dollars again. You do my poor lonely soul a favor now, and do like I say.

Allie

Dear Allie,

I ought to have sent the money back to you, but I'm keeping it. Just this once. I gave it to Ruby and she went to market with it. Not that any of us was going hungry, mind you, but it was marketing day, so we bought us some extras — fresh peaches, a tub of sour white cheese, a rhubarb tart, and such like that. I only did it for Ruby. This one time and that's all.

Cass

❧

Some parts of Copper Crown were as familiar as my dreams. When I stood out in the west planting field, the jimsonweed and milkplant growing up between my feet, I felt like I had been standing there my whole life, the seasons passing over my head in a narrow strip of boiling clouds and inching stars and night rolling into day, and all the while the land staying just the same. The trees lined themselves up along the edge of the field in the same way they'd been lined up since the start of time — two birch, one elm, two birch, two pine — their branches setting against the sky like so many outstretched hands, frozen in the moment of their first desiring. And me, standing in the field so still as a tree myself, so permanent, the toes of my shoes dug under the crumbling red earth like the start of hot, blind roots sinking into the unseen coolness below.

But the people were more fragile than the land, and the people of Copper Crown were changed. Some of them aged, some of them gone. Aunt Pauline had died five years back, and Uncle Jensen had all but abandoned his farm to the hands that worked it. Old man Lubbock was still hiring himself out at planting and picking seasons, but Lubbock's family and mine always thought they knew one another good enough not to be liked. When I walked past him on the Valley Road, he looked at me steadily through his half-shut eyes, but he never raised his hat. I was beginning to think that God had made it so I'd be a stranger every place I set foot.

And then I saw her. Come Saturday, I watched a colored woman walking out the door of the milliner's, her arms full of sundries all packed in a box. She was wearing an aged, out-of-style, broad-brimmed hat with dark veiling on the edge, and the angle of it hid away her eyes. But through the fine netting, I saw her mouth — the lips full and sorrowful as ever they were made, sensuous and sad where they turned down at the corners.

"Maggie," I said. And she turned to look.

❧

When Maggie threw her arms around me, the air filled up with the smell of cloth-soap and oranges — a laundry smell that rose up like perfume off the pores of her skin.

"I would've hardly knowed you," Maggie said. "Child, you is so much changed."

"The years have done it against my will," I said. Maggie laughed, her teeth showing even and white from the shadow under her hat. Her acorn eyes were light and determined, with small flecks of brown spilling out from the centers. "*You* don't look different, though," I said. "Your beauty hasn't left you, inside or out."

"No," she said. "I's aged and I's glad of it. It's made living easier on me."

It was true that Maggie appeared wearier by a few years — but not by nearly so many as had passed since we were together. Something in her form was turned ancient — the thinness of it, I guess. Her arms and legs had lost the flesh to shape them, and they extended out from her body at hurtful angles, the joints appearing outsized and swollen. But you hadn't to watch her take two steps to know that she'd kept her grace. The way she held up her head, the space she put to her stride — they were markers of her dignity that couldn't be starved or wearied away.

"Has you come back to stay?" she said.

"No," I said. But then I thought better of it. "Maybe. My mama, she's got pneumonia, and she's been needing Ruby and me to set by her nights."

"Ruby come with you?" Maggie said.

"Mm-hmm," I said. "All grown now."

"And the last time I seen her, she wasn't two days old," Maggie said. "Fresh orphaned and crying and desperate for my breast."

❧

Saturday next, Maggie came up to the house. There was a man with her. I saw them both from the upstairs window — Maggie wrapped up in her paper-yellow dress, no bigger than a child, and the man lording over her, bent and swaggering at the shoulder. For a minute I was wondering had she got herself married again, but then I saw that the man was young — still fighting the awkward ways of his newly long limbs, still contemplating where he ought to hide his man-sized hands. And when he came to the front door, I saw that his eyes were drawn from the palest shade of sky. Then I knew it was Lloyd. Maggie caught a hold of the wonder in my face.

She said, "Would you ever expected I could've growed a child so high?"

"He's nearly twice as tall as you," I said. Lloyd looked down on us and smiled, showing a set of teeth that were just like Maggie's, white to distraction. I held out my hand to him and he took it up inside his giant, man-sized palm.

"Hello, ma'am," he said.

"Hello, Lloyd," I said. "I have seen you once before now, but I don't guess you remember me." Lloyd winced the bone-brown skin around his eyes, like if he only tried hard enough, the remembrance would be sure to find him.

"You ain't going to recall it," Maggie said to him, laughing. "You was only a few days old at the time."

"Well, then you can't keep me responsible for anything I might said," Lloyd told me.

"Nobody held your cries against you," I

said. "Yours nor Ruby's neither."

"Ruby?" Lloyd said.

"My girl Ruby," I said. "She was born the same day as you." And even while I said it, I heard Ruby's foot on the staircase.

"Same day as Lily Mark died," Maggie said. "A beauty, she was." Ruby reached the bottom of the stairs, her blue-black hair falling loose about her shoulders. At the sound of her step, Maggie turned towards her. I heard the high, rising note of a gasp. "Oh my heavens," Maggie said. "She's Lily Mark all over."

Ruby turned her eyes on me, keen and bright where they traveled into mine. "Who's Lily Mark?" she said.

❧

There wasn't ever any excuse for the deceit, I guess — and still I clung to it all the same. Nothing had been difficult about it. Not the wishing, not the telling, not the being believed. I only had to make up one or two details about the birthing — how I lay fourteen hours in labor, how the doctor came the next day and found out my breasts were dry. Ruby didn't ask for any more. Didn't need any more, most likely, when she saw how much I loved her.

But when once Ruby asked me, "Who's Lily

Mark?" I thought to scream or cry out or faint away. Just to hear her lips moving over the sounds of her mama's name made me wish I was deaf. Me not birthing her wasn't half so painful as now pretending that I had. All I could do was to stare at the floorboards at the front of Ruby's feet. The toes of her two wine-colored shoes looked eatable as apples, rounded and shining where they walked across the floor.

"I'll tell you about Lily Mark some other time," I said. "She's just somebody that used to room with the family."

While I talked, I could see the surprise at my words washing its way over Maggie's face. She blinked her eyes real fast for a bit — like the light indoors had changed of a sudden and she was trying to adjust her vision. But then she recovered herself, smiling broadly and pressing Ruby's hand. "If you let me stay awhile," Maggie said, "I promise as I won't be talking no more about folks you all don't know."

❧

When I asked Maggie what was Lloyd doing for his living, she said that he was working with paints. So naturally I thought he was painting the sides of houses and barns and such like, but Maggie said no, it wasn't that kind of painting.

I said, "When it comes to painting, how many kinds are there?"

She said, "It's *picture*-painting, what Lloyd does. Oil painting on a canvas."

"Picture-painting?" I said.

"That's right," Maggie said.

"Pictures of what?" I said.

"It's people he paints mostly," Maggie said. "He makes portraits of them, portraits of the most beautiful kind. Most folks say he's looking through the skin to find the very soul in a person. Most folks say he's seeing with the eye of God."

"Will he paint one for the asking?" I said.

"Sure enough," Maggie said. "You only got to ask him once."

"Because I'd love to get me a portrait picture of Mama. I'd find a way to pay you all for it."

"No, you wouldn't," Maggie said. "Lloyd don't take no money for his painting."

"Not ever?" I said.

"No."

"But I heard you say that painting was his living," I said.

"And that what it be," Maggie said. "His living or his life, don't make no matter what name you put to it. He doing it because he been called to do it. And once you see his working, you going to stop wondering what I mean."

❧

Lloyd brought over a canvas that had already been painted on. It measured three and a half foot by four and a half foot and when he carried it between his arms, it seemed like it swallowed him whole from his head to his knees. He ought to have been turned sightless by it, on account of him not being able to see anything but the patch of changing ground which moved past his feet. But in spite of my conjectures, he never tripped nor fell nor ran into anything, at least not as I could see. He must've walked three miles to get to the house that Sunday, on a road that twisted and turned and twined its rocky way from out of the town. He held the canvas up in front of his face as solid as a wall, and him taking those lean, long strides over the ground without a hesitation, without a faltering — just as easy and smooth as he climbed the stairs up to Mama's bedroom — guided forward by nothing but the need to get somewhere and the eyes of a merciful God.

"It's already been painted on," I said, pointing at the canvas.

"That's all right," Lloyd said. "Don't hurt none to paint over what's already been put down." Lloyd looked at me with his clear eyes, pale as the high sky, and from somewhere I thought I heard a wind traveling across them. His face was touched by a strange-colored peace. In the bed, Mama was curled up in the shape of a child — tiny stick-legs pulled up to her sunk-in chest. I went away and left them alone. At the end of the day, I came back to find Mama sitting upright in her bed. Her and Lloyd were talking and laughing, their eyes fixed on the fresh-painted portrait that was drying in the corner.

"Look at what Lloyd has done," Mama said. "Isn't it a miracle, one side to the other?"

I looked at the canvas. At the one end of it, Mama was nested in her bedclothes, holding like a girl, open-handed, to a porcelain cup and saucer. And at the other end stood her papa, wide-hatted and blue-glowing, his girlish silk beard streaming down to his waist. He was pouring out tea from a high copper kettle into Mama's waiting cup, wearing a smile he must've kept hidden except just for her when the two of them were alone.

"Just look at my papa!" Mama said. "Have you ever seen him appearing so fine?"

❧

Lloyd left the portrait with us three days and nights. Me and Mama and Grandaddy fussed and clucked over it with such a pride that an outsider looking in would have thought sure that one of us had painted it ourselves. Ruby was the only one who didn't say much on it. Her blue-black brows sank down over her eyes like they were somewhere between lost and wandering. "Who's that glowing man?" she was wanting to say. But her shyness held it back.

On the fourth day since we called the portrait ours, Lloyd came to fetch it away. He stood over me at the door, bent-shouldered and swaying, like a sapling tree in the wind.

"You want it back?" I said. "I thought you gave it to us for permanent."

"It's going to stay in your mind's eye for permanent," Lloyd said. "I just going to take away the portrait, not the remembering you's got for it."

"But why?" I said. "What use have you got for it now that you should take it away from us? We're the only folks can appreciate it."

"I need the canvas mostly," Lloyd said. "I has already promised I'd paint a likeness for somebody else."

"Well, haven't you got more canvases than just the one?" I said.

"No, ma'am, I ain't."

"Then I'll go out and buy you another," I said.

"No, ma'am," he said. "You won't find another canvas that shapes the paint as good as this one."

"That shapes the paint?" I said.

"Yes, ma'am," Lloyd said. "It's the canvas does most of my seeing for me."

And so I watched him take it away. He held the picture out in front of him, his head bowed forward against the bleach-white back of the stretch cloth. His legs folded into the distance, overlong and foreign-elegant, like some high-stepping bird. He walked off as fast and sure as if that canvas had been a window frame, its center clear like glass, and all the sights of the world passing before it and away.

❧

Maggie'd worked Olson's laundry these last twenty years. She said she hadn't minded it on account of it kept her hands busy and her mind free. Sometimes, her ankles got swollen from standing up all the day. But some folks said such swelling came from all a body's tears that hadn't ever been cried — by which reason you ought never be holding back your rain, because it was all going to end up pooling at your feet, the one way or the other. And Maggie owned that it might have been true. She wasn't sure. All she knew for certain was that on Sundays, with her feet propped up high on a chair pillow, and the songs of churchgoing still singing themselves through her mind, she didn't know much of grief nor swollen ankles neither.

The years when neither she nor Lloyd could go out on the street for all the hooting and name-calling and brick-throwing that followed, they were past and done with. When she talked on them, she called them the anger years, and an expression that looked for a moment like she might still have been living them put out all the light in her face. "The anger years was come," she said, "and the anger years was gone. And I ain't yet found the reason to either one."

"Just so long as they have left you," I said. "You've got all the rest of the years of your life to live the way you want them. That's miracle enough."

"How you know so much about anger time?" Maggie said. "You talk like it's been periling you your whole life."

"Not my whole life," I said. "It's only just

now that I'm finding it out."

❧

"Maybe it's not that Allie doesn't care for me anymore," I said. "Maybe it's just that she can't abide by my color."

"By principle," Maggie said, nodding her head, the brim on her hat taking away her eyes and then bringing them back.

"By principle," I said. "Those sound like the words that Warren used to use. *By principle, by rights, by what ought to happened . . ."*

"She wrote me about it," Maggie said. "In a letter."

"I haven't got anything to say to her can make her change her mind," I said. "I've said it all before now."

"That don't make no matter," Maggie said. "You got to keep on saying it. You got to say it fresh. You got to find you a different way."

"I can't push myself where I'm not wanted," I said. "I don't have it in me."

Maggie said, "Girl, I has made my hair white pushing myself forward in a town where didn't nobody want me." She reached around her head and pulled off her yellow faille hat. In one of her hands there shone a pearl-tipped hatpin, long and gleaming as a needle. At the top of her head, I saw one broad-laid shock of aching-white hair. All the rest of the strands were black, and it appeared like that one white-laid shock was just a part of her that had been killed overnight, from a sudden surprise or grief turned out in an ill-going dream.

"Oh, Maggie," I said. "There isn't any talking past it. I have lost my surest friend in the world."

"Only if you let her go," she said.

❧

Maggie brought over an old hatbox filled up brimming with letters from Allie. She sank her hand down through the envelopes and when it came back up, it was holding five or six of them, tied together in a packet by a piece of cooking twine.

"These is the most recent ones," Maggie said. "If you ain't seen them yet, you ought to be seeing them now." She handed me the packet and then she set back down in her chair. A small cloud of dust rose up from the seat cushions, and through it, Maggie was staring at me, like she might've been appreciably far away.

"You going to leave them with me for a couple days?" I said.

"No," Maggie said. "I going to wait right

here whiles you reads them all."

"What for?" I said.

"Girl, once you reads them, you going to want to talk to me. I's just saving myself another trip," she said.

So I opened up the first one.

Dear Maggie,

I hasn't knowed what is the far side of grief till now. I hasn't knowed what is the shadow of sorrow. Warren is left me and what can I do? I has prayed to God until my voice gone dry, but God, He don't hear me. I has said, Bring him back and I do anything You want me. But I is only speaking to the earless dark.

And you know what's cutting me to the root of my soul? The same day they come up road and killed him, the same morning they done it, the same dying hour, I told him he'd got to be more respectful to the white peoples, more bowing-down. Specially after the way that poor man lost his hand in Warren's tractor, and even though it wasn't none of his fault. Be respectful, I told him, and they going to forgive you, the smallest single bit at a time.

I said, You bend the branch a inch a day and it going to train itself to a new direction — you bend the branch a yard at once, it going to break off in your hands.

He said, A inch a day? That what you think? Woman, I ain't going to live long enough for a inch a day. I ain't got myself enough years for that kind of one-day waiting.

Maggie, I been a fool not to believed him. Because it wasn't a hour passed before the earth was taking up his blood as easy as if it been rain. And I stood there and watched his life stream full away, him what I always thought been in too much of a hurry. He lay down at my feet and proved me wrong.

And at the end of the day, the sun falled down out the sky and left me standing in the dark — me, waiting by myself, I don't know for what, next to a man who just that morning been wanting so many things and now was wanting nothing at all.

Allie

❧

Dear Maggie,

I wish Warren would've left me some children. We tried to start us a baby, but my belly just stayed hollow. I's had me a womanly figure since I was no more than fourteen years old, and the monthly since two years before then, and I never thought it would trouble me to turn out as many children as I been wanting. But God ain't prepared me my disappointments.

The only thing of Warren's I got to remember him by be his ideas. When he was living, I ain't give him the satisfaction of taking up his thinkings for my own. But it seems like the least as I can do now that he be gone.

One time he said to me, Allie you been cooking for white peoples since you was ten year old.

I said, Yeah. Long as I can remember.

And you still doing it, he said.

Doing more of it now than I ever has, I said.

What for? he said.

How you mean?

What for you doing it now? he said.

I like cooking, I said. I got a talent for it. I take to it better than I take to doing nigh on anything else.

So you take your talent, which most folks and not leastwise me can tell you it's considerable, and you give it away.

I ain't *giving* it away, I said. Folks is paying for it. Good money, too.

Ain't coloreds got good enough money for your cooking?

The money be all the same one person to the next, I said. But you can't go serving a colored the same time you is serving a white.

Then serve your own kind, he said. If you's got to make yourself a choice, serve your own kind.

For a long time I went on like before, setting out dinners for two hundred peoples a day, and not a colored one in sight. But then Warren's talkings come back to me, sounding through my head over and over like they'd got nowhere else to go. And sometimes when I set my fixings down afront of a stranger, I seen a red sunburned neck and a head of shortcut yellow hair and I wondered if he could've been one of the very same mens that took my Warren down not six months back, and me standing there serving him his supper while Warren lay unbreathing and soil-bound, waiting on me to do him right. And my wondering turned to suspicioning and my suspicioning turned to knowing, and it wasn't long before every man that come to eat at my tables had got hisself involved with killing my husband one way or the other. They was guilty by their paleness, and they all looked the same.

So I closed the restaurant down. The mens and the womens, they come banging on my doors for hours at a time, but I turned them all away. They left angry. They said, Wasn't we paying out enough for whatever all food you give us? Don't you know how good you had it, girl?

After a month, they didn't come back no more.

When I opened back up, I only took in coloreds. I cut my prices down to where all of them could pay. It ain't been a couple months yet and already I's feeding as many peoples as I ever done before. I sleep silent now on account of Warren's talkings is going away from my head. When I do hear him, he only be laughing, quiet and deep, whispering love-words as I can't quite decipher, like was always his way when he been pleased.

Allie

❧

Dear Maggie,

Has you seen a sign of Cass? Her and Ruby has left me for to go back to their old house at Copper Crown, and I thought as maybe you would have come across them by now. They ain't took much money with them when they went away, and even though I mail them twenty dollars by the week, often as not they send it back with a note on how they ain't needful. Which is a lie.

I's trying to pretend I ain't missing them, but my pretending don't go too far. If you see them, you write me on how they is. Soon as you can.

Allie

❧

Dear Maggie,

Pack up your articles. Yours and Lloyd's both. I want you to come up town. Girl, I is lonely for company and only the best kind will do me.

I wake up in the morning to the house gone quiet around me, and I think, in the wakeful dreaming of my mind, that maybe it's the hour of quiet when them you love is still sleeping at their beds. And then my reckoning dissolves itself. Because aside of me, wrapped in the bedsheets where my fingers is grasping to find it out, there be a nothing where Warren ought to been. And down the hall, in rooms where the first of the daylight come trembling in like water, green against the tree-shadow walls, there be a nothing where Cass ought to been. There be a nothing at the pillow where Ruby laid down her head for so many years, not even the hollow of the round, not even the last of the heat of the thousand breaths that warmed it. And the house is gone quiet with a quiet worse than death, with a quiet that is nothing.

I going to lose all my reason if I's left to my ownsome this way.

Tell Olson you has give enough years to his laundering, and you is retiring out. You and yours won't want for aught with me because I has plenty.

I is waiting on you.

Allie

❧

I turned to look on Maggie. Her head was bowed, the brim on her yellow grain-ribboned hat covering all but her turned-down lips. There were bunches of tiny bluebonnets playing over the yellow cotton field of her dress, and the folds of it hung loose over the withered-skinny body underneath. She held herself proud-upright, the bones at her spine pulled straight towards the ceiling. She set so still she might not have been breathing and, except for the blue veins at her ankles, flowing like rivers under the crepe-skin brown, I might have feared she'd died in the interval since she'd spoken to me last.

"So Allie has asked you to go up and stay with her," I said. Maggie's hat tilted up slow and even. It looked to be the only part on her that moved.

"Yes," Maggie said.

"Are you going?" I said. Her hat nodded up and down.

"I's tired," she said. "I need the rest."

"I expect it'll be a comfort to her," I said. "Getting the house peopled again." Maggie's wide, sorrowing lips sank down deeper at the corners. Their color kept moving somewhere between mauve and blue and they were alive in her face like a wound.

"Us being there won't make up for her lack of you and Ruby," she said. "When she's feeling stronger, she going to ask you to come back to her as sure as she's missing you now."

"Maybe she will," I said.

"No maybe about it," Maggie said.

"But a person can't come running back just for the asking," I said.

"I'd like to know why not," Maggie said. "I always done it, and long as them that's asking be doing it with love, I ain't found a whatfor in the world to make me ashame."

❧

My life got almost as quiet as Allie's must have been, what with Maggie and Lloyd gone away from me. The day they went, Maggie stepped onto the bus carrying nothing but two wide-band hatboxes and a purse stuffed full with an extra dress. And Lloyd brought his fresh-painted canvas, which the driver tried to make him put underneath in the baggage hold but which Lloyd said might ruin all the baggage down there on account of the paint not being entirely dry. So the driver let him hold it on his lap. Maggie let down the window on her side and raised her lips up to the high square of wind that the glass had slid off of.

"Write me," she said.

And then they pulled out, the voice of the bus pitched high and whining while the monster that was the dust swallowed it up from behind.

Back at the house, Mama got worse. She couldn't set up to drink her tea in the mornings anymore, so Grandaddy fed it to her from the cup, one spoonful at a time. Sometimes a dark, milky drop rolled from the spoon out onto her cheek, where it set as round and perfect as a tear until Grandaddy wiped it away with the curled end of his girlish beard. Her breathing turned to labor, a swampy rattle coming from her lungs in a sound that was much bigger than the child-sized ribs surrounding it.

"I'm taking too long to die," she said. "I'm sorry to make you all wait on me this way."

"We aren't waiting on you to die," Ruby said. "We're waiting on you to get better."

"Bless you, now," Mama said. "When I die, I *am* going to get better."

"You talk like you know it for sure," Ruby said.

"I do," Mama said. "And the moment I leave this world, you're going to find it out for yourself."

❧

The man standing in the doorway of our house had got himself what sounded like the killing lung. He was half-coughing, half-expiring into the flying, white-wing folds of his handkerchief, and when he brought his lips away from it, there was all that red. He looked out at me from his sunk-in, crab-veined, animal eyes, intent and weary, as if I ought to have known him.

"Yes?" I said. "Is there something I can be getting you?"

"Am I changed that much for you not to be knowing your own relation?" he said. He stepped closer, into the light. I saw a sloping forehead, bulging forward just above the brow. The rest of his face was in shadow, even the caved-in eyes, shining out with fever or desperation in small rounds of animal blackness.

"Uncle Jensen?" I said.

"The selfsame one," he said. He pulled out a new handkerchief from the inside of his coat, and coughed into it twice.

I stared at him silently, not opening the door any wider than I had done to start.

"I'm sick," he said, touching his chest with

the waving white cloth. "Blood in the lungs and there's nothing for it."

"You looking for a bed to stay the night?" I said.

He stepped back from the door, stuffing the cloth into an unfilled pocket. "I'm not wandering," he said. "I've got me cash money, fine clothes. I've got property." His voice was raised, and all of a sudden a wind of sour liquor hit me full in the face.

"Then what do you want with me?" I said.

He staggered once against the porch rail before he set down on the step. His head nodded itself over his shoulders with the proud-angry motions of a man that thought he deserved to be setting at the center of the world.

"I am trying to locate someone," he said. "Someone that maybe you all know."

"Who?" I said.

"There was a nigra woman used to work for me," he said. "Up at the house. She lived on the tree side of Marston's hill. Jenna Farrell was her name."

"I know who you mean," I said. And up from my remembering came Allie's mama, limb and sloe-eyed, lying in her sickbed while she watched Remy through the window, eating flowers. "She's been dead a long time."

Uncle Jensen nodded again. "She had herself a couple kids," he said.

"One of which you strung from a rope as I remember," I said.

"That wasn't none of my doing," he said. "That boy brought it on himself."

"I can't say as we all saw it that way," I said. But Uncle Jensen went right on, acting like he didn't hear.

"There been a girl was his sister, though," he said. "Kind of pale as nigras go."

"So?" I said.

"You knew her?" he said.

"I knew her," I said.

"You know where she's at now?" he said.

"Depends."

"On what?" he said.

"On why you want to find it out."

Uncle Jensen pulled back his head to look on me, his narrow weasel eyes glistening from out of the dark. "Ain't a man got a right to know where his own children is at?"

He was sneering now. His lips were swollen up with drink and sickness and they curled up high off his teeth.

"Allie isn't any of yours," I said.

"It's Allie, is it?" he said. "Them nigras always pick out names ain't no regular person has got. Allie." And he rolled the sound around in his mouth like it was a backwoods liquor he was tasting for the first time.

❧

Uncle Jensen, he wouldn't go away until he got it out of me. The address, I mean. He just set at the doorstep, coughing into waving bits of cloth pulled out from his pockets. And in between the coughing, he talked on how Aunt Pauline, which he spoke on with reverence now that she was dead, couldn't carry a child three months without the bleeding would start severe. Matter of fact, she'd lost six of his children in just that way, he said. And after that, the doctor told her she ought not be trying to grow any more. Barren was barren, and like as not would always be. 'Course, there *were* other children, by nigra women mostly, but he never followed them up. And now they were grown and gone, and him not knowing even the first thing about them, not even their names.

He said if he ever found out the whereabouts of one of them, he'd keep himself apart. He wouldn't even get so close as to converse with them, probably. He'd just look on them from a distance, and take a satisfaction in perceiving that his seed had taken a hold somewhere. That's all he had a need of, he said, just perceiving that his seed had taken a hold. Such a knowing became important to a man that had the killing lung, a man like himself, that wouldn't outlast two, maybe three months.

So as I couldn't see the harm in it, I told him. *137 Halliday Road, Victoria County,* I said. And after I'd spoken, he stood up from the porch and walked away, a dozen white bits of handkerchief waving from his pockets like so many moths, thinking to help him get to wherever he was bound.

❧

God gave Mama back the prophecy. Just for the final few hours of her life, but He gave it back to her all the same. Her fever rose so high that her skin burned our fingertips when we touched it, and from her mouth came fast-falling words, loosed in a whisper that flew straight to our souls and waked them. She spoke soft-voiced, confused truths, the meanings of which we could hardly guess.

"And eyes are going to open on my dying, so that the dying is a gift to them that's left behind. And the children, they cry, but their crying is blind, because God takes the soul without any sadness. And who's going to know me when I've passed over except them that have loved with an untouched heart. There's a wholeness to it that can't be explained.

There's a wholeness that's beyond understanding."

While she spoke, Ruby and me ran cloths wet with rubbing alcohol over the steaming course of her limbs, now starved into sticks, with the joints resting huge and bulbous. On her back, her ribs were raised to where they stretched the skin — each bony finger pushing out from its confines so that together they were a terrible opening hand. And I got the idea that when the hand was opened all the way, she would be dead inside its palm — wet and curled and broken like the tiny boneless fish that children caught in still-water ponds.

Late in the last day, she set straight up in bed. Her perspiring rolled down her neck and onto her nakedness in a fan of drops, like her skin itself was crying. But as to her eyes, they were wide and clear, their gray-green color as depthless and sad as the earth must've been on the day it was first set up in the sky.

"Oh, Cass," she said. "You're going to come so soon after me."

And then she laid herself back down, the sheet floating up around her in a wind that settled at the same time as her breath, noiseless and forever.

❧

Ruby said, "My gramma is a spirit."

❧

Me, I was grieving so hard I didn't see Mama get up off the bed and walk away. Ruby saw it, though.

"God Amighty," she said. I rubbed my eyelids with my fingertips, the skin there swollen and tight. When I looked out into the room, nothing was changed. Mama's form lay quietly on the mattress, pale and graying and even smaller than before, what with all the air gone out of her lungs.

"I saw her rise up from where she was laid," Ruby said. "She rose up and she went out the door, upright and walking, same as you or me."

"Just now?" I said.

"Not ten seconds back," Ruby said.

"Oh, child," I said.

"I didn't imagine it, Mama. It was for real, I know it was for real because I looked away once and then looked back again and she was still there, standing in blue, all of her in blue, even her hair," Ruby said. And she sank her head down into her hands then, a sheet of her raven hair falling forward in a net. Her crying came out in tiny coughs, like her breathing and her tears kept getting tangled somewhere in her thin ivory throat. Her hands were pressed so tight against her face that the fingertips were all turned white.

"Ruby girl," I said.

"Maybe it sounds crazy, but I didn't imagine it," she said. "She rose up off the bed and walked on out the room, and me watching her all the while, so I know it was for real, because I was watching it, Mama, really I was."

"I believe you," I said.

"What?"

"I believe you," I said.

"You do?"

I said, "Girl, your eyes have opened."

❧

Mama got put to ground quietly, just like she said she always wanted. Only people at the burying were Ruby and me, along with the Reverend Carstair of course, who disapproved of the fact that we were without hymn singing and store-bought flowers. But the reverend wasn't really a reverend by my way of thinking, since he ran the millinery six days a week and only wore his reverend-of-the-Lord collar on Sundays and even then it was mostly attached crooked on his neck. So I wasn't afraid of his disapproval.

I guess I never took to what people might call organization religion, what with a whole town gathering one day out of the week to set down at the inside of a church and get pious. Those that go to services regularly, every Sunday out the year, are supposed to be holier than those that don't, but my mama hadn't gone to church a day in her life that I could remember, and it seemed to me that she was one of the holiest people I ever knew.

I wished her spirit would appear itself to me, because I had got questions to ask her. Like was being a spirit what all she expected and could she fly up into the sky when she wanted, just like a bird, and was that why people had dreams at night that they could fly above the treetops, their naked toes skimming the leaves, because really it was their souls that were flying, practicing for the day when they'd pass over into a state of grace.

But Mama kept herself hidden from me, and my questions lived silently inside my mind, tossing and multiplying, wondering if they'd ever get answers to them without I would have to die and find them out myself.

❧

Two days after the burying, a letter from Maggie came in the post. It said,

dear cass,

how is your mama? i been waiting to hear. why hasn't you wrote me?

lloyd and me has got ourselves settled to where it seems we has lived our whole lives in this house. i know just how the floorboards going to creak when i step on them, i know just where the wood swells in the window frames when it rains, and i know all the linens on all the beds in all the rooms on account of every Saturday i wash them myself, this being the only thing allie suffers me to do for upkeep. my hands is kept free all the day, and i like to set rocking at the porch, a sweet lemon ice at my side, listening to the wind moving in the trees.

girl, what a forest you has planted! half of them trees has outsized the house by twice, and they ain't reached their limit yet. if them that knows how to grow things is gifted by the favor of god, you got all the gifts of a hundred mens and womens boiled down to one. and there is spirits living in them trees, dozens of them, and don't you go trying to tell me there ain't because i has seen them myself, shining in the night as bright as a city in blue. and lloyd has seen them, too. which i know on account of the paintings he been setting to his canvas. every morning he disappears into the woods with a old painting and every evening he appears hisself out of the woods with a new one. last five days in a row, he been painting a young woman spirit, skinny-figured as a boy, with a great, gleaming knot of hair she wears on the top of her head. it's oloe! young and fragile-made as the day she died. and lloyd has took to her like a boy full in love.

only bad thing that happened since i got here been uncle jensen. he's boarding at a sleep-house down the road and on days when he ain't too sick to get out of bed, which i thank to God it ain't too many, he comes out to the restaurant asking after allie. he keeps talking on how he be her daddy, but i think he be a crazy man to say so. a line like his can't be hid, and anybody can see allie don't have a drop of his mean spirit inside her. not a single, only drop. don't nobody believe it except maybe allie herself, because she locks herself in her room upstairs everytime he comes by, and she don't let nobody in, not even me. i tell her he be a crazy man, but she don't answer me none. so we all just sets around listening to his rantings until he goes on away.

i got to finish now. you write me soon, or i going to worry on you to where i has to come see you myself.

love,

maggie

p.s. — i regret i got to tell you your old horse died. the spotted one with all the height on him. last month it was. one night he just laid hisself down on the barn floor and he wouldn't get up again. guess he was just tired. allie called the rendering service and they come out to get him. it took five growed mens to carry him away.

p.s. also — allie give me twenty dollars to put at the inside of this letter in case you might be needing it. so here it is.

❧

I got myself sick. Not bad sick, but sick all the same. There was a heaviness down below my collar, like somebody had weighted my breathing with a brick. Ruby acted as panicked as if I was going to die tomorrow, and I would've set her straight except the next day there were two bricks holding down my breath and I couldn't raise my voice loud enough to convince her I was as sound as I'd ever been.

She made me take to my bed, and she wouldn't hear any of the objections I gave. She said, "When you're sick you've got to do like I tell you. When you're well again you can revenge yourself on me for being such a pinch-nosed, bossy girl. You wouldn't have taken ill in the first place if you hadn't set up at dawn with Gramma so many times, drinking tea in the shivering dark."

She didn't go on to say I'd probably caught myself the same pneumonia as Mama'd had, but I could see she was thinking it by the way her hands trembled when she filled up my water glass. "As if there wasn't another time when you could've had yourselves a pot of tea!"

❧

I put myself a pen to paper. I said,

Dear Maggie,

Mama has died. It's been about one week now. On the last day of her life, she went out of her head. She talked on things that were going to happen, but she talked on them in a language of tongues, the words all strange and misordered so we could hardly understand her. I wished I could've said goodbye to her while she was still in her rightful mind, but by the time we knew she was fading, she'd stopped recognizing Ruby and me. When she spoke her wild words, she looked through us to our souls, like all our clothings and skins and standing bones were no more substantial than the air. And then she left us completely, her spirit, too, because I haven't seen her all these seven days.

Yesterday, I fell sick myself. It's nothing that you should pay me any never mind, though. A cold in the chest, that's all. But who do you think should come through my bedroom door this early morning except the spirit of my grandaddy, toting a cozy of his wild, spice tea. The same as he did for Mama all those weeks she was bedridden. At first I thought to turn him away on account of maybe his tea-bringing was a practice he saved for the dying. But then I caught a sight of his face — his eyes pale like eternity and endless as water, just like my mama's — and all I wanted in the world was to have him setting beside me, pouring out cream and spooning in sugar with his dainty blue fingers, long and slender as a woman's. There for an hour or two I wished he were my own daddy, which to my remembering had never shown me a gentle word or way excepting he showed it to Oloe first. But the past, it can't be touched by wishing.

And that holds true for Allie, too. If Uncle Jensen is her daddy, there isn't any amount of wishing in the world can undo it. But cruelty doesn't have to run like diseasing from one kin to the next. And if the sins of the fathers are visited upon the children, she has paid his debt ten times over. Maybe twenty. And somewhere in heaven that number is written down. You tell her I said so.

Love,

Cass

❧

The bricks at my chest, they got heavier. Ruby set in a chair by the window all the night long, counting how many times I breathed in a minute. In her small hands, she held to a silver-blue watch with a fine-link chain which I thought I'd once spied in the palm of my grandaddy while he timed his steeping tea. Outside, the moon shone as bright as a half sun, which I knew on account of the shadows moving across the cloth of Ruby's dress — tree shadows with the leaves in shapes of hearts and empty bowls, almonds and beads. They netted her in their shifting patterns, a gray mosaic on blue cotton skirts.

Ruby was looking out the window to the road below, making up stories about the slow-passing cars.

"It's a sedan," she said. "So shiny you could probably see all the stars reflected in the hood. It's got a three-window cab with a face behind each glass, and everybody is wearing a hat, even the child. Who knows where they are heading to."

"Where do you think?" I said. The car must've been past now, but Ruby still looked to where it disappeared itself, in some dusty, moon-touched corner of the road.

"They are probably heading to the ocean," she said. "For a weekend with a breeze, wading in the Gulf in their new-bought swimming things."

"Just like you ought to be doing yourself," I said. "Instead of nursemaiding all day and night." But Ruby kept her eyes set out to the road, not answering. In a little while, she leaned forward in her chair, her hand put up to shade the reflection in the glass.

"Someone else is coming now," she said. "It's not a car."

"They walking?" I said. "This time of night?"

"No, they're riding a horse," she said. "And Mama, if you could only see! It's a horse as tall as the lower trees! And painted! I would've thought it was Remy if I didn't know better." A chill ran across my neck while she spoke.

"Who's riding him?" I said.

"It's a woman," Ruby said. "Wide-set and wild-haired. All dressed in blue. She's riding right up to the house."

"What's she look like? Can you see?" I said.

"No, wait," Ruby said. "The blueness isn't her dress. It's all of her. The hair, the face, the hands. If only you could see. She's just glowing in her color! Same way that Gramma was when I saw her rise from death."

"Ruby girl —" I said.

"She's facing the window now. She's facing straight up, her eyes full toward me," Ruby said. "And Mama, you'll never guess! She looks just like me!"

❧

Lily Mark came into the room with her hair a mass of blue-set curls, falling halfway down her back and trembling like so many garden snakes when she tossed her head. She wore a cloak that reached from her neck to the floor, and a yard of it trailed after her, like a moving pool of the bluest rain. One naked foot appeared itself from under a fold in the cloth, and I could see from where I lay that all the little toenails there were the purest white, like beach shells or bones. She walked on towards Ruby, her arms branched out in front for to fold her child to her breast.

But Ruby had backed herself away. She stood wedged in a corner, direct in the window light, her eyes blinking from the strange glare. On her cheek, there fell the shadow of a tree leaf in the exact shape and size of an apricot. Her eyes in their fear were opened almost as wide.

"Who is she, Mama?" Ruby said.

"It's all right," I said. "Let her come to you. She's a relation."

And Lily Mark surrounded her then, her cloak spreading out as thin as mist to cover my Ruby's shoulders, her neck, her pale frighted face, all of her that lived and breathed, so that in the end, it was like looking at them from across a great distance, through the fog-thick air over marshes and valleys I'd seen before, and rivers too wide to swim.

❧

I said, "Child, I have lied to you."

Ruby said, "By what way?"

I said, "There was a girl once, fifteen and buxom and black-haired and with child. She was angry when I knew her — angry from her struggling and having so little to show for it."

"And that girl was Lily Mark?" Ruby said.

"You just wait and see what I tell you," I said. "The girl had a name to herself, that's true. But this isn't a story about names. It's a story about a single only girl, and for all of fate's workings, she might've been you or me."

"All right," Ruby said.

"Because the point I am making is that the girl was all alone, see?" I said. "Without her own people and without her own man. And the time came when she bore her child, but the birthing went hard with her and she died after on."

"Oh, Mama, what a shame," Ruby said.

"And in the few hours before she died, she held her baby girl to her breast and she knew the sweet pull of that life. And the part of her that was that single only girl with no one to need and no one to be needing back, that part of her was taken away."

"And what about the baby?" Ruby said.

"The one that cared for the baby wasn't any more than a girl herself," I said. "Big-hearted and skinny-ribbed and sixteen years old. And she loved that baby to where she looked on it like her own creation. She bathed it. She kissed it. She circled it in clean wrappings. And when the time came for the baby to speak, the girl whispered 'Mama' in her tiny ear, and in a few months passing the baby said it back."

"Oh, Mama," Ruby said.

"And the baby, she said it just like you."

❧

Lily Mark lived her nights in a high, bright magnolia. Her blue skirts flowed rounder than the trailing silver strands of the tree's leafy hair. In the wind, she looked like a giant floating balloon, tied to earth by a thin string of bark. Ruby's bedroom had a window that faced out onto the tree direct, and in the early hours of the morning a set of wooden fingers tapped against the glass. Then Ruby rose herself out of bed to lift the lower panes, and in came Lily Mark, her substance flowing like the skin of the balloon when the air is running out from its center. When she'd settled herself inside the room, there was always a spray of white magnolia blossoms at her bare blue feet. Lily Mark liked to gather them up to float in Ruby's bathwater, in small blooming islands that smelled of ripe peaches and sawdust. Later, when Ruby brought me my breakfast, I smelled the flavor of the blooms on the bare skin of her neck, and in the wet streaming of her hair. It was beautiful, that smell, but I couldn't help thinking how it was the smell of somebody else's mothering on the child of my own.

❧

I kept waiting for Ruby to rise in her anger against me, to scold and scatter me up and down for letting her think I'd been her real mama. But she never did anything of the kind. She said, *Have some more soup, now* and *Why don't you turn your head to the side so that I can brush out your hair,* but she never said, *How could you do me the way you've done?* She left me to ask that question to myself, and that's just what I *did* ask in the quiet of my bedded days.

Once Ruby said, "Mama, you have such a wondering expression in your eyes. What are you thinking on?"

I said, "I'm wondering at how you still call me Mama. At how good it feels when you do."

Ruby said, "What else could I ever call you? What other name could ever do you right?"

❧

I wasn't accustomed to thanking God for any favors He'd done me, but I did say a thanks for Ruby. I spoke it out loud in the middle of the night with the dark falling all around my head in its cool and breathless colors.

I know maybe I don't talk to You as much as I ought. But God, You've got to admit You haven't talked to me much either. Not directly, I mean, like You used to with Mama. I guess I would've tried to pray oftener except I kind of had the feeling that I was talking to myself, that You must've been somewhere else, out of listening distance, helping out righteous people with their righteous problems. Like presidents maybe. And priests.

Anyway, I'm not calling on You this time to ask You for anything. I'm just calling on You to say thank You for seeing fit to have Ruby keep on loving me like I'm her mama, even when she knows I'm not. It's a generous thing, Your having her keep on loving me — generous and merciful and I didn't expect either one. Ruby, she doesn't seem to mind having two mamas, even though to me it's a plain excess. She says love doesn't hold any limits, but I guess You know that already.

One thing I'd like to know about, God, is how come my child has grown up wiser than me.

May it be Your will to bless me and mine.

❧

When my sickness got worse, I put my pen to paper for one more time. My writing was cramped and odd-angled, and I had to try hard to get the letters to look like themselves. I said,

Dear Allie,

So we have had us a silence. Has it done you any good? Me, I thought the quiet was likely to make me deaf the way it filled up my life with all its empty spaces.

I am writing you from my bed, which I haven't got up out of for two weeks now. After Mama died, the sickness climbed inside of me, too. And Allie, now I'm thinking maybe it's going to take me in just the same way. When I breathe, I hear the sound of a snake-tail rattling through me, like stones rolling through a casing. I try not to be afraid.

Girl, I am sorry for the wrongs I've done you, and this is what I want to say. I didn't want Warren killed and I didn't have anything to do with those that killed him, but all the same, I wasn't sorry when he died. I know how it must pain you, but that's the way it was. Warren, he disliked me for my kind. And me, I disliked Warren for seeing kinds instead of persons, types instead of people. He ought to have known there was a difference between the way I was sometimes bound to act and the way I might've wanted to. But he always treated me like they were the same thing. I couldn't get me any room for understanding.

But Allie, I'm guilty all the same. Because even though I didn't want Warren hurt, I was hurting him all the while in my mind — turning him into a nothing, a nobody, an absence. I wanted things to be like they were before he ever came — when you and me and Ruby didn't know any divisions amongst us, when we didn't know any hurt or spite from each other that couldn't be mended with a laugh. And to my mind, Warren was always putting himself in the way — always bringing up differences where I wanted there to be sameness, always bringing up injuries where I wanted there to be healings.

The thing is, part of me knows now that Warren was right. That people have got cause to be separate if they want — even if her that wants to keep herself separate is *you,* who I love as much as I ever loved my own sister. So, now I am sorry, maybe too-late-sorry, but sorry just the same, and I hope you feel the words as truly as I write them. Forgive me my dislikes, if you can. Forgive me my wantings. I still care for you, girl, now and in the next life.

Your Cass

❧

I don't remember the day particular that Allie came to me. The days fell into each other, losing their edges and their names. So I don't know the day itself and I don't even know the time, except it was in that hour of the afternoon when the sun reached its shining through the windows in thick, gold wedges, like pieces of an airy pie. And I recall the sun because Allie was standing right in amongst the wedges, scattering their color, when I first saw her. There was yellow by her shoulders — the yellow of hayfields or fire — and all around her hair, there was white — white like the hollow of the sky on the hottest, newest day. Her earrings blazed in the shapes of fish, hinged on metallic, scalloped scales.

"Cassie," she said. "I want you to come home."

"Oh, I didn't ever think to hear you say it," I said.

"Will you?" she said.

"Yes," I said. "In whatever way you'll have me."

So her and Ruby packed the necessaries. They folded my dresses into a traveling trunk, and then they put in the dishes with the china-blue flowers growing at the borders, which had been me and Mama's favorites so far back as I could remember. They put in the silver-blue glowing watch that belonged to my gran-daddy, and I tried to raise my voice to stop them, but with all the clattering of dishes and the closings of cupboards, didn't anybody hear. And they settled the tea cozy right on top of all the rest, embroidered thick and green with a tin clasp at the top that made it look like a giant purse. Then they slid the trunk down the stairs, the two of them pulling and straining and wondering out loud on how everything weighed so much. When they came back up to the room, Allie took me under the arms and Ruby took me under the knees and they lifted me up. Outside, my head fell back and I saw the trees where they cracked the sky. Somehow, they reminded me of the forest I was going to — wood fingers reaching across the blue egg of heaven — and I couldn't help but smile.

Allie and Ruby, they laid me out on the backseat of the car. The drive was seven hours long and the road was irregular. At the first, all the mudded bumps and ruts, they shook me from my rest. But after a time, I didn't feel them anymore. It seemed like somebody lifted me up off the seat to cradle me in his quiet arms. And once, when I rolled over in my sleep, I was sure I felt the long silk beard of my grandaddy, resting on my shoulder in its cooling blue curls.

❧

Mondrow's wall had weathered some. When I looked at it through the car window, I saw the brick had turned a burnished red — dull and hot-looking, like the glow from a dusty coal. Over the top row of cement, the forest waved its emerald arms. And then we were past the gate, and the wall moved away from us, and all around us, there were only trees. The sycamore and the pepper trees had grown high and lush, their jewel-leaves shifting against the blue. And over the drive, two winding sets of purple elms laced their woody hands together. Up by the house, there were the two blooming bell trees that Allie and me had planted ourselves. Their trunks were planted close and even, and it looked to me like they circled round one the other at the middle. I couldn't tell which blooms belonged on which tree, and at the ground, the petals all fell the same — in one wide circle of scattered pink-and-white silk, like the skirts on a young girl's dress.

The house was as beautiful as I ever remembered. Over the honey-wood floors, there were silk rugs in colors like spring — peach and white and pale, budding green. And in every room, there were great glass vases filled with flowers — dozens of high, white roses, sheaves of lilacs with their pearl-tight blooms. On the walls were china cabinets stacked with porcelain, and Allie showed me the shelf where my mama's pattern of blue flowers would go. It was a high-up shelf with mirrors in the back and the cabinet that contained it was dark and fine cherrywood, the grain polished clear.

In my bedroom, the linens were fresh. They felt cool on my legs when I slipped in between them, and they smelled like citrus and bleach, like Maggie always smelled when she came from Olson's laundry.

And after the unpacking, Allie and Maggie came to set by my bed. They didn't say anything. They just set there, bending over me like two mothers, watchful in the darkness, until finally I closed my eyes and left for sleep.

❧

And when I woke they were still beside me. Allie looked down on me with the roundest jewel eyes God has ever made. Her hands twisted one the other in her lap. Her palms were the color of baby skin, pink-white and tender-looking, and from one inside finger, there shone her wedding band in a dull curl of silver.

"I missed you," she said.

"I've been hoping you would," I said.

"Has you missed me, too?" she said.

"Yes," I said. "Even when I told myself I oughtn't."

Allie's hands fidgeted with her dress, plucking up tiny mountains of cloth and flattening them again on her lap. Maggie watched her.

"You sent Uncle Jensen to me, didn't you?" Allie said.

"He came to me and asked where you were," I said. "He seemed so sick, I guess I thought he couldn't do you any harm."

"Did you know he claimed to be my daddy?" she said.

I didn't answer. I watched her thick, baby-skin fingers plucking at her skirt.

"Claimed to be my daddy and he didn't claim it only to me," she said. "He talked on it to everybody he seen — to Maggie, to Lloyd, to the customers that passed by him at the gate."

"Oh, Allie," I said.

"And when he got too sick to come out to the gate," she said, "he stayed bed-rid at Tamry's boarding house just down the road.

And every day, he told it to the boarders. 'I has a nigra daughter lives not a mile away from here,' he said. 'But she won't come to see me. Even now when I is dying.' "

"Allie, I wouldn't have told him where you were if I had known what he had in his mind," I said.

"I ain't blaming you," Allie said, "so don't you say a word. You just listen and I'll tell you how it happened."

"All right," I said.

"Keep quiet now, and you'll see how everything come to pass," she said.

❧

"Well, I hated him, I guess you know that. Not only for the way he done Clyde and Carlyle, and not only for what he must have forced on my mama while she worked inside his house neither. No, I hated him mostly for being part of me without my allowing — for giving me his light skin and his thick-veined hands and his angry heart. I hated his blood that run through me, his murdering thoughts that sprung to life in my mind.

"And I remembered all those nights I prayed that God would learn me who my daddy been. If I only would've knowed I was praying on my own misery.

"So I stayed away from him. I shut him out. Every time he come to the house, I closed myself in my room and I bolted the door. And then when he got bed-rid, I thanked to God and I prayed he'd die without I would set eyes on him again.

"But Cassie, the strangest thing did happen. I clumb into bed every night only to be waked by close-by spirits. There was mens and womens, some of them as I recognized and some of them as I didn't. And all of them, shining in their forms and loosing low whisperings from their lips, all of them lifted me up off the bed and carried me out the window. I floated down the street, just like I been a spirit myself — eye-level with the treetops and breathing in the high wind. And where do you think them spirits took me but to where Uncle Jensen been dying — through the second-floor window of Tamry's boarding house and into the same room with him. The sheets was rounded like a mountain across his belly — and the mountain rolled when he coughed, though it never once waked him. At his bedstand there was blooded handkerchiefs, all crumpled into balls like red and white blossoms that had lost their stems. The air been sour with alcohol.

"I watched over him while he slept, that's all. I watched over him and sometimes I felt sorry for him, dying there in the night without a friend to help him through it. At dawn, the spirits come back to carry me home, and the next night we done the whole thing over again, same as before.

"Only after a while, something strange happened to me. I lost my hating for the man. I don't know how. It dropped out of my pockets. It slipped through my hands. I forgot it in a stranger's house and I don't remember the stranger's name. So that when he died, I was glad only for the end to his suffering. I lay awake in bed at night, imagining the spirits would carry me to wherever his soul been took. But it never happened. And the only spirit hands that touched me was in my remembering, cool and quiet as wings.

"A week after they buried him, a solicitor come up to the house. He give me some papers with seals pressed into the corners. Land deeds, he said, for all that Jensen owned. He said Jensen didn't have no other children to leave things to. Just me — a no-count, half-blood colored, and a woman on top of it. Don't it make you laugh? And now you and me got to figure out what to do with all that property. I figure as it belongs to both of us, since we is cousins. Cousins, Cassie, just think of it! Cousins, after all this time!"

❧

Allie, she held my hand inside hers. The backs of her hands were dark, but her palms looked pink and undressed, like the bareness of babies.

"I'm sorry for the way I done you," I said.

"No need," Allie said. "We has spoke our sorries already and I don't intend that we should keep on speaking them."

"If I had it to do over again, I would've moved away when you first married yourself to Warren," I said.

"I don't guess I would've stood for it," she said.

"Yes, you would've," I said. "On account of you loved him as much as anybody can love anybody. And whatever me and Ruby and the rest of the world had done, it wouldn't have concerned you for more than a minute or two. Because love would've pushed it out of your head."

"Well, I expect it would've," Allie said. "It don't mean I cared for you any the less."

"No, of course it doesn't," I said. "Not that I can speak from experience since I never had a man to love me like Warren did you. I always was expecting to find one, but I never did.

It's been one of my recent disappointments."

"You got time yet," Allie said. "You only thirty-four years old."

"Is that all?" I said.

"Girl, you ain't even reached to your prime!"

"Well, then I'll wait on feeling deprived," I said.

"You ain't even reached to your bloom!"

Allie's laughter played around her face and then left. First her cheeks were high and round like fruits and then they were planed and hollow, like the bowl the fruits had been taken out of. She touched her hand to my forehead, leaving it awhile to feel for dampness and heat.

"Maybe I ought to called the doctor," she said.

"You and Ruby and Maggie are doctors enough," I said.

"We trying to be," she said.

"I can't open my eyes without one of you is tending me," I said.

"That's fine then," Allie said. "Just fine."

❧

The next day, Allie and me figured out we had us more land and cash money than we knew how to tally. What with the restaurant bringing in eighty clear dollars a night, and

Jensen's property turning over a thousand bushels of cotton a year, we were the richest women in Victoria County, and probably Wharton and Liberty and a few more after that.

"But the being rich don't matter much without we has some way to make use of it," Allie said.

"Like what way?" I said.

"I don't know," Allie said. "Seems a shame that my mama and Clyde couldn't have lived to see the day when Jensen left the land to their very own kin. He made them suffer over that soil. Made them suffer till their backs was bent and their souls was aged."

"And now I bet they've been replaced by others that work just as hard and sleep just as heavy," I said.

"The foreman, he's got to hire fifty or sixty pickers at the harvest," Allie said.

"At the least," I said.

"I wonder what *they'd* be like to do with a thousand bushels cotton."

"The pickers?" I said.

"Mm-hmm."

"They'd lay floors down in their houses. They'd buy thick-soled shoes for their children. They'd raise pork pigs in their yards."

"Sounds nice, don't it?" she said.

"Sounds beautiful."

"Girl, I expect we would make a sorry pair of cotton farmers anyway."

"Pitiful," I said.

"Then it's settled," Allie said. "I'll call up that lawyer man tomorrow."

❧

It was time for the ripening of fruit and the darkening of leaves. Out in the yard, chestnuts fell to the ground in a rain of brown stones, making dents in the soft summer earth. Ruby and Lloyd were to have themselves a birthday.

Allie set herself to baking a cake. She bought walnuts to shell and rum to pour and chocolate to melt over boiling water. Lily Mark, who had shown up on Remy just two days behind us, spent all her time with a brush and comb in her hand, running the both of them through the sea of black hair falling down Ruby's pale neck. Like she could make Ruby more beautiful by the hundred-stroke. Maggie, she laundered everybody's dress clothes, soaking them in scented water and fine soap. And when she came to ask me what was I going to wear for the party, I told her my old wedding dress was all I had. So she took it out the closet and ran her hand over the fine-stitchings and the yellow lace. The skirt had a ripped hem from when Skeet had torn it, but outside of that, it wasn't much changed.

"This going to be fine," Maggie said. "All that yellowing going to come out when I wash it. You going to be so glorious turned out, you'll put the rest of us to shame."

❧

They dressed me in my bed, Maggie and Allie and Ruby. They drew the skirts down over my head in a cool white tunnel. Then they rolled me over and fastened the seventy-two cloth buttons, lined up like small round candies across the length of my back.

"You beautiful," they said. "You a brand-new, first-time bride."

❧

Lloyd, he'd fallen to loving Oloe. I don't know how it happened, except he was taken with her girlish spirit. She was so tall and frail when she had been alive, her thick auburn hair piled into a towering knot on the top of her head. And now that she was made over in blueness and mist, she appeared more delicate than ever before, like she was a single reed growing on the bottom of the sea — like she was a cold rose growing on the surface of the moon.

Lloyd, he painted her day in and day out. He painted her while she was sewing new dresses, with yards of the palest blue cloth spread out about her feet. He painted her while she was sleeping, her sweet blue lips breathing out the bluest air. He painted her while she let her hair down, unrolling her bun like a weighted skein, in the moment before it got taken up by the wind. He even painted her on the morning she came into my bedroom with her silk threads and her mending needles to close up the tears in my wedding dress while I lay inside it.

"Hold still," she said to me. And her voice was underwater, rich and liquid-sounding. "Hold still while I mend you right."

❧

Everybody came to the birthday party. Lloyd and Humberto, they carried my bed downstairs and set it out on the lawn. Allie, she brought out the cake lit up by a city of candles and Lloyd and Ruby made themselves a secret wish before blowing them out. I was just thinking of what their wishes might have been when a crowd of spirits appeared themselves. They came walking out from under the shade of the trees, their blueness hanging in the air like a fog, swirling and damp despite the heat of midday. My mama appeared to me first, her white hanks of hair falling easily over her shoulders. Her eyes were wet and gray and deep, like the place where all of life began, and when I looked into them, I spied an eternity, seamless and miraculous-made. My grandaddy was there, too, smoothing his beard down his shirtfront and looking out shyly from under his straw hat. And behind him were Lily Mark and Oloe, and my daddy, and Clyde and Carlyle, standing toothless and dignified. And Maggie gave cake to them all and everybody stood around quietly, holding to their china-blue plates with both hands, and listening to the sound of peace in the trees.

Out by the road, Mondrow's wall closed us in. And I thought how it was a shame that none of the world knew we were here. And while I was thinking it, I was staring at the arms of my white-blooming bell tree, bending and bowing in the late summer wind. It wouldn't be much time before that tree leaned towards me, its petaled fingers reaching to take me in. All of a sudden the blooms would open around my face, trembling against my ears and neck like petals of hair. And the tips of my toes would sink down deep in the earth — into the cool and the black and the wet, like roots. And when I turned to look, my hands would be leaves — pale and alive and silver on their undersides.

Allie would watch over me while it happened, while the circling, sweet wind pulled me up into the trees. The forest would clap its hands for joy and the leaves would fill up with laughter. While the high, clear sky welcomed me into it, my branches would arch in their heaven.

And after I died, I would recollect my life and the way I passed through it. I would think on all the things I had yet to do. Under the soil, my roots would edge towards Mondrow's wall, where I would finger the bricks to find their cracks and loose edges — ones that the other trees hadn't found yet. In five years or ten, this wall would give way under us — crumbling by pieces, one stone at a time. When that hour came, we would pull up our roots and walk out over the ruins, out towards the waiting world.

Because a love like this, it can't be contained.

The employees of THORNDIKE PRESS hope you have enjoyed this Large Print book. All our Large Print titles are designed for easy reading, and all our books are made to last. Other Thorndike Large Print books are available at your library, through selected bookstores, or directly from us. For more information about current and upcoming titles, please call or mail your name and address to:

THORNDIKE PRESS
PO Box 159
Thorndike, Maine 04986
800/223-6121
207/948-2962